Vanda dared not look. Not at first.

After a few seconds, she had to. Just a quick glance. He might not notice that. Might not see she was awake. She turned her head toward where she guessed he'd be. Ever so slowly, ever so gradually. Opened her eyes a fraction. Looking from beneath her eyelids. Then wished she hadn't.

He was standing close, no more than six feet away. Still masked, but wearing some sort of loose-fitting robe. He was aware she was watching him. He stooped and set the object he was carrying on the ground. An object she recognized immediately. An object that raised her terror to even higher levels. Two feet high, four inches wide, painted drab green. A can that would hold five gallons of liquid: usually petrol....

BILL KITSON

Bill Kitson, a retired finance executive, was born in West Yorkshire. He is an avid fan of cricket and cryptic crosswords and is also the former chairman of the Scarborough Writer's Circle. *Identity Crisis* is the sixth instalment in the Mike Nash series, following Kitson's gripping thrillers *Depth of Despair, Chosen, Minds That Hate, Altered Egos* and *Back-Slash*.

IDENTITY CRISIS

BILL KITSON

W♦RLDWIDE®

TORONTO • NEW YORK • LONDON
AMSTERDAM • PARIS • SYDNEY • HAMBURG
STOCKHOLM • ATHENS • TOKYO • MILAN
MADRID • WARSAW • BUDAPEST • AUCKLAND

For Violet Alice, my mother-in-law
(1927–2010)
'So proud'

Recycling programs
for this product may
not exist in your area.

ISBN-13: 978-0-373-06292-8

IDENTITY CRISIS

Copyright © 2013 by Bill Kitson

A Worldwide Library Suspense/December 2013
First published by Robert Hale Limited.

www.Harlequin.com

Printed in U.S.A.

IDENTITY CRISIS

Acknowledgments

So many people are involved with each new Mike Nash book—assisting with advice and patient counselling to ensure the accuracy of my plots—it is impossible to name them all. With *Identity Crisis,* however, there are certain people who must be mentioned.

Lindsay McKenzie and his wife, Vanda, for their generosity and allowing me take their names in vain.

Steve and Heather Bell, of J M Bell & Sons, and Graham Parkin of Leeds Commercial, for their expert advice on vans and trucks.

My tireless in-house editor, Val, for keeping me on the right lines.

Everyone at Robert Hale Ltd for their continued help, support and patience.

And to my readers, whose names I do not know, whose demand for more Mike Nash thrillers is inspirational.

PROLOGUE

March 2004

IT WAS RAINING. Not warm summer rain, but cold, driving rain. The sort that wets you through to the skin and chills you to the bone. She huddled miserably in the less than adequate protection of the bus shelter. All pleasure at the shopping expedition long gone. This country had its good points. A cold, wet, March night was not one of them, nor was the less than adequate bus service. She had been waiting for the best part of three-quarters of an hour, getting wetter, colder and more miserable, when a passing car stopped. The driver glanced up at the sign over the shelter. 'Not waiting for that bus are you?' He indicated the destination board.

She nodded, her mind too numb to form the words.

He shook his head sadly. 'Not tonight, love,' he told her, the cruel message not alleviated by his cheery tone. 'You been reading that?' He pointed to the schedule in the case alongside the shelter.

She nodded again.

'Out of date, love. That's last summer's schedule. Management,' his tone took on a sneering contempt, 'haven't got themselves off their fat arses to change it yet. Probably hoped to leave it for another month until the summer schedule restarts. Sorry, love. Looks like you're stranded. Either that, a taxi, or Shanks's pony.'

Unfamiliar with the expression 'Shanks's pony' she

guessed it meant she would have to walk. She hadn't planned on anything other than the bus ride. The taxi fare lay in carrier bags at her feet. She looked down at them and sighed. Nothing else for it, she told herself. At least the walk will warm you up. And the carriers aren't too heavy.

She had reached the edge of town when another car pulled up. Normally, she would have ignored it. Particularly in the dark. Particularly as she was in a lonely spot. But as it coasted to a halt, she recognized the occupant and relaxed. She wasn't going to have to walk after all. She was cold, wet and tired. The rain had started again. And it wasn't as if the driver was a stranger, not a total stranger that is. She knew him, had seen him earlier in the day.

Normally, the last thing she'd do was get into a stranger's car. And it was. The last thing she did.

February 2005

IAN WALTHAM STARED out of the window. Hoping to see her. Hoping she would come striding up the gravel drive. But knowing it was not going to happen. Where had she gone? And why? He thought he and Sally were happy. What reason had she to leave? Why depart so suddenly without even taking her clothes or her passport? He'd heard of such things happening with women, but not his Sally, surely. His vision blurred with tears and he turned away. It had been over three weeks, three long, weary, sleep-bereft weeks, and still no news. No sightings, no word; not even a phone call or a note. The police had been of little use; clearly, they were more inclined to think of it as domestic disharmony. Or, that he'd done something to her.

Ian was so immersed in his thoughts that he failed to see the postman's van pull up at the end of the drive.

Failed to see the driver or hear him walking up the gravel drive. The clatter of the letterbox startled him. He went to the other door and picked up the envelope, without much thought as to its contents. Even as he opened it, he had no foreboding as to what might be inside.

He removed a piece of paper and unfolded it. Even when he read the message, he failed to understand it. Then he saw the photograph. Nausea threatened. He swallowed, but hot bile raced into his throat. He reached the kitchen sink and vomited. Eventually, a measure of calm returned. He noticed there was something still inside the envelope. He inverted it and shook it, staring with fresh horror at what fell on to the palm of his hand. Ian groped for the phone, his eyes blurred with tears: the first of many. After some time he managed to get through to the detective handling Sally's disappearance. 'I've had a packet delivered,' he told the man. 'There's a message inside it.' He could feel his voice rising towards hysteria, could do nothing to prevent it.

'What is the message?'

The detective could barely make out what Waltham said, he had to ask him to repeat it. As if once wasn't bad enough.

'"What others created, I cremated". And,' he sobbed, 'there's a photograph of Sally. Naked on some sort of table. But there was something else. Something far worse. Her wedding ring. I know it's hers. It has our wedding date engraved in it. The thing is,' fresh tears flowed as his voice trembled, 'it's been sawn in two.'

The final horror came two days later, when more photographs arrived.

ONE

SERGEANT JACK BINNS looked up as the door opened. He was used to all manner of visitors entering the reception area at Helmsdale police station. A small boy, whom Binns guessed would be about five or six years old, came through the door first, holding it open for an elderly lady, who was struggling to get a large suitcase through the narrow aperture. Her efforts were hampered by her reliance on a walking stick. Binns hurried from the reception desk to assist. They didn't fit readily into any of the usual categories.

'How can I help you?' he asked once they were inside. His guess was that they were tourists, either seeking directions, or a recommendation for somewhere to stay. Both had happened before, more than once, and it was the height of the tourist season.

'We would like to see Detective Inspector Nash, please.'

The woman's request surprised him. Obviously, his guess had been wide of the mark. 'I'm afraid Mr Nash isn't here at the moment. Can anyone else help you?'

'When will he return?'

Binns glanced at the clock. 'He went through to Netherdale Headquarters for a meeting with the chief constable, so it's difficult to say. An hour, certainly, maybe more. Are you sure nobody else can assist you? Perhaps if you were to tell me what it is in connection with, that might make it easier.'

'Thank you, but we have to see Inspector Nash. Is it in order for us to wait?'

The old lady's English was impeccable, but Binns thought he detected an accent, although he was unable to identify the source. 'If you wish, although I should warn you those benches are a little uncomfortable.'

The woman smiled and signalled to the boy to sit down. So far, the child hadn't spoken a single word.

Time passed slowly. Even the normally unruffled sergeant was becoming flustered as Nash still hadn't appeared long after the hour had come and gone. Binns had made several attempts to engage the visitors in conversation, partly from courtesy, more from curiosity, but without success. He had even tried to get the boy to speak by offering him a drink. Instead, the boy looked at his companion who declined the offer on his behalf.

Eventually the outer door opened and Binns looked up, relief obvious on his face as he saw the new arrival. 'Mike, visitors for you. They've been waiting a long time.'

'Thanks, Jack.'

Nash turned to inspect the couple. The old lady struggled stiffly to her feet, leaning heavily on her walking stick for support. Nash's glance went from the woman to the child. Something about him, his blonde hair and blue eyes, the shape of his face, seemed familiar, but Nash couldn't think why. 'I'm Detective Inspector Nash. What can I do for you?'

'May we speak to you in private, please?'

'Of course, if you prefer.' Nash glanced over his shoulder. 'Either of the interview rooms free, Jack?'

'Both of them are,' Binns replied. 'If you leave the suitcase here, I'll keep an eye on it.'

Once inside the room, they turned to face Nash, ignoring the chairs he offered them. The woman's free hand, he noticed, was resting protectively on the young boy's shoulder. The boy was clutching her leg, standing so close he was almost hidden in the folds of her skirt. His eyes were wide and fixed on Nash, his face bore an expression that could have been fearful, but was most certainly apprehensive. 'What can I do to help you?' Nash asked.

FORTY MINUTES LATER, Binns looked up from the desk as Nash walked swiftly across reception and headed for the stairs to the CID suite. 'What's it all about, Mike?'

Nash continued up the stairs, ignoring the uniformed officer. Binns stared after him, 'What have I done?' he grumbled aloud. 'Why is nobody talking to me this morning?'

Inside the CID suite, DS Mironova and DC Pearce were struggling with paperwork ensuing from arrests made over the previous weekend. Clara looked up as Nash entered the room. She was about to comment on his timekeeping, when she saw the expression on his face. She stared at him as he went into his office and closed the door. 'What's biting him?' she asked.

Viv Pearce looked up. 'I didn't notice. What are you on about?'

'Mike came in, looking as if he'd seen a ghost, and went straight into his office. That's most unlike him. He always says hello, if nothing else.'

'Maybe God gave him a chewing about something.'

'You shouldn't refer to the chief constable in such an irreverent way. I don't think Mike would be worried. Apart from the fact that he's her blue-eyed boy, our conviction statistics are good. I'll have a word with Jack. If anyone knows, he will.'

A couple of minutes later, Clara put the phone down. 'Jack's as mystified as us. Apparently, Mike has a couple of visitors waiting in one of the interview rooms. An old lady and a small boy.'

Inside his office, Nash dialled Netherdale and asked to speak to the chief constable. 'Ma'am, something's cropped up, and I need to take some leave as a matter of urgency.'

'That's sudden, why didn't you mention it at the meeting?'

'I didn't know about it then.'

'When are you thinking of?'

'Immediately.'

'Immediately as of tomorrow, or next Monday?'

'Immediately as of this afternoon.'

'You'd better explain.'

Nash hesitated, but knew he had no choice. The explanation took some time. When it was over, he put the phone down. His sense of relief was short-lived. Now he had to brief Clara, who would be in charge during his absence. Telling the chief constable had been easy by comparison. He opened the door and called her into his office. As she went in, Clara noticed his serious expression and wondered what was wrong. Something had clearly upset him.

'I've been speaking to the chief. As of now, I'm on leave. That means you're in charge. I'll be away for a month, but if there's an emergency, and I mean a real emergency, I've agreed you can contact me and I'll come home early.'

'Come home? From where? Where are you going?'

Nash got to his feet. 'France. Come with me. I've someone I'd very much like you to meet.'

Pearce watched them pass through the CID suite, his curiosity by now thoroughly roused.

Clara glanced at the elderly lady and the small boy

waiting in the interview room. She noted the elegance of
the woman's clothes, and was in the process of smiling
politely at the boy when Nash began to make the introduc-
tions. 'This is my assistant, Detective Sergeant Mironova.
Clara, allow me to introduce Madame Mirabelle Collin.
Mirabelle is Monique Canvey's aunt. And this is her great
nephew Daniel. Daniel is my son.'

It was almost half an hour later when Clara returned
alone to the CID suite. Viv noticed she looked close to
tears.

'Well, are you going to tell me what's going on?' he
asked.

Clara looked at him but her gaze wasn't focused. 'Do
you remember Monique Canvey?'

'The girl Mike was sweet on. She went to live in France
didn't she? She was nice.'

'That's right.' Clara bit on her lip before she continued,
'Sadly, Monique died a few months ago. She was working
in a hospital and picked up an infection of some description.' She paused and took a deep breath, emotion threatening to overcome her. 'Well, I've just met Monique's
six-year-old son. The boy's name is Daniel, and Mike is
Daniel's father.'

Pearce looked at her, startled. 'Good Heavens! That
must have come as a shock and a half.'

'I think that's putting it mildly. You should see the boy
though, Viv. Daniel is just like a miniature copy of Mike.
The same fair hair, blue eyes, shape of face, the lot. Oh,
but Viv, I felt so sorry for the poor little mite. He looks
so bewildered, and helpless and frightened. He's just lost
his mother, and now he's been brought to a strange country, to live with a father he's never met….' Clara's voice
tailed off into a fresh bout of tears.

NASH HAD ONLY been gone a couple of days when DS Mironova had a visitor. She looked up as the door to the CID suite opened, her surprise and delight obvious, as she recognized the familiar figure of former Detective Chief Superintendent Pratt.

'Tom, great to see you. And looking so well, too. How are you?'

Tom did indeed look well, far more so than before the heart attack that had caused him to take early retirement.

'I'm as fit as a fiddle.'

'Have you been on holiday?'

'The sun tan, you mean? No, that's down to golf and gardening. I saw the doctor last week. Not because there was a problem, just for the routine MOT. He's really pleased, reckons I'm fitter than I've been for years.'

'That's terrific news. Is this a purely social call, or did you have something specific in mind?'

'A bit of both really. I was hoping to have a word with Mike, but Jack Binns told me he's away.'

'That's right. Did Jack explain why?'

'No, I think he was about to, when a bloke came in to report an attack of vandalism on Westlea estate.' Pratt smiled. 'Nice to see some things don't change.'

Mironova explained the reason for Nash's absence. Pratt smiled thoughtfully. 'How did he take the news that he's a father?'

'Well, obviously it came as a heck of a shock, but once he got over that, I think he was secretly rather thrilled at the prospect. But you should have seen the lad, Tom. He looked so lost and helpless, it was all I could do not to pick him up and comfort him. He's the spit and image of Mike, too.'

'It's going to be hard for them both,' Pratt agreed. 'Mind you, it'll curb Mike's hyperactive social life.'

'So, what was it you wanted Mike for, or is it personal?'

'Not really. The thing is, I'm bored. I've got my golf handicap down as far as I can, and there isn't a weed dare show its face in the garden. Plus I've decorated every room in the house, and now I reckon I'm starting to get on the wife's nerves. Jack told me there was a vacancy for a part-time civilian clerical officer, and when I saw my doctor, he agreed I was fit enough to put in for it. What do you think?'

'Are you sure about this? I mean, from our point of view, you'd be ideal. We wouldn't have to train you, you've forgotten more about admin than most of us will ever know. You'd be great at preparing paperwork for CPS and so forth. However, I can see all sorts of snags. You'd need to take a medical, and there would be the question of insurance, and how it would affect your pension, and more besides, I expect. Plus, how would you feel about taking orders from us, when you've been the one in charge?'

'That wouldn't be a problem. Nor would the medical, for that matter, and I'm sure we can sort things like the pension out.'

'Then why don't you fill in an application form and I'll give it to the chief constable. I'm due to see her the day after tomorrow, and I could sound her out then.'

Pratt smiled. 'I anticipated that.' He reached into his jacket pocket and produced an envelope. 'I picked up a form at Netherdale this morning.'

AT FELLING PRISON, the visitor looked round the depressing room and greeted the prisoner respectfully. 'This is bad'—he indicated their surroundings—'seeing you in a place like this, amongst people such as this.' His gaze strayed to the next table, where a prisoner was being harangued by a raddled-looking blonde woman. The man on the receiving end of the tongue-lashing was big in every direction. His height couldn't be disguised, even seated. His girth was even more obvious. He overflowed from the chair, more with muscle than fat. Despite his awesome appearance, he had obviously taken on one or two superior opponents in his time. Several jagged scars bore witness to the fact. He was all but hairless, the skin on the top of his head being the only visible part of his anatomy that wasn't adorned by tattoos. 'It seems all wrong, you being in here. It must be hell.'

The prisoner's smile was bitter with irony. 'You should try it from this side of the table, Tony. On the other hand, I'm learning all sorts of useful skills and you never know when the ability to hide a packet of drugs in a condom and then swallow it might come in handy. However, I'm hopeful that you're about to set the ball rolling to end all that for me. It might take a while, a long, long while, but not as long as the sentence they gave me.'

'What have you got in mind?'

'I understand that you're a free agent at the moment?'

'If that's a polite way of saying I'm out of work, you're right.'

'What went wrong?'

'I was working for a private security company. We'd been given the job of ferrying this lot'—he indicated the prisoners who were receiving visitors —'to and from court. One of them tried to escape and the management felt I was a little over-enthusiastic in the way I dealt with him. That was it. In these days of political correctness'— Tony sneered as he delivered the phrase—'the prisoner's rights come before those of the general public. So I'm now being paid a pittance by the government for doing nothing.'

'It must be tricky making ends meet on what they dole out? How on earth they expect you to manage on the paltry sum, especially when you've kids to support, is beyond me.'

'Tell me about it! But you didn't bring me all this way to listen to your impersonation of my wife, did you?'

'Hardly, that was a bonus for you. Listen carefully and I'll tell you why I did ask you to come.'

The prisoner leaned forward, his voice dropped to little more than a whisper as he recounted what he'd been planning. He spoke quickly, the urgency of what he had to say somehow emphasised by the quiet tone. Although he was only conveying the outline, it was some considerable time before he sat back in his chair and asked, 'Any questions? Anything you reckon I might have left out or got wrong?'

The temptation was to give a knee-jerk response, but that wasn't Tony's way. He thought about what he'd been told for several moments, running through the practical elements of what he would have to do. 'Recruitment is going to be the big thing. I don't need numbers, but getting the right calibre of men is the tricky bit. That might take as long as the rest of it.'

'Maybe, but it's crucial to get it right. More important than rushing it. It's a long time until Christmas, but I'm rather hoping it will be the last one I spend in this place, so I need you to succeed in order to stand a chance of getting out.'

'The other big problem that springs to mind is communication. One visit a month and a few phone calls isn't exactly conducive to the success of the operation.'

'That's why I need you to get something for me.' He told the visitor what he had in mind.

'How can I do that? I can get it, that's no problem. But how do I deliver it?'

The prisoner's voice was barely above a whisper by now. 'You need to find someone who's due for sentencing soon. Promise you'll pay their wife's rent or mortgage for six months, a year even. Tell them if, and when, I get it I'll authorize payment.'

'What if you don't get it? What if they're caught?'

'They won't get caught, I'll see to that. Nor will they refuse—if they know what's good for them.'

'This could take some time.'

The prisoner glanced at his surroundings. 'Yeah, well, I've got plenty of that, haven't I? A lifetime of it.'

'What do I do about money? This is going to cost to set up and I'm not exactly rolling in it.'

'Go see my accountant. He'll be expecting someone to contact him. Mention my name.'

'Is that all?'

'He'll ask you for a password.'

'And the answer?'

'Tell him, Kosovo 1996.'

The visitor smiled. 'I might have guessed it would be something like that. Is there anything else I should know?'

'Only a warning. Watch out for the police. Don't fall into the trap of underestimating your enemy. I did, and that's why I'm here. One sniff of their activity and I'll want to know as a matter of urgency. Especially if it's a bloke called Nash. He's the bastard who put me away and crippled me into the bargain. That's a score still to be settled.'

The rest of the hour-long visit was spent in planning. Even then, the time was too short. But then, they had lots to discuss.

EDDIE MICHAELS WAS a career criminal. As such, it was hardly a prosperous career. If the police were to set up a squad to deal with disorganised crime, Eddie would have been one of their prime targets. A succession of bungled burglaries, slipshod shop-lifting, luckless larceny and failed felonies had resulted in several custodial sentences.

As he stood in the dock aware that another enforced absence from hearth and home awaited him, Eddie's main concern was for his partner Rosie and their large brood of offspring. Eddie wasn't getting any younger and his prospects weren't getting any brighter. He knew, sooner or later, he'd have to throw in the towel and try to earn an honest living. That looked like being later rather than sooner, given the sour-faced judge who'd been allotted his trial. From what Eddie had seen of the miserable old bastard, he reckoned he'd dish out the maximum sentence. His only cheering thought was that they'd dispensed with the death penalty.

Eddie hadn't anything put aside for a rainy day and it looked as if it was about to start pouring down any minute. Nor would Rosie be able to supplement the meagre amount the state allowed convicts' wives during their incarceration. In the past, she'd been able to draw a reasonable income by entertaining a select clientele who would pay handsomely to share what was Eddie's by right. However, her looks were fading and her figure now distorted by repeated childbirth so that was no longer an option.

In the sparsely populated spectators' gallery, one of the few attending the session studied the defendant, oblivious to the progress of the trial. The small, fat, balding felon would be ideal for his purpose, he decided. In fact, he'd already made a tentative approach to the man's partner.

Jerry Freeman, following instructions, had been visiting the court on and off for a few weeks before settling on Michaels to undertake the task. He had already rejected a number of candidates, whose unreliability was evident by their manner. Their unsuitability was down to a number of causes, either their offences being drug-fuelled, or down to personality disorders. Eddie Michaels was, strange though it seemed, a much more stable character, albeit a loser.

He glanced to the left, where Rosie was seated with two of the oldest of her brood. He wondered idly how many of them were Eddie's, and if Eddie knew, or cared. Given Rosie's former profession it seemed unlikely that Eddie could claim parentage for all of them. He smiled to himself as he recalled the opening of his conversation with Rosie. She'd been under the misapprehension that he had a totally different proposition in mind. However, once he made his intentions known, her enthusiasm was undoubted. Likewise, he felt sure of her ability to persuade Eddie to do the right thing.

For the man about to be convicted, a few hours' discomfort was a small price to pay in return for payment of their rent for a year, together with a small allowance to secure Eddie's silence and a bonus for the successful delivery of the mobile phone. As long as the prison authorities didn't suspect anything and carry out a rectal examination, all would be well.

He caught Rosie's eye and nodded. She smiled brightly at the man who'd made her the offer. She made a slight upward gesture with one thumb. That was it then: it was all systems go.

IT WAS FEBRUARY, nearing the half-term break. DS Mironova entered Mike Nash's office late on Wednesday afternoon. She stared at the floor, then at her boss. 'You're not bored by any chance, are you?' She transferred her gaze back to the DI.

Nash smiled. 'However did you guess?'

Clara indicated the dozen or so paper aeroplanes scattered around the carpet. 'Deduction, I'm a detective, in case you'd forgotten.'

'I've almost forgotten I'm one myself,' Nash grumbled. 'I'm thinking of going out and committing a crime just so I've something to detect.'

'Nothing to distract you? No eager women falling at your feet? No little assignations to look forward to?'

Nash winced. 'Don't remind me. Things are that bad I nearly asked you out.'

'Thanks for the compliment. Put so flatteringly; it would have been difficult to turn you down. You're so out of practice you're even losing your natural charm. No numbers in your little black book? Better buy yourself a computer and try one of those online dating agencies. I understand there are some that specialize in the over forties.'

'Now that's below the belt. Anyway, was there a reason for you disturbing me when I'm so busy, or have you just come in to be impertinent?'

'I wanted to ask if you'd anything for me to do. You're not the only one who's bored. Viv's been monopolizing the computer most of the day. I've just found out he's playing sudoku online. That's how slow things are.'

'Things might get a bit busier for you from tomorrow. You haven't forgotten I'm taking Daniel to France. We're leaving tonight, so I'll be away until Monday.'

Clara smiled, Nash the devoted parent was still a novel idea to her. Over the preceding months she had grown fond of Daniel, having on numerous occasions had to act as babysitter or to collect the boy from After-school club, or the registered child minder Nash had selected, as he struggled to fit in his parental duties with that of a full-time police officer. On occasion, the strain had shown, and Clara was aware that part of Nash's concern was the imperfection of the arrangements and the effect they might have on Daniel. Although Clara had no great love for the concept of boarding schools, Nash's plan to send Daniel to his old school as soon as the boy was old enough, seemed to her the only solution. 'No, I've not forgotten. Is he looking forward to the trip?'

'Mixed feelings, I'd say. It must be difficult for a youngster. First, his mother died, then he was brought to a strange country to live with a father he'd never met, only heard of. I think the saving grace was that Monique told Daniel before she died that she wanted him to come and live with me and get to know me. Apparently, she used to talk about me a lot. Quite honestly, I'm astonished he's settled as well as he has. I just hope he doesn't grow to resent me. Just as he's settling in and getting accustomed to his new life and different surroundings, off he goes, back to France and what must be painful memories.'

Clara hid a smile. Although Nash couldn't see it, to even a casual observer it was obvious that the boy adored his father. Clara certainly wasn't about to tell Nash that. 'Are you sure it's the right thing to do?'

'Yes and no. To be honest, Clara, I'm learning as I go along. But I promised his great aunt I'd take Daniel to stay with her for the two weeks of half-term. She's far from well, and I think she's scared if she doesn't see him this time there might not be another chance. I can't deny her that, or Daniel either. He may not be looking forward to it at present, but if he didn't go and anything happened he'd feel rotten about it later.'

'Have you checked the ferry sailings? In view of the weather, I mean?'

Nash grimaced. 'They're all right, as far as I know. The south coast seems to have escaped the brunt of the gales. The worst part might be the drive down.'

'One good thing, this weather seems to have kept all

the villains indoors. In their own doors, I mean. I've not known it as quiet as this for a long time. I even had Tom Pratt asking me if there was any filing to do. He's bored stiff with no paperwork to deal with.'

Nash winced. 'I thought you'd know by now, Clara, not to tempt fate like that.'

Mironova threw up her hands. 'I know, I know,' she mocked him. 'Sod's Law and all that. Listen, why don't you get yourself off now? Before the phone rings, I mean.'

'I think I will. Even if it does ring, it'll probably only be the chief. She promised to let me know when she's heard who our new superintendent is going to be, but she thought it would be more likely next week rather than this.'

TWO

THE WEATHER THROUGHOUT February had been wilder than for many years. Heavy rain, brought sweeping in from the Atlantic by storm-to-gale-force winds, lashed the north of England for much of the month.

The last Thursday in February was no exception. As night fell, the wind picked up. On the outskirts of Helmsdale in Wintersett village, close to the edge of Helm Woods, the small cottage, sturdily built though it was, received a continuous battering from the wind and lashing rain. The only occupant was watching television. At the window behind her, she could hear the leaves and branches of the ivy tapping and scraping against the glass. She felt the hairs rise on the nape of her neck. She cast an involuntary glance backwards, towards the window, but could see little but the raindrops on the panes. On the TV, the forecaster was promising gales. No kidding, she thought. She began to relax, laughing a little at her fears. It had all been her imagination. She was sure of that now.

Again the tapping sound. Again the wind howling through the nearby trees. She stirred, she wished Brian were here. Normally, being alone didn't worry her but tonight, things were different. Tonight, for some reason, she felt—not afraid—but unsettled.

She got up and went into the kitchen. She hated cooking for one. She wondered fleetingly if Brian would phone, then dismissed the idea: he was on a golfing holiday. That would be his excuse. Not that he actually made excuses.

Not anymore, obviously didn't think it was necessary. She wondered again about these frequent jaunts of his. Was he really that keen on golf? Not that she cared. She preferred it when he wasn't there. And that said more about the state of their marriage than anything. She knew she'd leave him if she'd anywhere to go, any money of her own. But he made sure that wasn't feasible. What was it they called people like that? A control freak—that was it. These days they were like two strangers sharing the same house.

She stopped torturing herself and tried to concentrate. Her back was to the kitchen window. That gave her no chance to see the face peering in. Nor did she hear any sound the watcher might have made. The howling wind saw to that. The figure remained, watching, impassive, until she moved. Half a turn was enough.

She wasn't sure why she looked out of the window. There was nothing to see. The night was pitch-black. She gave a shrug that was as much mental as physical, and turned back to her ingredients. Immediately her back was turned, the face reappeared. Watching: watching and waiting.

She felt restless and decided to delay preparing her meal until after the programme she wanted to watch on television. She poured herself a glass of red wine, returned to the lounge and settled down to watch her favourite soap. The familiar theme tune was just ending when the phone rang. She muttered something impolite and got up to answer it. She was halfway across the room when the ringing stopped. Whoever had been calling had changed their mind. Either that or it was a wrong number.

The wind was picking up, getting ever stronger. Now it was collecting small bits of debris, hurling them against the cottage walls, the doors, the windows. That must account for the new sounds she could hear. Mustn't it? Or was it something else? Something more sinister.

Stop it, she told herself severely. You're getting yourself worked up over nothing. Then she heard it again, a squeaking sound. It came from the back of the house. It could be the sound of ivy against the kitchen window or a hinge creaking. That was it, surely. It couldn't be anything else. Could it? She ought to go and check, but dare not. Fear was beginning to take over: irrational, but undeniable. It held her in the chair, unwilling to move.

All her senses were at fever pitch. Her ears strained for any sound that might not be connected to the storm. Was it her imagination, or did it seem a little colder in the room? Had a door been opened letting in the cooler air? There! What was that? A footstep? Something moving outside? Or inside? She became aware she was gripping the arms of her chair, her eyes fixed on the lounge door as fear escalated. She glanced down; saw the knuckles white with stress. This is ridiculous, she told herself.

She looked back at the door. Fear turned to terror. The handle was moving. The door opened. As she saw the figure standing in the doorway, her terror multiplied. She screamed. 'Who are you?' she screamed and screamed again.

NASH GLANCED ACROSS at his companion. The boy was small, fair, almost angelically so, with blue eyes. Anyone seeing them together couldn't doubt their relationship. Many had commented on the fact but Nash himself couldn't see it. To him, Daniel was so much like his mother, although time was beginning to blur Monique's memory. When he'd mentioned this to Mironova, he'd been taken aback by her laughter. 'Nonsense, Mike,' she'd told him briskly. 'Daniel is like a miniature version of you.

Hair, eyes, shape of face, that's only part of it. He's even picking up your mannerisms.'

'Such as?' Nash was intrigued. Like everyone else, he wasn't aware he had any.

'Staring off into the distance as if you're not listening, when in fact you're picking up every word, is one. Tilting your head slightly when you're puzzling something out is another.'

Nash recognized that one. Not from himself, but from his son.

He looked at the clock. 'Time to go, Daniel,' he told him gently.

The boy looked up from the book he'd been pretending to read. The antics of the mouse and the Gruffalo were fun, but not at the moment. 'Must we, Papa?'

'You know we must,' Nash's voice was quietly firm. 'I promised tante Mirabelle you could spend this holiday with her. Remember? She's not well, and she's old. You wouldn't want to deny her the chance of seeing you, would you?'

France, the place of his birth and his home for all his life until his mama had died, suddenly seemed a long way away, alien almost. 'No, Papa, but I don't want...I mean... it's a long time.'

'A fortnight will soon pass when you get there. Don't forget, I'll be taking you there and coming to bring you home again.'

Daniel got to his feet and looked round the room. His new home, the home he'd shared with his papa for the last few months had come to mean a lot to the child. 'Come on, son.' Nash stretched out his hand. Daniel held it tightly, his small fingers gripping those of his father. 'You're sure you've got everything?'

Daniel nodded, too choked-up to speak. His small suitcase was already in the back of Papa's new car. One of the first things Nash had done after Daniel's arrival was to sell his motorbike, his beloved Road Rocket. In its place in the garage was a Range Rover. The car had become important to the small boy. He felt sure his papa had bought the car solely for his benefit.

He cast a wistful glance back at the flat as they drove away. It was all right Papa saying it would soon pass, but two weeks seemed an awfully long time to the six-year-old.

FRIDAY IS THE worst day of the week on the roads. Especially if your journey is a long one. Everyone wants to get away, to get home for the weekend, to get to that last business appointment, to get to the supermarket, to get to school and pick up the children. The main roads and motorways are clogged with heavy goods vehicles and a host of others whose journey must be completed before close of business on Friday evening.

That is without taking the weather into account. If the weather is good, Friday is still a difficult day to travel. If it's bad, Friday on the roads is a nightmare. For Doctor Johana Grey, travelling from Cornwall to North Yorkshire, all these elements combined to make her journey close to impossible. There may be worse routes to contemplate taking on such a day, but off the cuff, Jo couldn't think of one. She was miserably reminded of the punch line to an old joke, 'If you're heading for Yorkshire, I wouldn't start from here.'

However, she had no choice in the matter. Free time was hardly in plenteous supply. It never is when you start a new job. The problem with taking up a new position late in the year is that everyone else has already booked their holidays, so you have to fit your own in as and when you can. She could have pulled rank, but that was not her way.

By the time she reached the Midlands, Jo had already been on the road for over five hours. The traffic bulletins were warning of a host of problems ahead but there was no way she could avoid these. The westerly gales that had struck that morning had brought with them prolonged torrential rain. Flooded roads had already caused her a couple of detours. Now, with no sign of the rain slackening, let alone ceasing, and the wind, to the dismay of the forecasters, strengthening rather than abating, the rest of her journey looked like prolonging her frustration.

She pulled into a motorway service area, as much for a rest as the coffee. As she waited for the drink to cool to a point where it didn't strip the skin from the roof of her mouth, she took the opportunity to phone her sister. There was no response from the landline. Jo frowned, Vanda was aware that she would be en route, why was she not answering the phone? She glanced at her watch. Perhaps Vanda had gone into Helmsdale. Good Buys supermarket was one of Vanda's favourite haunts. Maybe she'd gone there to stock up for their girlie weekend.

Not that this was the only reason for the visit, in fact, it wasn't even the main one. Jo had arranged it earlier in the week. It would give her a chance to collect the personal possessions she'd left with Vanda following her transfer a few months back. Even then, she wouldn't have made the journey if Vanda's husband had been at home. But that was only because Jo detested him.

She tried Vanda's mobile. It went straight to voicemail. Jo's frown deepened. That was unusual. No, she corrected herself, not unusual, more like unheard of. Although she was over thirty, Vanda had embraced mobile phone technology with all the eagerness of a teenager. Jo settled for leaving a message. She returned to her coffee, which was by now approaching drinkable temperature. As she was sipping cautiously at it, she reflected on the message telling Vanda about the delays, warning her that she would phone again when she got nearer. She did a quick mental calculation and reckoned she would probably reach one of the service areas around Sheffield somewhere close to 7 p.m.

Unfortunately, her sums did not allow for the carnage the weather was about to cause on the motorway ahead and it was past 8.30 p.m. before she pulled into the service area south of Sheffield. By then Jo was unutterably weary as she reached for her mobile. All tiredness fell away however, when she again failed to get a response.

It was at this point that the concern turned into heightening anxiety. Where was she? Was she ill? Worse still, had she suffered some form of accident? Jo thought about Vanda's house. Its location, in the centre of woodland, was remote, too remote for someone who might be in difficulty. Suppose the gales had brought one of those massive trees down on the house. She thrust that thought firmly away. Undeterred, it returned. She tried to recall how close the trees were to the house. Too close, she felt sure. A hundred nightmare scenarios flashed through her mind. Ignoring her own weariness, she buckled her seat belt and turned the ignition.

As she drove, her thoughts centred on the possible reasons for Vanda failing to answer. If the power was out, the phones wouldn't work. And if Vanda had been without power, she'd have no means of charging her mobile. Even if it was charged, the nearest cell might have had its mast damaged. All logical reasons, all perfectly feasible. None of them easing her anxiety in the slightest.

As she approached Netherdale at the gateway to the

dale, a series of bright flashing red and blue lights warned her of yet another incident. A tree was blocking the road.

'I'm afraid this road will be closed for several hours,' the police officer told her. 'Your only alternative is to turn round, go back to the last junction and take the Bishopton road. That is, if you want to reach Helmsdale before morning.'

'I'm actually heading for Wintersett,' she told him. 'Have you any idea how conditions are the other side of Helmsdale?'

The officer scratched his chin thoughtfully. 'I don't know about that, not for certain,' he told her apologetically. 'My information is a couple of hours out-of-date and, the way the weather is, things are changing almost minute to minute. I'm not sure if Winter Bridge is passable. The Helm is running about five metres higher than normal in places. If that's the case, all the low-lying ground near Winter Bridge could be under several feet of water by now.'

'I shall have to risk it. I've driven all the way from Cornwall and I must get to my sister's house tonight, somehow or other.'

Jo watched sympathetically as the officer fought his way to the next vehicle in the waiting queue, staggering as each fresh gust blew him off course. She put the Mercedes into gear and swung into an adjacent gateway leading to a farmer's field, before turning to head back for the Bishopton junction.

She reached Helmsdale without further mishap, although several times she had to inch her way through puddles that threatened to meet in the centre of the country road. On two occasions, her headlights failed to pick up the danger in time and the steering wheel bucked and twisted in her hand, almost breaking free as the Mercedes ploughed into the floodwater at too high a speed.

She pressed on, switching the radio on, partly for comfort, but mainly to try to catch local news and traffic information. She blessed her own laxity. She had not retuned the set following her move to Cornwall, and Shire FM was still one of her pre-set stations. She was in time to catch the eleven o'clock news. The bulletin contained little else but reports of the great storm and its effects nationwide. From the local section of the bulletin, she learned that the River Helm had indeed burst its banks as the traffic officer had predicted, but that it had happened further downstream. The overspill had flooded a wide area of farmland and threatened homes in three or four villages. Although Jo felt momentary sympathy for those affected, she was thankful that the incident had relieved the pressure on Winter Bridge and the surrounding land.

THREE

IT WAS NEARING midnight when Jo turned into the lane leading to Vanda's cottage. The drive meandered for almost half a mile before sweeping round behind the property. Beyond it, the stream that served as a tributary to the Helm ran within fifty feet or so of the house. Jo was crawling forward now, her speedometer registering no more than five miles per hour. She tried to remember if there were trees alongside the drive. She could only recall high hedges, but wasn't in the mood for taking chances. As she neared the end of the drive she passed the old mill. The business had closed long ago, the mill itself was little used, but the property Vanda and her husband had bought still bore the name Mill Cottage.

As she pulled to a halt at the rear, before she even got out of the car, one glance at the house told her something was wrong. The place was in darkness. Complete, inky-black darkness. Her headlights reflected back from the double-glazed windows, mocking the darkness beyond, taunting her mind to fresh levels of fear and concern. Aware of her impending arrival, Vanda would have left the outside light on. More than that, the kitchen, which stretched over half of the back of the building would have been ablaze with light. Even if the power was out, Jo knew her sister would have lit a collection of candles. Living out in the sticks, they always had a good stock to hand for precisely an event such as this.

She switched the ignition off and got out of the car.

Her first impression was of noise. The roaring of the wind through the bank of high trees at the far side of the stream was amplified by the rushing torrent of water over the weir above the mill. Rain splashed spitefully into Jo's face as she bent against the gale and forced her way to the dim outline of the large porch at the back of the building.

She knew the approximate position of the doorknob, yet the darkness was so absolute Jo had to fumble for several seconds to locate it. She cursed her stupidity in not leaving her headlights on. The knob moved easily and she stepped into the porch, shutting the outer door with some difficulty against the wind. She groped for a light switch and after a couple of seconds found it. The porch light barely rewarded the effort. The globe above the kitchen door provided little more than a dim glow for a few seconds. This gradually strengthened and Jo realized Vanda must have fitted energy-saving bulbs.

She reached forward and grasped the kitchen door handle. It was then she noticed the first sign of trouble: the glass in the pane next to the handle was missing. Or rather, most of it was. The pane had been smashed. By accident, or something more sinister? Steady, Jo, she told herself, Vanda might have locked herself out, nothing worse than that. The handle turned easily and a second later, she was in the kitchen, blinking in the sudden brightness of the dozen or so ceiling lights. The room was empty, although there were the components of a meal on one of the worktops.

As she moved swiftly across the room, panic gripped her. Whatever straightforward explanations there might have been, had all been dismissed. There was power, therefore, the phone would work. The house was warm and dry, therefore the gales hadn't brought any trees down on it, nor had the stream flooded the building. With the outer and kitchen doors closed, the sound of the gale was muted to a whisper. Inside, the house was silent. She opened the door into the hall. Apart from reflected light from the kitchen, it too was in darkness.

All the doors leading off the hall were closed. She opted to try the lounge first. As she opened the door, a sudden noise startled her. Jo was weary, her nerves already stretched. Then she recognized it. She took a deep recuperative breath. It was the sound of a phone ringing. Four times it shrilled before Jo reacted. She started forward, flicking the light on as she passed, hurrying towards the sound. As she did so, it stopped, there was a short silence, then a voice said, 'Who are you? Who are you?'

Jo strode forward and yelled at the room's sole occupant. 'You bloody stupid idiot! You frightened the shit out of me! Where's Vanda?'

'Where's Vanda? Where's Vanda?' he mocked her.

She glared at the speaker, her gaze travelling from the black, razor-sharp beak to the brilliant flash of red on its tail that contrasted with the grey body and wings. 'Shut up, Coco, you bloody moron.'

The African Grey parrot blinked nervously and shuffled from foot to foot on his perch. Jo looked round. Her gaze dropped to the floor. She looked in horror at the carpet. The biscuit-coloured pile was disfigured with a large stain: a large red stain. Panic overcame her. She turned and bolted back to the kitchen. She snatched the phone off the wall, stuck it against her ear and began to dial 999. It was several seconds before she realized something was wrong. Several more before she worked out what. There was no ringing tone. She jiggled the receiver rest; no dial tone either. She fumbled in her coat pocket and pulled out her mobile phone, her hands shaking so violently she almost dropped it in the process.

She took a deep steadying breath. If she had dropped the phone on the tiled floor, it would have smashed. That would have been the last straw. She took several more deep breaths. Only when she was calmer did she start to dial once more.

After several fumbling attempts, she heard the ringing tone, and waited for the emergency operator. It seemed an age before the call was answered. She asked to be put through to the police and explained the nature of the emergency. After some intensive questioning, which Jo guessed hid their reluctance over what was likely to prove a false alarm, she was asked to hold whilst they connected her to Netherdale police station. Why not Helmsdale, Jo wondered? Then she realized, a small town station would probably be closed at night.

THE EARLY HOURS of the morning were agreed upon as the best time to send and receive messages. As part of the terms of his incarceration, the prisoner was kept in solitary confinement. That suited him fine, for he was not in the slightest bit anxious to fraternize with other inmates. Not only that, but with the acquisition of the mobile delivered by Eddie Michaels, he was able to communicate with his lieutenant as freely as the prison service would allow. The pre-arranged time for receipt of texts was 1 a.m. It was a couple of minutes after that on the Saturday morning when the message arrived. The prisoner studied it with subdued excitement. The plan was to be carried out that evening. The lieutenant promised to report again on Monday night. The prisoner smiled in anticipation. It looked like his men were in for a busy weekend.

DS MIRONOVA WASN'T sure what had woken her. She could hear the gentle breathing of her companion. Her fiancé David, usually the lightest of sleepers, a habit that stemmed from his military background, had not been disturbed. Then she heard a muted throbbing sound. She frowned, trying to work out where it was coming from. Not the central heating. She glanced at the clock, no, definitely not the heating. The sound stopped, then started again. She sat upright and thrust the duvet back. Alongside her, David mumbled a protest in his sleep.

Clara got out of bed and switched the bedside lamp on. She'd not rest until she located the source. She dragged her dressing gown from the chair, wrapped it round her and opened the bedroom door.

Behind her, David sat up. 'What's wrong?' he asked, more curiosity than alarm.

'I heard a noise. Can't work out what it is. I'm going to find out.'

He yawned. 'Probably a couple of cats fornicating in the street.'

'Men! One track bloody minds, the lot of you.'

As soon as she entered her sitting room, she located the source of her disturbance. She'd left her mobile on the table by her armchair. Although the phone was set to silent, she'd put it into vibrate mode when they'd got to the restaurant. One of the penalties of being on call. After the meal she'd forgotten to change the setting back. As she approached it, the phone lit up and began to dance around the circular tabletop. Clara seized it before it nose-dived on to the carpet and pressed receive. 'Mironova,' she grunted.

'Sorry to disturb your beauty sleep, not that you need it.'

She recognized Sergeant Binns' voice. 'What's the problem, Jack?'

'I've been trying to reach you for twenty minutes. Your landline's dead.' The reproach was mild. 'What's the matter, wouldn't the gallant major let you answer your mobile?'

'The gales brought a whacking great tree down two doors away, so that's probably knocked out the phones. I had the mobile on silent,' Clara explained.

'I've had a call from a Dr Johana Grey. She used to work at Netherdale Hospital, but now she's based in Cornwall. She's come back north for the weekend, visiting her sister. Or rather, that was the plan. She arrived at the house this evening, late on. The place was in darkness. The back door was open, one of its panes smashed. No sign of her sister – name of Mrs Vanda Dawson. She was on her own, husband in Spain on a golfing holiday. Dr Grey couldn't find any trace of her, but there was what looked like a large bloodstain on the lounge carpet. I've checked with Netherdale General and the ambulance service. No record of Mrs Dawson at the hospital or any call out by an ambulance to Wintersett, which is where she lives. With it being a doctor who phoned it in, and by the sound of her, not the sort to panic, I thought we should treat it as urgent, and you were my last resort, if you get my meaning. What do you reckon?'

Clara thought for a moment. She was aware that Binns had more on his mind than he'd said. 'It doesn't sound good,' she ventured.

'I agree, it doesn't sound as if there's an innocent explanation.'

'Let's not get ahead of ourselves.'

'What do you want me to do? Bear in mind I'm not overwhelmed with men waiting for something to do.'

'Can you spare someone in a patrol car? It might calm Dr Grey a bit until I get there.'

'I've nobody free, but I can leave one man in charge

here, and I'll nip through and keep Dr Grey company until you arrive. Will that do?'

'That's brilliant, Jack. Right, let's have some directions.'

As she was taking the details down, Clara saw movement out of the corner of her eye. David, sleepy-eyed and yawning, was leaning on the bedroom doorpost. She put the phone down and explained.

'Do you want me to ride out there with you?' He yawned as he was speaking.

'No, there's no point both of us losing sleep. I'm just sorry it's happened this weekend, right at the start of your leave. If only Mike hadn't buggered off to France.'

'You can't blame him for taking leave. He's stood in for you lots of times when I've been home,' David pointed out.

'True, and to be honest, until Daniel came to live with him I can't remember the last time he took a break. Forget it; I'm just grumpy at being woken up in the middle of the night.' She sighed. 'Better get cracking. The problem is I don't know how long this will take.'

THE HOUSE WAS silent. Jo waited, leaning against the kitchen unit. 'Wait where you are,' the officer had told her. 'Don't go anywhere, try to avoid touching any surfaces, just to be on the safe side. As soon as I've contacted someone, I'll ring you back.'

The call took her by surprise, even though she was expecting it. By now, the combination of tiredness and shock had caused her nerves to be stretched almost beyond endurance. 'Sorry for the delay,' he apologized. 'Detective Sergeant Mironova has asked me to pop out until she gets there. In the meantime, she wants you to go back to your car and be careful what you touch. Leave the house exactly as you found it.'

'I've turned most of the lights on, should I go back and turn them off?'

'Best not. Sergeant Mironova gave me some instructions for you. Are you ready?'

Jo obeyed Binns' instructions to the letter. She looked round the kitchen and picked up a tea towel. She draped it round her hand and opened the kitchen door then paused in the porch, delving into her pocket for the Mercedes keys. She could hear the wind-driven rain lashing against the window, could hear the gale howling through the trees. She gave an involuntary shudder. Despite the short time she'd been inside the house, she'd all but forgotten the atrocious weather. She braced herself for what the elements would throw at her and reached for the outer door handle.

Outside, the force of the blast made her stagger. She crouched low and thrust her way towards her car. Once inside, Jo remembered what Binns had told her. She needed little encouragement to switch the ignition on, turn the heater to full blast and tune in the radio. For good measure, she flicked the headlights switch and activated the central locking system.

The combination of light, heat and sound comforted her, much as Binns had hoped it would. The extra degree of security from the locked doors helped. Jo reached across to the back seat and took a pad and biro from her briefcase. Before she started to list her actions within the house, she glanced at the dashboard clock. She stared at the digital display in momentary disbelief. She'd left Cornwall midway through Friday morning. It was now into Saturday morning. During that time, Jo had been without food or rest. Despite this, she didn't feel the slightest bit hungry, and the weariness that had all but overcome her earlier had vanished. Adrenalin, she supposed. She shook her head and began to write.

She checked her notes, trying to recall if she had left anything out of her account. There was something…something in the kitchen. Then she remembered; she had tried to use the landline but couldn't get a dialling tone. She added that to her list.

Her task done, she wondered how long it was since she had spoken to the police. She could check her mobile, she supposed. That reminded her. He wanted her to write down the times of her abortive calls to Vanda. She took the details from the mobile phone memory, noting in passing that she had been waiting over an hour. Where was he? Why had no one arrived?

The music and the sound of the presenter's voice on the radio had soothed her to begin with. Now, they were becoming an irritant. She switched it off. Now, all she could hear above the low hum of the engine was the sound of the wind and rain. She hastily switched the radio back on. As she waited, she got a measure of the strength of the gale, as even the sturdy, low-slung Mercedes rocked slightly on its suspension.

Without warning, her rear-view mirror shone with the dazzling, dancing reflection from full beam headlights. Jo suffered a moment's heart-stopping panic before she saw the accompanying red and blue flashing lights. Almost immediately, the driver appeared by her window, a torch beam pointed upward, displaying his uniform and face.

Binns walked round the front of the car, his shadow elongated by the headlights. He waited as Jo unlocked the doors. 'Dr Grey?'

She nodded.

'Very sensible precaution,' he said approvingly as he slid into the seat alongside her. 'I'm Sergeant Binns. Although most people call me Jack.' He flipped open his warrant card for confirmation.

'Thank you for coming,' she gasped, the relief echoing in her voice. 'You've no idea how glad I am to see you.'

'I'm sorry it's taken so long to get here. We're short-handed due to the storm. Added to that I'd to take a detour: fallen trees. Helmsdale Road's completely blocked. Heaven knows what time they'll get it open again. The fire service has any number of emergencies to deal with. Every one of their men and appliances are out.' He paused and added sourly, 'They're lucky they've got the manpower to call on. I had to come here via Wintersett.'

'I'm just glad you got here,' Jo told him. 'What do we do now?'

'My orders are to stay with you until DS Mironova arrives.' Binns smiled at her. 'I spoke to her whilst I was on my way, to warn her about the road conditions. She'll be at least another half an hour. Would you like to fill me in on the details whilst we're waiting?'

Binns listened to Jo's story in silence. 'What do you think?' she asked when she'd finished.

He hesitated before replying. 'It isn't easy to imagine an innocent explanation,' he told her frankly. 'I'm not the detective though, and any speculation we indulge in might be totally off the mark. We'll leave the detective work to CID. I can tell you that I checked with Netherdale General and the cottage hospital at Bishopton, just to be on the safe side, and there have been no patients admitted in the last week matching your sister's description.' He paused. 'Not unless she was having a baby,' he added with a smile. 'I hadn't time to widen my enquiries further afield because I thought it was more important to get out here. I can organize that fairly quickly though, if needs be. One thought that did occur to me as I pulled up. There appears to be no sign of another car, apart from yours, I mean. I take it your sister must have one, living out here?'

Jo looked round for a second, perplexed. It was almost as if she expected Vanda's car to materialise out of the darkness. It was a measure of her state of mind that she hadn't thought to check. 'I didn't look,' she confessed. 'They both garage their cars in the old mill. Vanda and her husband, that is.'

'Is it that building I caught a glimpse of as I came down the drive?'

Jo nodded. 'It used to be a corn mill, but the building has been disused for years. The doorway where they loaded the flour sacks on to wagons is ideal for cars, just like the entrance to a double garage.'

Binns was about to say something, when the glare from a set of headlights signalled Mironova's arrival. 'DS Mironova's made better time than I thought,' Binns said.

FOUR

CLARA SWUNG ACROSS the front of the Mercedes and parked at right angles. Her headlights illuminated the back of the house. She waited for a few seconds, her hand hovering by the ignition key as she surveyed the scene, assessing the house and surrounds. Take your time, she thought. Work through it like Nash would do. Pretend you've to report back to him. Which, she added mentally, you might have to yet.

'What's she doing?' Jo asked Binns. 'Why hasn't she got out of the car?'

'At a guess, I'd say she was weighing things up, assessing the scene.' Binns narrowly avoided adding the word 'crime'.

He might not have said it but Jo didn't miss the significance.

The first thing Clara noticed was the milk bottles. They were in a small crate with four partitions, two of which contained full pint bottles. Helmsdale and the surrounding district was one of the few remaining areas that boasted a doorstep delivery service. Even the mighty supermarkets hadn't been able to devise a way of supplying a host of remote properties regularly, so it was left to the traditional milkmen. Assuming that the local supplier delivered daily, those bottles would have been on the doorstep since Friday morning. That meant Dr Grey's sister had either forgotten to take them in or…Clara's lips tightened as she considered the alternative. Which in turn, meant that whatever misfortune had befallen Mrs Dawson had taken place as early as the previous day.

She stared at the gravel on the end of the drive and the approach to the house. The large chippings were more the size of aggregate. Their normally chalk-white colour was stained a muddy shade of brown in places. Clara looked across towards the bank of the stream, partly in shadow, partly lit from the headlights of both cars. The level of the water, she could just about make out, was close to the top of the bank. Although the water was contained now, it was less than twenty-four hours since the River Helm had been in danger of flooding this area. Clara guessed this stream, a tributary to the Helm, must have been far higher. Was this significant? Could it have any bearing on what had happened to Mrs Dawson?

Clara was about to turn the ignition off when her attention was drawn to something moving in the wind. She flicked the headlights to main beam and concentrated her gaze on the back wall of the house. It was a few seconds before she saw the movement again and this time she was able to identify the source. It was a piece of cable, unattached, swinging loosely in the wind. TV aerial? Exterior light? Certainly her arrival hadn't attracted the attention of a motion-sensitive security light.

Her gaze travelled upwards. She leaned forward in her seat, unbuckling the seat belt so she could get a view of the wall right up to the eaves. Her expression took on a grimmer cast. The cable was neither from a TV aerial or an outside light. It was the telephone line. But what had caused it to split? Most people would have identified the storm as being the prime suspect. But Nash had trained her not to think like most people. She now had two mental notes. One, to check the milkman's delivery schedule. The second, to check that loose wire; find out whether it had snapped, or whether it had been cut. Clara reached over to the glove compartment and took out a large torch. Only then did she get out of the car.

As soon as she saw Mironova emerge, Jo struggled out of the Mercedes. Binns followed suit. 'I didn't know what to do,' Dr Grey told Clara, shouting over the noise of the wind. Her voice conveyed her fear, her pent-up stress and her concern for her sister.

Clara put a hand on the woman's arm, comforting as best as she was able. 'Don't worry, Dr Grey. It might be a lot of fuss over nothing. Let's get on with it. Sergeant Binns and I need to go through the house, examine everything in detail. In normal circumstances, I'd insist you wait in the car, but as long as you obey our instructions, I think on this occasion, we can bend the rules a bit.' She smiled. 'After all, you've already been inside, and you might be able to help.'

Waiting outside, inactive, alone, with only her most morbid thoughts for company was the last thing Jo wanted. With an effort that was almost as much physical as mental, she pulled herself together. 'Yes, of course, if you think I could be of any use.'

'You know the house, we don't,' Clara told her. 'I don't just mean the layout, but you'd know if things were out of place, or if there was something missing. Bring those notes Sergeant Binns asked you to make.'

'Clara, before I come in,' Binns said. 'I'll go across to the old mill and see if there are any cars parked there. Dr Grey said her sister uses it as a garage.'

'OK, then come and join us,' she yelled.

Mironova walked round to the rear of her car. The rain had ceased temporarily, which was a blessing, but the wind was blowing just as hard. She fought to open the boot and delved into her crime-scene bag. She slipped a

few evidence bags into her coat pocket then removed three
pairs of latex gloves and plastic overshoes. She passed
one set of each to Binns before taking Dr Grey's arm and
guiding her towards the house. As they walked across the
gravel, she handed Jo the protective clothing.

Jo took them, hating what they represented. 'I want
you to follow what I do and where I go,' Clara told her.
'I'm going to attempt to avoid walking where anyone else
might have walked, and I want you to do the same. I'm
sure you've seen the drill on TV; and I'm not trying to
insult your intelligence. That way, if a crime has been
committed here we stand less chance of contaminating
any trace evidence.'

'It's all right. I understand.' Jo had gone from close to
hysterical to subdued now, overwhelmed by the horrific
insinuations of the detective's actions and words. The routine donning of protective equipment, the matter-of-fact
assumption that they were entering a crime scene was
overpowering her already overstretched nerves.

'I'm not saying this is a crime scene,' Mironova startled her by saying. It was almost as if she had read Jo's
thoughts. Or, possibly the fact that she was more accustomed to dealing with relatives than professionals in just
such situations. 'All I mean,' she continued, 'is that it
would be too late once we're inside.' Clara paused outside the porch. 'Did you do anything apart from switch the
light on and open the door? Wipe your feet, for instance?'

The question was a simple one, yet Jo couldn't for the
life of her remember. 'I…I'm not sure,' she answered
slowly. 'I might have done.'

'Not easy to remember. A straightforward act like that,
it's a reflex action. The brain hardly registers that it's happened.' Mironova opened the outer door with her gloved
hand; the bulb glowed as feebly as earlier. Clara muttered

something mildly impolite, which as far as Jo could gather
was directed at global-warming activists.

Mironova stepped over the threshold in to the wide
porch, paused on the doormat to pull the overshoes on,
then took a long stride that carried her beyond the direct
route between the doors. Whilst she waited for Jo to follow suit, Clara examined the broken pane in the kitchen
door using the strong beam from her torch to supplement
the overhead light. She turned her attention downward,
playing the beam here and there in an attempt to pick up
reflections from broken glass. There were one or two,
certainly not a significant amount.

When Jo was alongside her, Mironova reached forward
and opened the inner door. The ceiling lights were bright
by comparison. 'That's better,' she breathed. Instead of
stepping into the kitchen Clara bent down and shone her
torch inwards, along the tiled surface of the kitchen floor.
The beam picked up a lot more glass fragments, confirm-
ing her suspicions.

'I'm sorry, Sergeant, I'd turned the lights on and didn't
want to go back to turn them off once Sergeant Binns had
phoned. The place was in total darkness when I arrived.'

'Don't worry about that, as long as we know.'

Mironova took another long stride into the kitchen and
waited for Jo to join her. When she did, Clara looked down
at the doctor's feet. Jo always wore trainers when she was
driving. Those, the jeans and the denim coat were almost
a uniform. 'You've very small feet, even for a woman.'

'Size five may be small, but my sister Vanda's feet
are even smaller. I don't know if she still does, but she
used to wear children's shoes. Said she got them a lot
cheaper when kids' clothing didn't have VAT on. One
thing about these trainers, they've a very distinctive pattern.' She pointed across the floor to a series of muddy

footprints. 'See those, with the diamond pattern on the sole. They're mine.'

'And,' Clara added, 'if you say Mrs Dawson's feet are smaller than yours, whose are the others? At a guess I'd say they're more like a size nine or even ten.' Which meant they were most likely a man's footprints. Mironova didn't say it. She didn't need to. 'We'll wait here for Sergeant Binns.'

As they did, Clara looked around the room. She pointed towards the corner by the kitchen door. 'The pane in the door was smashed from the outside. Afterwards someone swept most of the fragments up. Probably with that dustpan and brush.'

She looked at the partly prepared food on the worktop. As Mironova pondered the implications of this, Binns arrived. 'The mill was all locked up, but I shone a torch through the window. There's a blue Peugeot 307 inside,' he reported.

'That's Vanda's car. Brian keeps the mill locked at all times. He told Vanda that he didn't want anyone nicking either car, and with the place being so secluded it would make an easy target.'

Clara saw the distress in her face. Better distract her, get her involved. Less time to dwell on things. Even as she thought it, Mironova was aware of the grave implications of their recent find. 'OK, we'll have to move carefully,' she pointed across the floor. 'I don't want to mess up those prints. So, we'll go round this way.' Mironova pointed round the back of the central workstation. She led the way, pausing by the food on the worktop. There was a piece of steak, lying on a sheet of kitchen roll. The meat juices had leeched on to the paper, leaving a dark brown stain. Clara bent and sniffed at it. She made no comment, but Binns noticed his colleague's expression was sombre.

Jo Grey was very much aware of the implication. They moved round the island and reached the entrance to the hall, where Clara stepped through. There were three doors leading off. Lounge, dining room and cloakroom, Clara guessed. Towards the front of the house were the stairs leading to the upper storey. 'Did you look in every room?'

Weariness and stress were making Jo tetchy. 'Of course I did. Upstairs as well as down.'

'Were all the doors closed when you arrived?'

'Yes. I left them open when I looked for Vanda. Why, is that important?'

'It might be. If you're staying in, you usually leave one or two doors open. Closing them is more the action of someone leaving the house. Is this the lounge?' Mironova gestured to the nearest doorway.

Jo nodded, not trusting herself to speak. Clara was heading towards the open door when she heard the sound of a phone ringing. As she thrust the door wider the sound ceased; a voice said, 'Who are you? Who are you?'

If Jo had been startled earlier, Mironova was shocked rigid. She took a deep breath. 'You might have warned me,' she muttered as she eyed the parrot.

'I'd other things on my mind,' Jo answered tartly.

Mironova inspected the room. Before she began to look closely, she tried to imagine how Nash would have tackled the job. She started by noting the position of each piece of furniture, then turned her attention to the smaller items. Her interest centred on the TV remote control. It was on top of the display cabinet located between the door and the TV.

'That's odd,' she murmured.

'What is?' Binns asked.

'The remote. To use it you'd have to get up and walk all the way across the room, whether you were in one of the armchairs or on the sofa. Which rather negates its purpose.'

Mironova stepped further into the room. From a different angle she could see the stain which had spooked Jo earlier. She walked slowly across the carpet, accompanied by the continuous interrogation from the parrot. 'Who are you? Who are you?' the bird screeched repeatedly.

Clara ignored the grilling at first, but eventually the significance of the agitated squawking attracted her attention. She paused and looked back at Jo, who was hovering anxiously near the door. 'Does that bird always ask the same questions when someone comes in the room?'

'I've never heard him do that before. It must be something new Vanda's taught him. He's only a young bird, still learning his vocabulary.'

Mironova turned to look at the stain on the carpet. Rich, dark, red. The colour of blood. Except... She reached down, prodded it with the tip of her finger and sniffed at it. Looked up and smiled encouragingly at Dr Grey. 'This isn't blood. I can't tell you for certain what vineyard it is, but it's definitely red wine. Blood would have turned dark brown by now, like that around the steak in the kitchen.' She shuffled sideways and caught the reflection of a stray beam of light on glass. 'The wine glass it came from is under there.' Clara pointed to the sofa. She looked at the TV listings magazine on the coffee table next to the armchair and examined it for a few seconds. 'Does your sister like soaps?' she asked. *Coronation Street,* that sort of thing?'

'Can't get enough of them.'

'OK, as far as I can tell, and it's only guesswork, I'd say whatever happened to Mrs Dawson took place somewhere around 7.30 on Thursday evening. 8.30 at the latest.'

'How do you work that out, Clara?'

'For one thing, it had to be early evening, because she hadn't cooked her meal. It had to be Thursday, because there wasn't enough for two people. It might have been a day earlier of course.'

'No, I spoke to her on Thursday afternoon,' Jo told her.

'How can you pin the time down?' Binns asked Clara.

'She was watching TV, enjoying a glass of wine. The listings magazine is opened at Thursday's page, which confirms what Dr Grey just said. Whatever happened, when the TV was switched off someone put the remote over there. Nobody does that whilst they're watching, otherwise they'd have to traipse all the way across to change channels. And given her liking for soaps, that's about the time they're on.'

'Is that it?'

'As far as I can see. My only question is, what did the parrot see? Was the bird repeating something he'd been taught,' Clara paused and added grimly, 'or something he heard for the first time on Thursday night.'

BY COMPARISON, THE dining room looked untouched. Mironova turned to Jo. 'I want you to sit in here whilst Sergeant Binns and I look round upstairs. Are you all right with that? It's just that if there is anything to find, I don't want to risk contaminating any evidence.'

'I suppose so,' Jo hesitated, 'but you won't be too long, will you?'

'We'll be as quick as possible, I promise.'

When Binns was sure they were out of earshot of the dining room, he said, 'That was very impressive. In the lounge, I mean. Just like Nash at his best.' He paused and looked round before asking, 'What do you think about all this, Clara?'

Mironova had reached the landing; she turned. 'It doesn't look good,' she admitted cautiously.

'I think you know what I mean,' Binns persisted. 'It's all getting to sound too familiar. From what I've read, that is.'

'The Cremator?' Binns nodded.

'I'm trying hard not to think that way.' Clara shuddered inwardly as she spoke. It was one of her abiding fears that she'd have to investigate a Cremator incident. The serial killer had struck four, or was it five times over several years? Clara couldn't remember and at the moment it didn't matter. Other serial killers had been more prolific, but the man dubbed the Cremator by the tabloid press was deemed to be one of the most sadistic in recent times.

The Cremator's nickname arose from his practice of placing his victims on an altar-like rock, pouring petrol over them and setting fire to them. All this he duly photographed. Those photographs, which had been studied by detectives time after time, revealed a man who hid his identity behind a mask and cloak, and who placed a series of black magic symbols around the site of the funeral pyre.

Other, yet more horrifying details of his crimes were less well known, although some journalists had broken them to their horrified readership. The fact that he sent the victims' partners a photo showing him raping their loved one, then a further one showing the actual murder, had been leaked to the media. Although, the fact revealed by pathologists that at least three of his victims had been alive when he set fire to them, was known only to the investigating officers.

'We don't want to have to face that, not yet at least,' Clara said firmly.

'You have to admit it's a possibility though. A woman on her own in a rural location taken at night. Everything about this bears the hallmarks of the Cremator's other abductions.'

'I know that, Jack. I just don't want to go there. Not until I've eliminated every other explanation.'

'There can't be many of them.'

'I know that, and with every fresh discovery the alternatives get fewer and fewer. If you're right, we've only got a limited period of time.'

'Before we get called to a dumpsite, you mean?'

'Exactly, although with our force not having been involved, I can't remember the precise details.'

'I suppose we should think ourselves lucky we've escaped.'

'Yes, and I'm hoping our luck hasn't just run out.'

MIRONOVA TOOK THE main bedroom first. There was nothing out of place. So much so that it barely looked lived in, more like a display unit in a furniture store. She walked carefully across to the large wardrobe on the wall furthest from the door. She opened the twin doors and stared at the clothing. There were seven suits, neatly stored in transparent suit protectors hanging from the top rail. Clara noticed that they appeared to be sorted by colour, from lovat green on the left, through brown to charcoal grey on the right. Alongside them, a further set of protectors contained a blazer and flannels, a dress suit and a sports coat.

Below these was a series of business shirts, again neatly organized. The shelves at the right-hand side of the unit contained casual shirts, an array of knitwear, underwear, handkerchiefs and socks. Looking at the base of the wardrobe, Mironova saw a collection of shoes on a rail. All were highly polished. 'That's curious,' she said, more to herself than Binns.

'What is?'

She turned on her heel. 'Follow me.'

Clara opened the door into the second double bedroom. The story there was completely different. On the chair by the window was a motley collection of discarded clothing. A denim skirt, a pair of jeans and a couple of tops, all accompanied by an assortment of knickers, three bras and a jumbled heap of tights. Mironova looked across at the bedside cabinet. She picked up the book that was lying on it. The author was a lady who had made an excellent living from writing a string of romantic novels. She looked across at Binns.

'Any thoughts?'

'Only to wonder what you're thinking,' Binns responded.

'I'm trying to work out what significance there is, if any, in the fact that Mr and Mrs Dawson don't share the same bedroom, and haven't done so for some time to judge by the evidence. And, how significant it might be that his room is spotless and dust-free whilst his wife's has a bit of dust on every surface. She keeps his room cleaner than her own, even when he's away. Is that out of love, I wonder, or fear? He's obviously obsessively neat and tidy, almost anal-retentive, you've only to see the way he has his suits filed to tell that. Vanda's bedroom is far more normal. I think a word with Dr Grey about the state of the Dawson marriage might prove enlightening. Whether it has anything to do with her sister's disappearance is another matter altogether.'

FIVE

CONSCIOUSNESS RETURNED. WHAT had happened? She opened her eyes. It had no effect. Darkness was absolute. Her head felt muzzy, her mouth dry. She tried to remember. She'd been at home. The storm: was that what had happened? Had the storm caused some sort of a blackout? She was lying down now. But where had she been before? The lounge—that was the last thing she remembered—being in the lounge. Had she suffered some sort of an accident? Why was it so dark? And why was she lying like this? She wasn't at all comfortable. Her arms were stretched above her head and outwards, diagonally. Her legs too were stretched apart. Why? She could feel some sort of cover over her and a soft surface below her body, could feel the soft material against her skin.

Shock gripped her. She was naked. But she was never naked. Not even in bed. Not even with her husband. Not that he'd have noticed. Hadn't noticed for years. The thought of her nudity, the alarm it caused made her move. Or try to. It was then she felt the restraints. Shock changed gear. Moved up to panic.

She tried to work some saliva into the arid wasteland of her mouth. Tried to call out. Partial success: the loud cry came out as a muted croak. It was enough. She heard the rustle of movement. Another level of shock. Someone was there in the room with her. But who? And what room was this? As if in answer to the questions that were racing through her brain, a light came on directly overhead, hurting her eyes. She moved her head to avoid the beam. Blinking; trying to focus. It was then she saw the room's other occupant. Dressed from head to toe in black, only the glitter of his eyes behind the slits in the mask showed he was looking at her. Him? There was no way she could be sure her captor was male.

The blanks in her memory filled in. She had been watching TV, had heard sounds. Had started to get up from the chair; to investigate. Then seen the door handle turning. Then he'd opened the door. Then she'd seen him: dressed as he was now. Masked, like now. Terrifying, like now. Then she'd screamed. Screamed, although there was no one to hear—except him. Screamed for help she knew wouldn't come. Screamed until he placed a pad over her mouth, her nose. She'd smelled something odd. That was her last memory. A chemical smell, she remembered thinking that before memory ceased. And that was all, until now. Until the terror returned.

Again, she tried to scream, to call out. No better than before. She took a deep breath; tried to moisten her lips. Her tongue felt wooden. Her lips parched and cracked. Tried to speak instead.

'Who are you? What have you done to me? Why am I here? What do you want from me?'

The mask moved fractionally. He tilted his head to one side, as if considering her questions. She wasn't sure he'd understood them; wasn't sure she wanted to hear the answers. She waited, trembling now. After a long moment, he moved forward. She shrank back as much as her restraints would allow. Looked wildly right and left; anything rather than look directly at him. It was then she realized she was lying on a bed. Her wrists and ankles secured to the metal frame of the bedstead.

She opened her mouth to scream again. Saw him shake

his head and she stopped. Disobedience wasn't an option. He pulled the duvet back. Stared down at her body. She squirmed, part embarrassment, mostly fear. He continued to stare. Despite the mask, she could tell his gaze was moving, shifting from one area to another, examining every inch of her. With her legs apart and her arms tied above her head, her whole self was exposed to his inspection. Somewhere deep within her, something curled-up in mortification.

HE NODDED. WAS that approval, admiration even? But she didn't want his approval. Didn't want his admiration. Didn't want him near her. Didn't want him looking at her. Didn't want to be here. Because any doubts about why she was here were long gone. But she'd known that. Known it from the moment she woke up. Known it, but didn't want to admit it, even to herself. She knew he was going to rape her. And worse. She was in the power of a sex maniac, alone and helpless with probably only a short while to live. Because she knew that was what they did. Once they'd taken all they wanted, once the thrill was over the victim had to be silenced. She had read so many cases and felt that easy sympathy for the victims that distance allows.

He had entered her home easily. Now, tied up, naked and defenceless, it seemed he would be able to enter her with equal ease. To do whatever his filthy, perverted mind could think up. As the thoughts whirled around in her head, one overriding fear came to the fore. Something she had read in the papers. Other women like her. Housewives; snatched from the safety of their homes only to turn up with their bodies burned almost beyond recognition. Her terror became absolute as she realized she was probably being held captive by the man the papers had nicknamed 'the Cremator'.

SUCH WAS THE state of Johana Grey's nerves that she flinched when the door opened, even though she had heard the officers returning downstairs. 'I'm going to call in a forensics team,' Mironova told her, 'even though technically this isn't a crime scene. We've no evidence your sister was abducted, however the circumstances are such that I think it better not to take any chances.'

She saw Dr Grey was about to object and added, 'I know what you're going to say, the broken pane in the kitchen door does tend to suggest that something has happened to Mrs Dawson, but it is only circumstantial. There have been cases where women have vanished, where all the evidence pointed to an abduction, only for them to turn up safe and well with an innocent explanation. As yet, we simply don't know enough to be sure, but we'll get SOCO to do a sweep of the house just to be on the safe side. Sergeant Binns has gone to phone for a team to come out. Meanwhile I need to ask you some questions. I'd prefer to do it here, but if you'd rather be out of this house we can go back to Netherdale.'

Jo looked around. It was obvious to Mironova that she wasn't easy in these surroundings, but she nodded agreement.

'First off, can you tell me if your sister has a mobile phone? And if she has, I'd like the number.'

'Yes, she does; won't go anywhere without it. She uses it as a diary, an address book, a camera, the works. I have the number in my phone memory. It's in my bag in the car.'

'Don't worry just now. I'll get it from you when we've finished. I take it she doesn't use a traditional diary?'

There was the briefest flicker of a smile before Jo answered. 'Actually, she does. I teased her about it. She has a filofax, although why she needs both I've no idea. She told me it was in case her mobile packed-in or got stolen, or she was in a bad reception area. I said she was getting as freaky as Brian.'

'Her husband?' Jo nodded.

'Freaky? In what way freaky?'

'I meant the attention to detail. With Brian, it's like obsessive-compulsive disorder. I put it down to his being an accountant at first, but now I'm sure it's more than that.'

Mironova nodded, trying to gain empathy. 'I'll have a look round for Mrs Dawson's mobile and filofax later; they may be in a drawer somewhere. Now, what can you tell me about the state of their marriage? Are she and her husband happy?'

Clara knew the answer long before Jo replied. Knew by her expression.

'No, not really,' Jo said reluctantly. It was almost as if she felt she was being disloyal saying such a thing in the circumstances, and in the couple's own home. 'To be honest, sometimes I wonder what it is that holds the marriage together. I'm surprised one or the other of them hasn't waltzed off with someone else long ago.'

'Any specific reason to say that?'

Again, the hesitation. 'Vanda's never confided in me, not that way. In fact whenever I try to broach it, she changes the subject.'

'Has it been like this for a long time, or has there been a sudden deterioration?'

Jo looked embarrassed and thought for a few seconds. 'Things changed not long after they married. Brian has, shall we say, a different agenda to Vanda. I only come here when he's away.'

'Why is that? Because you don't like him?'

'You could say that. And partly because there isn't room anymore. The fact is that Brian and Vanda no longer sleep together.'

'And you've no idea what caused this?'

'I have my suspicions,' Jo replied cryptically.

Clara raised an eyebrow. Failing to gain a response, she encouraged her. 'Anything you can tell us, even if it's only your opinion, might be helpful.'

'Brian started spending more time away from home. Business trips, visiting clients, golfing holidays, that sort of thing. Trips where Vanda wasn't invited. It made me wonder if he was seeing another woman.'

'Was that purely your suspicion, or did your sister think it as well?'

'I don't...I'm not sure,' Jo ended lamely.

Clara had a flash of inspiration, the sort she felt Nash would have been proud of. 'Or was it that you suspected it was Vanda who was seeing someone else, not her husband? Is that it? Was your sister having an affair?'

There was a long silence before Jo replied. Getting her story right? Clara wondered cynically.

'Yes, I did think that,' she said eventually. 'I didn't have the nerve to challenge her about it, though. I'd never do that, not unless she volunteered the information.'

'And she didn't?'

'No, Vanda's always been a bit secretive. Vanda wasn't the type who.... Well, she liked attention, especially male company. Before she was married, I mean. She was never short of boyfriends before she met Brian, and she was fairly keen on, well, the physical side of her relationships, if you get my point. That was why I couldn't understand it when they stopped sharing the same bed. Along with that, she became more timid, subservient. Almost as if she'd done something wrong and was nursing a guilty secret, or that Brian had found out something and she was trying to make amends. But the clothing, that was very unlike her.'

Mironova frowned. 'What do you mean?'

'Ever since things started to go downhill Vanda stopped caring about her appearance. Wearing jeans to go shopping, not bothering to get her hair done as often. Little things like that. Almost as if she wanted to avoid making herself look attractive.'

'Do you think her husband cared about her?'

There was a flash of anger in Jo's eyes as she replied, 'That's impossible to say.'

'OK, that'll do for now. What I'd like you to do is go back to Helmsdale. You must be exhausted. If you don't feel up to driving, I'll get Sergeant Binns to take you. You can collect your car later. I'll get him to ring one of the hotels, they're sure to have rooms available at this time of year. You might not get much sleep, but you need the rest. Then you can come into the station in the morning to give your formal written statement, unless we've news for you before then, in which case I'll let you know straightaway.'

Jo refused the offer of a lift and set off for Helmsdale in the Mercedes. Once the tail lights of the sports car disappeared round the bend in the drive, Mironova turned to Binns. 'What's the form on SOCO?'

'They'll be here as soon as they can, that's all they said. They've to come from York. The Netherdale team is tied up with a domestic; Lisa Andrews is handling. Apparently, the couple had been arguing and he decided he ought to bury the hatchet. Unfortunately, he chose to bury it in his wife's head. It could be an hour or two before they get here. What do you want to do in the meantime? I could get a uniformed man to stand guard duty if you want? I really ought to head back.'

'I will want a uniform on duty, but not just yet. I'll remain here at least until SOCO arrive. I want to have a word with the milkman, if he delivers today. I also want to see what the postman brings.'

'Milkman?'

Clara pointed to the small crate by the back door. Binns noticed the two full bottles for the first time. 'I want to know when he left those,' Clara told him. 'If he delivers here every day; that means Vanda Dawson could have been missing since before Friday morning.'

'Unless she's having it off somewhere with her fancy man whilst her husband is playing golf in Spain.'

'She'd have to be a raving nymphomaniac or have the worst memory in history to be doing that when her sister is due to arrive for the weekend.'

'What you said about waiting for the postman, why do that?'

'Photographs,' she replied pointedly.

'I see. You think that might be the case?'

'I don't think we can afford to overlook it.'

'I'm not comfortable about leaving you here alone.'

'Thanks, Jack, but I won't be alone. Not for long anyway.'

Binns looked at her enquiringly.

'I'm about to make a phone call. I'll dig Major Sutton out of his bed: my bed, actually. He can come out and keep me company until the forensics lads arrive. When you get back I think you'd better phone Pearce and get him to go to the station.' Clara thought for a moment. 'No, on second thoughts, ask Viv to come straight here, he's big enough to take care of himself. I should be at Helmsdale to coordinate things. It would be useful if Tom was able to come into work today as well, but you'd better leave that until a less anti-social hour.'

WHEN BINNS HAD left, Clara phoned David's mobile. It took a few rings before he answered, his voice heavy with sleep. She explained the situation and gave him directions. 'Sound your horn when you arrive. I'll come out to you. I can't let anyone else into the house until the scene of crime people have been through it.'

Knowing he was on his way cheered Clara up. She wasn't scared, but would feel more comfortable when he arrived. Until then, she decided to try and find Vanda Dawson's filofax or her mobile phone. She met with partial success. In one of the kitchen drawers she found the filofax. Mironova took out a plastic evidence bag from her pocket and dropped the diary inside. She sealed the bag and laid it on the worktop before continuing her search. Following her original pathway, she looked through the house, opening drawers, cupboards and every imaginable storage space. Hanging beneath a coat in the hall, she found a well-used handbag containing car keys and a purse with bank cards and cash. Despite her extensive hunt, she found no trace of the missing phone.

Mironova returned to the kitchen and stood by the worktop, a puzzled frown on her face. Something was niggling at the back of her mind. Something she should have seen, but hadn't. As she waited, her own mobile bleeped. At first she thought it was a text message coming in, but one glance at the screen showed her it was a low battery warning. She'd left the phone on the table in her lounge instead of plugging it into her charger, and now she was going to pay the penalty. She was about to curse her stupidity when she stopped. That was it! That was what she'd been trying to remember! Not only was Vanda Dawson's mobile missing, but Clara had seen no sign of a charger either.

There was no chance to dwell on her discovery as she saw the lights of an approaching vehicle. Clara hurried to the back door in time to see the milkman emerge from the cab of his pickup. She hailed him and walked across the gravel towards him, relieved to find the storm was beginning to abate. In the glare of the headlights, she could see the driver's puzzled expression. He might have been used to being greeted by a female, but this obviously wasn't the woman he expected to see.

Clara identified herself and showed the man her warrant card. In response to her question, the milkman confirmed that he had left the two pints the previous morning.

'Was everything as normal?' Clara asked.

He scratched his head thoughtfully. 'As far as I remember. I mean, I'd have noticed if anything was out of the ordinary. What's the fuss about?'

Clara smiled. 'I can't tell you that, not at present. Did you collect any empties?'

'Ooh, that's a tricky one. Let me think. I can't be absolutely sure,' he said after a moment or two, 'but I don't think there were any. Why? What's the problem?'

'I'm afraid I can't say. When did you last see Mrs Dawson?'

'I waved to her on Thursday morning. Is she all right?'

'As far as I'm aware, she's absolutely fine. You might be needed to make a statement at some time. What's your name?' Clara waited, biro poised over her notebook.

'McKenzie,' he said after a second's hesitation. 'Lindsay McKenzie.'

If she hadn't been waiting to take the name down she might not have noticed it. Natural reluctance, or something else? She wasn't sure. 'And your address and phone number?'

This time there was no hesitation. Mironova wrote the details down before looking up. The early morning light was sufficient by now for her to see the man's expression clearly. It was of concern, no more. 'Have you had this round long?'

He smiled. 'Only a couple of years. I moved here from Cumbria. No work there. Most milk deliveries used to be by farmers using milk from their own farm. We even used to make and sell our own cream and cheese. But that's all changed. Nowadays everything goes to a central depot and then they bring me the bottled product back for delivery. It's known as progress.'

Clara smiled at the irony. 'If you don't agree with it, why not opt out?'

'Regulations!' There was no mistaking the disgust in his tone.

'Health and Safety, Food Hygiene, DEFRA, and that bloody lot in Brussels. They bring in all these fancy rules and regulations without giving a thought about how much they cost to enforce. Talk about a nanny state! How many times have you heard of someone being poisoned with a pint of full-fat milk?'

'Put like that, I can't think of one.'

'Right! You know something? I was talking to a French cheese producer at a conference last year and he was laughing at us. Laughing, because he said we British are the only ones who pay any heed to those EEC Directives. It made my blood boil, I can tell you.'

'I can see that,' Clara said soothingly. 'Thanks for your help, Mr McKenzie. If I need anything else, or if you have to make a statement, I'll be in touch. In the meantime, if you think of anything else that might be helpful, give me a call at Helmsdale. If you remember any strange vehicles you might have seen in the area for example.'

'I will that.' He halted, one hand on the doorframe of his pickup. 'I hope nothing's happened to Mrs Dawson. She's a right nice lady.'

After the milkman left Mironova paused, undecided what to do next. She was reluctant to go back inside the house. Any further intrusion risked contamination of what she was increasingly convinced was a crime scene. She decided to wait in her car and think through what her plan for the day should be. Locating Brian Dawson, putting an alert out for the missing woman, those had to be top of her list. If they could persuade Tom Pratt to come into work rather than play golf that would be immensely helpful. Reluctant though Clara was to admit the thought, she knew she should contact the other forces who had dealt with Cremator cases, to get them to e-mail their files to Helmsdale. If she had those to compare with, she might be able to judge if the serial killer had snatched another victim or if they were dealing with something altogether different.

Her musings were interrupted by the sound of a car engine and a tooting horn. Glancing in her rear-view mirror, Clara was pleased to see her fiancé's car pull up behind her. As David got out, she was even happier to see the flask in his hand. 'Bless you, David,' she greeted him as he opened her passenger door. 'That was extremely thoughtful.'

Major Sutton grinned. 'Got to keep the troops happy. First rule of any officer. What's the latest?'

They had finished their mugs of coffee and David was on the point of asking Clara if she wanted a refill, when Pearce arrived, followed swiftly by the van containing the SOCO team. Mironova explained the situation and instructed Viv to ensure he intercepted any mail that was delivered. 'I'm going back to the station,' she told him. 'If anything comes with what looks like photos inside put it straight into an evidence bag and make sure you get the postie's identity, in case we've to eliminate his prints. Let me know when the forensic lot are done and I'll get Binns to send a uniform to stand guard on the house.'

She thought for a moment. 'Actually, as soon as the boffins allow you in the house, see if the bunch of keys hanging in the kitchen fit the outer doors. If we can secure the place it will save on manpower we don't have.'

'In the meantime, I'll take a wander along the bank of the stream—and hope I don't find anything,' he added grimly.

Clara turned to get into her car. Sutton smiled at her across the vehicle's roof. He was aware that in the last few minutes Clara had completely forgotten he was there. Some men might have felt threatened at being ignored, but David appreciated the single-minded approach she had to her work. It was the sort of attitude he spent a lot of time trying to instil in the men he commanded.

'Sounds as if you've quite a day ahead of you.'

'You're not joking! Look, I'm sorry, David. It isn't quite the relaxing start to your leave we had in mind.'

'Don't worry about it. Work comes first, for both of us. We knew this sort of thing was likely to happen. I've been thinking whilst you were drilling your troops.' His light-hearted comment made her smile. 'It's market day in Helmsdale, so I reckon if I go shopping this morning I can prepare something for tea, and make sure it's something that won't spoil if you're an hour or two late.'

'That won't take too long. Won't you be bored stiff?'

David shook his head. 'There's rugby on TV this afternoon. I'll be quite happy watching that.'

'Okay, if you're sure.' Clara watched him get into the driving seat when she remembered something. 'Will you do me a favour? Go to the flat before you do your shopping and pick up the charger for my mobile, then drop it in at the station when you're in town?'

'No worries, see you later.'

Sutton had just cleared the drive when Mironova heard

the crunch of gravel that announced the arrival of another vehicle. She thought for a moment that David had forgotten something and returned, but as the vehicle swung round the end of the house, she saw it was a van, not a car. A greengrocery van she recognized. She'd met the owner a few times. Nash's drinking pal, Jonas Turner, supplied the greengrocer with produce from his allotment. She had been introduced to the man when she'd gone to the pub with Nash. Unlike Jonas Turner, the driver had no trouble getting her name right.

'Sergeant Mironova, what are you doing out here?'

'Hello, Eric.' His surname was Fields, which made the company title *Fresh Fields* an obvious one. She explained the situation in as much detail as she dared.

Fields whistled with dismay. 'I hope nothing's happened to her. She's a lovely woman, Mrs Dawson.'

Another unsolicited testimonial, Clara thought. Mrs Dawson seemed to be popular with all those who knew her. 'Do you deliver here every Saturday?'

Fields nodded. 'Summer and winter alike. Mrs Dawson prefers my stuff to what she can get in a supermarket. She says you never know how long they've had it in cold store.'

'And she's always here when you deliver?'

'Always. It's a pleasure coming here, to be honest. Mrs Dawson puts the kettle on as soon as she hears the van. I start by going to the wholesalers at 4 a.m., then pick up from Jonas, and after that it's non-stop until three o'clock in the afternoon, so a morning cuppa's a real treat.' His face clouded over. 'Of course it's all different if her husband's at home.'

'Why do you say that?'

'If he's here I don't get a cup of tea, and hardly get two words out of Mrs D. She dare not say boo-to-a-goose when he's around.'

'I take it you don't like him?'

Fields grinned. 'That obvious is it? I'm not saying there's owt wrong with him, he's just not my type.'

SIX

WHEN MIRONOVA ENTERED the police station, she saw Tom Pratt standing by reception talking to Jack Binns. Clara smiled in appreciation of the ex-superintendent, now civilian support worker's, sacrifice. 'Good of you to forgo your round of golf, Tom,' she greeted him.

Binns laughed. 'That wasn't hard. The course is closed because of the floods, so don't let him fool you. All Tom had to look forward to was several hours of supermarket shopping.'

'Nevertheless, not many civilian officers would be prepared to give up the weekend.'

'That's habit, I suppose,' Pratt admitted ruefully. 'Once a copper, always a copper even after you've retired.'

Clara turned to Jack Binns. 'Shouldn't you be at home now? All tucked up with your cocoa.'

'I thought you might want me to stay on, with Mike being away and all that.'

'If I need you, I know where to find you, OK? Now, home!'

'Yes, boss.' Binns gave Clara a reassuring smile as he headed for the locker room.

When they reached the CID suite, Tom Pratt headed for the small desk in the corner of the outer office that Nash had allocated him. Tom had always been a good administrator, and despite the fact that he handled all the unit's paperwork, his desk was commendably neat, especially compared to the untidiness of the trio of detectives. Tom pointed to the computer monitor. 'I've typed up the text for a flyer and a bulletin regarding the missing woman from the details Jack gave me. Hopefully, it might not be needed but I thought it would save time later on. I could do with a photo and a description, though.'

'We might have to rely on the missing woman's sister, Dr Grey, for those,' Clara told him. 'She should be coming in here sometime this morning.'

'I've also started compiling a missing person form in case that's needed. That was about all I could do until I spoke to you and found out what you need me for.'

'Thanks, Tom. It saves me having to think of these things when you're about. The main objective today is to locate the missing woman's husband. His name is Brian Dawson, and he went to Spain sometime last week on a golfing holiday, so I'm open to any bright ideas about how we trace him.'

'It could be dead easy,' Pratt told her. 'If it was a trip organized by his golf club, which a lot of them are, someone at the clubhouse will know where they're staying, how long they went for, that sort of thing. If it was a privately organized trip it could be a bit more difficult, but it should still be possible. The airlines will know who they've taken that had golf clubs in their luggage, as they are subject to special regulations these days. I assume Dawson is a member at Netherdale?'

'I've no idea.'

'I'll start with them. I play there, and although I don't know Dawson, the club secretary should. Failing that I'll try the other clubs in the area.'

'One other thing, I know it's hardly likely to give us anything meaningful, but check Dawson out on the computer, see if he's got form.'

IT WAS SOMETIME later after SOCO had left and Pearce was about to lock the doors, when he heard the sound of a vehicle. He saw the logo and the sign on the panels. Good Buys Online was the internet-shopping arm of the local supermarket chain. Pearce showed the driver his warrant card, a man he recognized vaguely, but couldn't place.

'I've a delivery for Mrs Dawson,' the man, whose badge proclaimed him to be Chris Willis, told Pearce.

'I'm afraid she isn't here.' Viv opted not to explain. He pointed to the paperwork the man was clutching. 'Can you tell from that when Mrs Dawson placed the order?'

'Should be able to.' Willis scanned the document. 'According to this, the order was received at 11.33 a.m. on Thursday.'

'Hang on a sec.' Pearce thought rapidly. From what Clara had told him, there was no sign of a computer in the house. 'Is it possible to tell how the order was placed?'

Willis frowned. 'I'm sorry, I'm not with you?'

'I mean, was it phoned in, or sent via e-mail or via your web pages?'

'Oh, I see. I'm not sure if it gives that info. Let me have a look.'

It took a couple of minutes of intense concentration before the driver found it. 'Here it is. The order was placed by Vanda Dawson, customer account number 75285 via a PDA using a Google Android platform, whatever the hell that means. Is that what you need to know?'

'It's a mobile phone with computer capabilities,' Pearce explained. 'Do you visit here regularly?'

'We usually get a large order every few weeks or so.'

'And is it always you who delivers?'

Willis grinned. 'Unless I'm on holiday, then the manager has to get off his fat backside and do some work for a change.'

'How long have you been doing the job?'

'Ever since the company set up the service—about three years ago.'

THE MOMENT SHE woke up, she was aware something had changed. The bed; this surface felt harder. She opened her eyes. The lights; they were different too. Further away, at the other end of the room. No longer directly overhead. No longer hurting her eyes.

Only, it wasn't a room. It was much bigger, and colder. That much she could tell without moving. And the ceiling; it was no longer a plaster ceiling. This place had what looked like metal sheets over a framework. What was it they were called? Corrugated. So, what was this place?

Curiosity made her try to sit up, to look round. But she couldn't. Her wrists and ankles were still tied. That hadn't changed. She moved as much as her bonds would allow. She could see there was some sort of structure running down one wall of the building. It looked like…? She frowned, concentrating, trying to think—stalls. Like they kept animals in. She sniffed the air, certain she was right. The building smelled of animals. She was in a barn. The straps securing her wrists were looped round iron rings attached to the walls. She wriggled slightly, trying to see how her ankles were tied.

That was when she realized why the room felt colder. She was no longer covered. Strangely, though, she could feel material beneath her shoulders. So the table, or whatever she was lying on, had been covered, but she hadn't. She wondered why that was then swiftly dismissed the thought. Not one she was keen to dwell on. The material felt soft, plush even. Not like a linen tablecloth at all. She squinted downwards and to one side. She could just see one edge of the fabric. It was the wrong colour for a tablecloth as well. Nobody used that shade of rich purple to cover tables—not since Victorian times. It was more like—her brain baulked at the final word, frozen with terror at the implication—an altar. Like the one used by the serial killer she had read so much about. He placed his victims on an altar surrounded by satanic symbols, before setting fire to them.

She hadn't spoken the word aloud, yet it was as if she'd given him his entrance cue. She heard a door open and close. Heard the sound of approaching footsteps. She dared not look. Not at first. After a few seconds, she had to. Just a quick glance. He might not notice that. Might not see she was awake. She turned her head towards where she guessed he'd be. Ever so slowly, ever so gradually. Opened her eyes a fraction. Looking from beneath her eyelids. Then wished she hadn't.

He was standing close to her, no more than six feet away. Still masked, but wearing some sort of loose-fitting robe. He was aware she was watching him. He stooped and set the object he was carrying on the ground. An object she recognized immediately. An object that raised her terror to even higher levels. Two feet high, four inches wide, painted drab green. A can that would hold five gallons of liquid: usually petrol.

She looked away, unable to stand the sight of it, of him, unwilling to let him see how afraid she was. After several seconds' silence, she heard a rustle of movement. Had to look. Didn't want to, but had to. Turned her head, wished she hadn't.

The sound had been him; removing the robe. Apart from the mask, he was as naked as she was. She couldn't bear to look, dared not look away. He stepped forward. Stood alongside her. Looking. Then he turned slightly and

bent his head. What was he doing? Praying? She looked
down. Another mistake. He certainly wasn't praying.

She looked hurriedly away, her heart thumping violently. He was preparing himself and she knew exactly
what for. She heard another movement and looked again.
As she did, he waved one hand in a strange sort of gesture. Was this part of some strange, sick ritual? Before she
knew it he moved again, quickly, mounted the altar and
straddled her. He was close now, almost close enough for
his body to touch hers. She shrank back as far as she could.
He moved closer. She could feel the warmth of his body
against hers, smelt his masculine scent. Saw the glitter
in the eyes half hidden by the mask. Then he was on her.

How long he lay there, she couldn't tell. Eventually
he raised himself from her, and climbed off the altar. He
stood beside her and waved his hand again, in that same
curious gesture. She saw him walk away. Saw him pick
up the can.

He stopped, his back towards her and fiddled with
something. Then he turned and she saw he had a carrier
bag in his hand. He collected his robe and put it on. Her
relief was beyond measure. He hadn't been able to do it.
Was that because of her? Did she fail to satisfy his libido in
some way? At that moment the reason didn't matter. The
violation she'd dreaded, the assault she'd been expecting
hadn't taken place. In fact, what had happened had been
more like a simulated sex act. Her relief was short-lived.
As he walked away he stopped and bent down and picked
up the can again. She watched, bewilderment and terror
mingled. Seconds later, she heard the door open and close.

She waited in silence, wondering what was going to
happen next. She didn't want to speculate but there were
few alternatives to distract her. The respite was temporary. Within minutes, he was back. Dressed in jeans, a

T-shirt and wearing a sweater over it. That was a relief. He was no longer carrying the petrol can, for which she was more than thankful. He was still wearing the mask, though. That puzzled her. Why was he wearing it? If he was going to kill her, why hide his face? Was it because he knew she would recognize him? But, if he was who she thought he was, he was going to torture her and burn her alive, so what did it matter?

She had no leisure for further speculation. He reached behind her and unfastened the straps securing her to the wall, then moved to the other end of the table and untied her ankles. He put one arm behind her knees, the other round her shoulders and swivelled her until she was sitting on the edge of the altar. Only it wasn't an altar, merely a sturdy trestle table with a piece of material thrown over it. Her captor bent down and picked up a small bundle of clothes. Her clothes. He passed them to her. 'Dress.'

Vanda realized with some surprise that this was only the second word he had spoken since he'd taken her prisoner. Again, she wondered if that was because he was afraid she might recognize his voice. She needed no encouragement to obey his command. She was acutely aware that he was watching her closely throughout the process, which took far longer than usual because her fingers were numb from the straps and her hands were trembling violently. She donned her trainers, all the time trying to avoid the question that burned in her mind, the question she could not dismiss no matter how hard she tried. 'What next?' It was so overwhelming she almost believed she had given voice to it.

'Drink.'

She looked up. He was holding out a small bottle with the cap removed; just as well, she was sure she wouldn't have been able to manage it on her own. She took it, sipping cautiously at the cold water; then swallowing deeper draughts as her thirst took over, until the bottle was almost empty.

He watched approvingly. He was just in time to take the bottle from her hands before she dropped it, just in time to catch her when she slipped sideways off the table, as the sedative again took effect.

THE FORENSIC REPORT from Mill Cottage had been both negative and puzzling. The officer in charge told Mironova they'd failed to find any fingerprints on the surfaces in the kitchen, hall and lounge, apart from those of Dr Grey. What they had found were several specks of white fibre clinging to the kitchen units, door handles and lounge furniture. They had tested the fibres, which they found to be impregnated with some sort of chemical. 'We haven't identified the chemical yet, and the samples are so small we might not be able to, but my best guess would be they're from some of those sanitised wipes used in kitchens nowadays. And I'd say they've been used specifically to eradicate any fingerprints.'

'That doesn't sound good. Not good at all,' Clara commented.

'No it doesn't,' the officer agreed. 'And what makes it worse is that we failed to find any material matching those fibres in the house. If they were used as we suspect, someone brought them into the house.'

His report decided Mironova to step the investigation up into a full-blown missing person's enquiry, even though the time-line set out in her guidance notes hadn't expired. When Dr Grey arrived later to make her statement, Clara managed to obtain a photo of the missing woman from her mobile phone. As she was providing this via a Bluetooth message, Clara was struck by a stray thought. During the time she'd spent examining the interior of Mill Cottage, she hadn't seen any photos of either Vanda Dawson, her husband, or the pair of them together. She was about to question Dr Grey about this strange fact, but in view of her distress, decided to leave the matter for the time being, merely making a note to mention it in her report.

Later that afternoon, Pearce returned and was deputed to assist Pratt in the hunt for Brian Dawson. Viv had already told Clara that the postman had delivered nothing more meaningful than a couple of items of junk mail, one from a power supply company, the other from a charity trying to flog raffle tickets. 'He got there just after you left.' He detailed the chat he'd had with the man. 'I asked him if it was his regular round, which it is. He's been on it a couple of years or so. His name….' Pearce consulted his notebook, 'is Glen Clarke, spelt with an E. He was very fussy about that. He lives in Helmsdale.'

'Any other visitors to the house?'

'One more, and it might be significant.' Pearce related his chat with the supermarket delivery driver.

At the end of it, Clara said, 'That confirms our worst fears, I reckon. If Vanda Dawson ordered all those groceries, she obviously wasn't planning to be absent from home.'

Pratt summed up the results of their efforts. 'Before I set about tracing Dawson, I checked him on the computer as you asked. There's nothing apart from a speeding fine he collected a few months back. As far as the golfing holiday's concerned, that's a real mystery. The secretary at Helmsdale Golf Club confirmed that Dawson is a member, but knows of no trips to Spain. Certainly not one organized by the club, and he hasn't heard of any group of members sorting their own trip out. After that, I started trying to contact airlines that fly to Spain. Unfortunately, most of the departments that could give me any information are closed, so there's very little I can do until Monday. I even tried the airports, but it's the same with them. However, those which could search their computers couldn't find any trace of Dawson on their recent flights. That's not to say he isn't in Spain, but I can't be sure one way or the other, until Monday at the earliest.'

'Oh great! That's absolutely brilliant! That means Vanda Dawson's gone missing and we can't even locate her husband to tell him. Tom, can you think of anything else that could possibly go wrong today?'

Pratt shook his head. He couldn't think of any way the day could get worse.

As TOM PRATT was leaving the station to drive back to Netherdale, he passed a group of motor cyclists heading through the market place towards the Bishopton road. Bikers were a common enough sight during the summer when Helmsdale was a favourite destination for groups from the West Riding and the north east, but at this time of the year they were much less in evidence. He gave no more thought to them than to wonder where they hailed from and where they were heading so late in the day, then dismissed them from his mind. It was not until much later that he remembered the group.

After crossing the market place, the bikers pulled into the car park to the rear of the High Street at the northern end of the town. When they'd switched their engines off, leaned their bikes on their stands and removed their helmets, the leader spoke to them. 'Right, let's be sure everything is ready. Have you got the kit in place?'

'All sorted. The vans are parked out of sight,' one of the men replied. 'The signs and barricades are ready to be pulled into place as soon as I get the word. I've concealed them behind hedges, but it's no more than a couple of minutes' work to get them into position.'

'I'll supervise the first part, the rest of you get on your way.' The leader looked at one of the men, 'Got your equipment ready?'

'Dead easy, I got it last week. I've tested it a couple of times. It'll work fine.'

'Right, you'd better get yourselves off. The signal will be when I pass you.'

WHEN CLARA TOLD David about her day, she described it as like trying to swim upstream in the River Helm after the flood. 'I'm afraid I have to go into work again tomorrow. I spoke to the Chief Constable and she agreed there wasn't much more I could do today, so she's called a meeting for nine o'clock in the morning; unless something else crops up in the meantime,' she added darkly. 'For now, I'm looking forward to nothing more taxing than a long hot soak in the bath, preferably accompanied by a glass of wine, then tasting this dinner that smells so delicious, and finally collapsing into bed.'

THE DRIVER OF the security van yawned. It was partly from boredom, mostly from weariness. Saturday evening always got him this way, recently, even more so. That was down to his boss trying to run the company on a shoe-string. The recession, credit crunch, call it what you like had hit all industry hard; theirs was no exception. The result was everyone competing for the same business, and cutting margins to the bone simply in order to secure the work. Slimmer margins led inevitably to demands for the overheads to be reduced. In the security business, that was a dangerous practice.

Guardwell Transport had operated a fleet of twenty

vans similar to his until eighteen months ago. They had provided secure transport facilities for banks and retailers throughout the north of England with a staff of over eighty men on the road, plus over half a dozen in the control room and several more at their central depot in Netherdale.

The rapid decline of the company was marked by the loss of their three largest contracts. This had been followed by a dramatic reduction in the number of vehicles and the workforce. Now, they had only six vans bearing the company logo with a mere fifteen crew members and one man in the control room. The reduction in crew size from three to two per van had been a source of great concern to the employees, several of whom had expressed their reservations at the perceived danger of this practice. Not surprisingly, the more vociferous objectors had been the first to lose their jobs.

Whereas at the height of the company's success they had worked twenty-four hours a day, seven days a week, the reduced demand resulted in them being on the road only five days a week, and only for twelve hours at the most.

Saturday was their busiest day, and as another economy measure, their boss had redesigned each van's route to include extra pick up points. That was all very well, under normal circumstances, but it didn't allow any margin for such things as exceptional weather. This week had been a case in point. The severe gales and floods had led to the postponement of several of their collections over the past two days, most of which had been pushed on to the Saturday round. Today had been a grueling twelve-hour stint already, and they still had these last two calls to make. Two more, then back to the depot to offload. Then home.

The driver had pulled into the delivery yard at the back of the Helmsdale branch of the Good Buys supermarket chain, reversed to the delivery door and checked all round to make sure there was no danger before releasing the lock to let his colleague out of the vehicle. As soon as the man was clear, he relocked the van and watched in his rear-view mirror until his colleague was safely inside the store. Only then did he relax and lean back in his seat. Further down, the yard was wider to enable maximum car parking space. In line with this, the dividing walls behind four of the units had been removed to provide parking for staff and disabled customers, not only of the supermarket, but also of the local branch of a national chemist's chain, a building society and one of the town's few residential hotels.

At this time of day, the yard had hardly any cars, which in turn had given three enterprising local lads the opportunity for a kick-about game of football. Watched by an indulgent parent, the trio even had the use of floodlights, provided by the motion-sensitive PIR lights attached to the buildings. The driver smiled, it was almost as if they'd brought Old Trafford to Helmsdale.

Turning to the more mundane task he was paid for, the driver got on the radio and reported their safe arrival at Helmsdale. He ended the call, wondering if the radio operator in their control room had woken up specially to take their call. He certainly sounded as weary as the driver felt.

Returning to the excitement of the live soccer, the driver saw the largest of the players break away and swerve neatly round a despairing lunge of a tackle. He approached the van, drew back his foot and shot for goal. The driver heard a slight thump as the ball struck the underside of the van; then the burgeoning Beckham gave him a cheeky grin, before peeling away to celebrate his triumph, arms aloft to welcome the plaudits of an imaginary crowd of devoted fans.

The lad's celebrations ceased abruptly when he reached the adult—surely the boy's father. The driver saw the up-raised hand and the wagging finger; he didn't need to hear what was being said to realize the young player was being berated for his thoughtlessness. The adult turned away from the crestfallen youth and approached the van. He signalled to the driver that the ball had got stuck under the van; then made a diving motion with both hands. Obviously, he wanted to scramble under the vehicle to retrieve the ball. The driver nodded agreement.

He heard a couple of small thumps before the man emerged. He was carrying the football in one hand, rubbing his elbow with the other. Apparently, the retrieval had been at the cost of a bruise or two. No doubt that would be mentioned to the goal scorer in addition to the previous telling-off. The parent made a thumbs up sign of thanks to the driver and walked off to shepherd his brood of footballers away. No doubt going home for their tea, the driver sighed wistfully.

As they reached the far wall the parent was talking to the eldest again, presumably reinforcing the earlier dressing-down. A few seconds later, the driver saw his partner emerge from the store with the strong box securely attached to his wrist. He let him into the back of the van and waited for his signal before opening the connecting hatch. The guard climbed through to the cab and attached the paperwork to his clipboard. The driver set off for their last call which was at the supermarket's Bishopton branch.

After leaving the car parking area, the boys hurried down the street with the adult strolling at a more leisurely pace behind them. Around the corner, he met their mother. 'The lads did very well, Mrs Michaels.' He knew she wasn't actually Eddie's wife, but that scarcely mattered. 'Very well indeed.' He took an envelope from his coat pocket. 'I'll be sure to report back favourably to my boss. And here's the money, as promised.' He smiled. 'I suppose that makes them professional footballers.'

SEVEN

THE SECURITY VAN was almost halfway to Bishopton on a straight stretch of road when the driver spotted a sign warning of a closure ahead. He pointed it out. 'I hope that's left over from the storm and they've forgotten to take it in,' he commented.

His colleague picked up the clipboard and thumbed through the papers until he found their daily instruction sheet. 'There's no mention of road closures on here,' he said. 'Do you want me to raise the office, see if they know about it?'

'No, we'll wait and see. Probably the council hasn't bothered to send someone out to pick them up. Idle set of buggers!'

Two miles further on they saw a second sign, and this time the guard did attempt to radio into their control room. All he got was background crackle and the hiss of static. 'Bloody thing's on the blink again.' He replaced the microphone in disgust. 'Five weeks ago I told them it wasn't working properly, and the mechanic swore he'd repaired the fault. Obviously, nothing's been done.'

'What do you expect? The bloody firm hasn't got tuppence to scratch its arse with. Certainly none to spare for such luxuries as maintenance.'

Despite his anger, he smiled at the driver's cynicism. As the man was speaking, they could just pick out an orange glow in the far reaches of their headlight beam. As they got closer, they saw it came from the luridly coloured set of temporary barriers placed across the Bishopton arm of the road junction. The diversion arrows pointed them to the north, towards Wintersett village. 'Damn and blast!' the driver exclaimed. 'That's going to add half an hour to the journey. Better try that radio again.'

He tried several times, but with no more success. They were a fair way along the Wintersett road when the driver noticed a set of headlights in his rear-view mirror. They appeared to be well back, at a guess probably as much as a mile. Switching his attention to the road ahead, he caught a brief glimpse of a single light, which was instantly hidden by the contours of the land. As they reached the top of the next incline, he saw it again. Was it a car with one headlight out? Whatever it was, it was coming towards them at a fairly rapid rate.

Their first intimation of trouble came when the headlight faltered, swinging wildly, first to the right, then to the left as the motorbike rider attempted to correct a skid. It plunged; then settled low to the ground as it slithered remorselessly towards them. The driver slammed the van's brakes on and the vehicle came to a shuddering halt. They could see the bike now, riderless, sliding on its side, the tank striking sparks from the road surface as it made spasmodic contact with the tarmac.

The bike came to rest no more than a cricket pitch length in front of them, its front wheel resting on the grass verge. The forks looked bent; the machine was obviously close to being beyond repair. But what of the rider? Further along the lane they could just pick out a motionless figure in the furthest reaches of their headlights: ominously motionless.

The van driver steered cautiously round the bike and inched nearer the fallen rider. He pulled up as close as he dared and they peered in horror at the torn, gashed leathers, the dented helmet, but most of their attention concentrated on the blood that was forming a pool on the road surface. Its source was the biggest gash in the leather tunic towards the rider's heart, close to the ground. The blood was still pumping, more spurt than seepage.

They stared in horror, the guard again tried desperately to contact his control room, to summon an ambulance, he told the driver. A hearse would be more appropriate, the driver thought. Failing yet again, the guard said, 'Keep trying them, will you. Let me out. I'm going to see what I can do for the poor sod.'

'We shouldn't. We're not supposed to leave the cab. You know the rules.'

'Sod the rules. Do you think that poor bugger gives a toss for the rules?'

'There's another vehicle coming up behind. Perhaps we ought to let the driver sort this out?'

'You think he'll be trained in first aid, like I am? You think it's likely to be a doctor on his rounds?'

The driver gave in, reluctantly. He pressed the release button for the passenger door and watched his colleague stride forward towards the downed rider, the green first aid kit gleaming in the headlights. His attention was distracted momentarily by the approach of the vehicle he'd seen earlier. As the headlights loomed larger in his rearview mirror, he was thankful he'd already switched his hazard flashers on. The squealing hiss of air brakes as the driver anchored up emphasized the wisdom of this decision. He saw the vehicle stop, too close for total comfort. Any chance of the joke about a country doctor being true vanished as the driver saw that it was what looked, in the darkness, like a removals van. Either that or—

He didn't have time to ponder the unlikely event of someone moving house at this time on a Saturday night because as he switched his gaze from the rear, he saw that the scene in front of him had changed dramatically in the brief instant he'd been distracted.

The bike rider was no longer lying in the road. He was no longer lifeless. He was on his feet. Any pleasure this gave the driver was more than outweighed by his dismay at the sight of the pistol the man was holding to his colleague's temple. The driver hit the alarm button. The wailing siren didn't seem to panic the biker, nor do much to excite the driver of the vehicle behind him.

The sound of that vehicle's engine made the driver look in his wing mirror. He saw the van swing out, obviously to overtake him. Meanwhile in the other mirror, he saw a lone figure collecting the battered motorbike and wheeling it along the road.

The scene was one of suspended animation apart from the moving vehicle. As it passed, the driver of the Guardwell van realized his guess had been wrong. It wasn't a furniture van. It looked more like a big cattle wagon. It passed the two men in the road before reversing towards the security van. The biker gestured him forward, reinforcing his message with the pistol. As he went to obey, he saw more men emerge from the cab of the wagon. Two of them lowered the tailboard, whilst another hurried past towards the man pushing the bike. All were dressed like the biker, even down to the helmets. Which made them totally unidentifiable.

Enough was enough; the driver, by now resigned to the hijacking, drove the security van forward as far as the ramp into the compartment usually reserved for the animals. He obeyed the signal to stop and applied the handbrake. One of the raiders appeared by his window, gesturing for him to get out. The futility of disobedience was emphasized by his colleague's keys, which the man dangled in one hand. More urgently, by the gun in his other.

As he climbed out of the cab, another man grabbed him and spun him round. His wrists were secured with duct tape, another piece was slapped none too gently over his mouth, before he was frog-marched towards a Transit van that had appeared seemingly from nowhere. As he went towards it, the driver saw more raiders pushing motorbikes towards the cattle truck. Then he was pushed inside the back of the Transit along with his colleague and a collection of diversion signs and temporary barriers. Nothing, it had seemed been left to chance. Although he was unable to see his watch, the driver guessed the whole operation had taken little more than five minutes. The only slight consolation the driver had in his misery was that the raiders had taken such trouble to remain anonymous. Surely, they wouldn't have done this had they intended to kill their hostages. Or was that wishful thinking?

The leader of the hijackers issued instructions to one of his men. 'As far as we know the jamming device worked, but we can't take that for granted. Drive the van inside the truck. You'll have to stay in the cab. Disable the GPS tracker. Look sharp about it.'

INSIDE THE CONTROL room of Guardwell Transport in Netherdale the radio operator was on his phone involved in losing a singularly pointless argument about his personal habits. The other protagonist, his long-term girlfriend, was protesting his habit of going out on Friday night and spending money they could ill afford on drink. Or as she put it, 'I'm sick and fed up of working all week to find the rent for this place, only to have you go out and piss the food money against the wall.'

As the debate, which was more of a monologue, grew

ever more heated his gaze, which had been concentrating on the bank of monitors and CCTV screens that surrounded him, flicked less frequently to the one to his right, a map-overlay that showed the position of their vans as tracked by the global positioning satellite beacon they all carried.

As it was, with only one van remaining out on the road involving a small rural pick up, it was scarcely priority to check the minute-by-minute progress of the vehicle.

Eventually, as she ran out of things to say, or more probably the breath to say them with, he seized the opportunity to begin the case for the defence. 'Look, I know I was late back last night, and I know I'd had too much to drink, but it's hardly fair to say I do that every week. Last night was a special occasion. It was Roy's birthday. You knew that before I went out. It's hardly like I was hiding it from you. We all had a bit too much, I admit, but I left ages before the others. I could hardly call in, have one drink, say Happy Birthday and walk out again, now could I?'

It appears he could, or so she thought. Her attempt to tell him so, cut short in full flow. 'Christ!' he yelled. 'Got to go! Emergency!'

He ended the call and flung his mobile on to the console. The Helmsdale/Bishopton van had disappeared off the screen. At first, he thought it might be the monitor playing up. He rebooted it, but with no success. He tried the radio. He called the van three times; his own voice, distorted by static hiss, was his sole reward.

Abandoning the attempt, he dialled his boss's home number. He got the voicemail. Trying the man's mobile gave him a similar result. He tried both numbers again, this time leaving messages. He was unsure what to do next. Their systems had been playing up recently, and he remembered there had been a few complaints recently about that particular van. Should he call the police? Thought of what would come down on his head if it were a false alarm unnerved him. Twice he picked up the phone; twice he replaced it. He glanced at the clock. He'd give it fifteen minutes. If he hadn't been able to raise his boss by then or hadn't been able to contact the van, then he'd ring the police.

In the meantime, he could call Good Buys in Bishopton. The van should have arrived, he guessed, if the manager could confirm it had then the panic would be over. He picked up his list of phone numbers. He had a frustratingly long wait before his call was answered. When it was, instead of the manager, he was only able to speak to a harassed sounding assistant, who promised she would get the manager to ring back if possible. Unwilling to settle for that, he asked if she could confirm seeing the van or any of their staff. She hadn't, but qualified the remark by saying she wouldn't be able to spot them from her position.

He watched the minutes tick by in a torment of doubt. He was about to ring the police when he was forestalled. The caller was the manager of Good Buys, who hadn't seen their van, and wanted to be off home, where were they? He was waiting to lock the store and wasn't at all happy at the delay.

Having fobbed him off, the radio controller was still unable to place his call as the phone rang again. This time it was his boss, who had at last picked up one of his messages. He came straight to the point, brutally so, demanding to know why the police hadn't already been called. Much put upon, the controller pointed out that if he'd had immediate guidance he would have done so. It probably wasn't going to make his career prospects any brighter, but he was past caring.

Ending the call, he immediately dialled 999. By the

time they took the call and acted on it, half an hour had passed since the security van had been hijacked. Two patrol cars were despatched with lights flashing and sirens wailing. They spent a further hour travelling at a variety of speeds up and down the full length of the Helmsdale to Bishopton road, the route the van would have taken. Their search was fruitless, because they were unaware of the temporary diversion, the signs for which were in the back of the Transit van together with the two kidnapped guards.

DC LISA ANDREWS was more than a little annoyed. Her plans for a romantic evening with her long-term boyfriend, Alan Marshall, were wrecked by the phone call. She listened to the reports from the traffic officers who had searched Bishopton Road as soon as she reached Netherdale station. The other officer who had been to Guardwell's depot was unable to give any more meaningful news about the disappearance of the van. He had been able to interview the company's managing director, who had informed him that the van would have been carrying something well over £½ million. Lisa whistled in surprise, so he explained what the director had told him. 'They're doing more collections per van on each trip. Cost cutting! They'd already been to a dozen sites. Bishopton was their final call. That's why there was so much money onboard.'

At that point, Lisa wisely decided more seniority on the case was called for. She dialled Mike Nash's number, and it wasn't until it went to voicemail that she remembered he was on leave. She muttered something decidedly unladylike and tried DS Mironova's mobile instead.

Clara had enjoyed her bath and had demolished the greater part of the dinner David had cooked. She was on the next to last forkful when her mobile rang. She checked the caller ID on her screen before she answered. 'Hello, Lisa. What's the problem, or are you just bored?'

Sutton watched his fiancée's expression change from relaxed, to tense, from astonishment to incredulity, before settling into a strange mixture of acceptance and disbelief. As she listened to the DC's explanation, apart from a series of grunts that might have signified yes or no, her only contribution was, 'I can't believe this. I don't remember breaking a mirror.' Eventually, Clara said, 'I'll join you as soon as I can get there. Give Pearce a bell, will you. I'll phone God. We need all hands on deck for this.'

When she'd finished, Clara stared across the table at Sutton, but David was well aware she wasn't looking at him, barely knew he was there. 'What is it?' he asked, 'What's happened?'

'That, David, is a bloody good question. I wish I knew. First, Vanda Dawson disappeared, probably kidnapped, possibly by a sadistic serial killer. Then we find out her husband has vanished without trace. He's supposed to be in Spain, but he could be anywhere. As if that wasn't enough for one day, we now seem to have mislaid a full-sized security van, complete with its two-man crew and the trifling sum of somewhere in excess of half a million pounds. Not bad in sixteen hours or so, don't you think? So, if you know what the hell is going on I wish you'd tell me because I have absolutely no idea. Unless Helmsdale has been twinned with the Bermuda Triangle, that is.'

CHIEF CONSTABLE O'DONNELL started the meeting promptly at 9 a.m. 'I take it there haven't been any further mysterious disappearances overnight?'

As the most senior of the trio of detectives there, Mironova answered her. She had never felt Nash's absence as keenly as she did at that moment. She felt exposed and realized how comforting it was having the cushion of a senior officer to report to. 'No, ma'am,' she replied. 'To be fair, I think at least one of the vanishing acts might have an innocent explanation, at least as far as criminal behaviour is concerned.' She noticed O'Donnell's frown and hastened to explain. 'Brian Dawson, the missing woman's husband. Although we can't find any evidence that he is golfing in Spain, which is where he's supposed to be from what his sister-in-law told us, that might have more to do with the state of the marriage than anything. We'll know for certain tomorrow.'

'It could mean he's implicated in his wife's disappearance, which would have very sinister connotations,' O'Donnell pointed out.

'Agreed, although I don't think it's likely.'

'Why not?'

'For one thing, he was well aware that Dr Grey was going to visit her sister this weekend. If he'd been intending to harm his wife I believe he'd have chosen a time when she wouldn't be missed as quickly. In addition to that, he wouldn't have needed to break a pane of glass in the back door to get into the house; he'd have a key. I know he might have faked it to look like a break-in, but he certainly wouldn't have needed to eradicate the fingerprints.'

'Sorry, you've lost me,' the chief constable said.

'The forensic team found that the fingerprints had been wiped from every surface in the ground floor of the house. They believe whoever did that used antiseptic wipes. Dawson wouldn't have done that. His prints had every right to be there.'

'That makes sense. So, where do we go from here?'

'I'm afraid we ought to consider the possibility that this is another of the Cremator's abductions. From what little I know about those cases, which is no more than has appeared in the press, it seems to fit the general pattern.'

The chief constable winced. 'I was afraid you might say that. I suppose we should consider ourselves lucky that he hasn't struck round here before. Has anyone got any alternative theories?'

Her question was greeted with silence. 'In that case I'll make it a priority to request copies of the case notes from the various forces involved.' She turned to Viv. 'DC Pearce, as our resident computer expert, will you download all the stuff that's on the PNC about the incidents. I believe there have been four, or else five.'

Pearce nodded his agreement and the chief constable continued, 'Maybe if we all look through the notes on each case we might come up with something that will lead us to this pervert before he can harm another victim. I certainly hope so. It doesn't help that it's likely to be tomorrow at the very earliest before the hard copies get here. That makes the computer files even more important.'

O'Donnell turned over a sheet of paper. 'Now, let's turn our attention to the case of the vanishing van. Lisa, will you tell me precisely what happened yesterday evening?'

DC Andrews related the events. When she'd finished, the chief constable said, 'I think the fact that the GPS tracker was disabled is highly significant. This doesn't sound like a set of amateurs. To me this looks like the work of a really professional outfit. I think it might be worth checking to see if there is any intelligence on the subject. Try the Major Crimes Unit first. Then have a word with Scotland Yard. If one of the big mobs has started operating in our area we've got to put paid to it immediately. Have you found out how much the van was carrying?'

'Just over six-hundred-thousand pounds,' Andrews said quietly. 'I had the MD of the security company phone all the clients where that van collected. It took him most of the night. The reason for the larger than normal amount, was twofold. One, Guardwell Transport has been laying men off and reducing their fleet size, so each van makes more collections. Two, there were very few collections on Friday because of the storm. A lot of retailers rang in to say they'd taken in so little that day they hadn't reached their insurance ceilings.'

Lisa noticed Pearce's puzzled frown. 'That's the maximum they can keep on the premises allowed by their insurance policy. If they go over that, the insurance company can disallow the claim if they are robbed.'

'Any thought that this might be an inside job? You mentioned that Guardwell are pulling their horns in. Does that mean the company's in trouble?'

'According to the Managing Director, things certainly aren't going well,' Lisa agreed. 'His comment was that with the recession, competition is savage, with everyone chasing a reduced amount of business. He said their actions were a prudent response to the state of the economy, which I took to mean desperate measures to stay afloat. As I see it, there are three possibilities to consider. One, that the MD has orchestrated this to raise desperately needed capital. Two, that the crew of the van are implicated, either acting alone or as part of a larger unit, or three, that it might be down to one or more ex-employees. They'd have a double axe to grind. Revenge plus gain: two very powerful motives.'

'There is a fourth alternative,' O'Donnell pointed out. 'That it is a totally outside job, organized and carried out by a set of professional criminals. Apart from the question of who did it, the other thing we need to find out is how. This is a supposedly totally secure vehicle on a lightly used road at a time on a Saturday night when there would be little, if any, other traffic about. So, any ideas how they did it? The first question I need answering is, what about this GPS tracker? What's the technology like? Is it possible to pinpoint the location of the vehicle when it was disabled? And how difficult is it to do that?'

'I've looked into that already, ma'am,' Pearce told her.

'Unfortunately, the system isn't the most sophisticated on the market. In fact, it's one of the very earliest models, which means it isn't that accurate. Nor did the manufacturers think it necessary to be too cunning when it came to protecting the tracker. I assume they thought it would be quite secure where they sited it. But once someone has access to the vehicle cab it would only take a few minutes to put it out of action.'

'Thanks, Viv, you're really cheering me up,' O'Donnell retorted. 'Did you think to check the MO out on the computer?'

'I did, ma'am. I widened the parameters not concentrating wholly on security vans, but there's nothing similar recorded.'

'How about this business of the radio not working?'

'There again,' Pearce told her. 'I had a look at the equipment they use: not brilliant. It might have developed a fault, but that seems a bit too much of a coincidence. Alternatively, if someone was close enough to the van they could jam the signal so that all the crew or their control room would hear would be static.'

'I think our first priority is to investigate the inside connection. Make that your priority for today. I'll talk to other forces, MCU and the Met about the gang theory. I suggest that unless anything crops up beforehand we meet again tomorrow at 9 a.m. By that time Nash should be back.' O'Donnell paused for a moment. 'I learned on Friday who your new superintendent will be. In view of what has happened, I've asked them to take up their post immediately. They should be available from Wednesday.' She looked up, noting their slightly apprehensive expressions. 'I realize you want to know who it is, but you'll have to wait. Seniority gives Nash the right to be the one to tell you.'

EIGHT

As SOON AS Nash reached the CID suite he knew something serious must have happened during his absence. Nothing trivial would have brought the chief constable from Netherdale at this time on a Monday morning. The presence of DC Andrews, also a rare visitor to Helmsdale, merely confirmed his suspicion.

The first part of the meeting was spent updating Nash on what had gone on over the weekend. The chief constable began with the security van hijack. Despite the cooperation of Scotland Yard and the Major Crimes Unit, she told them there was nothing to suggest that known organized crime gangs were operating in their region.

Nash's contribution was immediate and positive. After listening to O'Donnell relating the events of Saturday night, he turned to DC Andrews. 'How many patrol cars went out?'

'Two, one from here and a second from Bishopton,' Lisa said.

'And how long after the van disappeared was it before our cars went looking for it?'

Lisa consulted her notes. 'About forty minutes after the controller spotted it was missing from his screen.'

Nash shook his head in disbelief and walked over to the area map on the wall. 'Going from the time that van made its collection at Good Buys in Helmsdale they should have reached somewhere around this point.' He indicated a spot more than halfway to Bishopton. 'That means the hijackers would still have to be somewhere along the Bishopton to Helmsdale road when our patrol cars started searching it. But the officers reported very little traffic, only a couple of saloon cars. So, if they hadn't got time to get clear, where did they go?'

'That's what we've been trying to work out,' Mironova said. 'Are you suggesting they went the other way, towards Bishopton? Is that your theory?'

'No. Why would they go that way?'

'Sorry, Mike, you're not making sense,' the chief constable's tone was impatient, waspish even.

'The road leads to Bishopton and Bishop's Cross, nowhere else. I don't think they'd risk going into what is effectively a bottleneck. They sound far too professional an outfit to chance trapping themselves like that.'

'All right, mastermind, you tell us where they did go.' This time there was no disguising the irritation in O'Donnell's voice. 'Or are you suggesting the van was abducted by aliens? Should we be looking for reports of UFO sightings?'

'What I'm suggesting is that they weren't on that road at all.'

There was a moment's silence before O'Donnell said, 'So where were they? On the M25?'

Nash grinned. 'Look at it from the gang's point of view. They need to complete the hijack with the minimum risk of being disturbed. They also want the vehicle to disappear without trace. However, the van has radio communication with a central control room, plus an onboard GPS tracker. The first thing they must do is disable the radio. There are two ways they could do that. Either with the cooperation of someone on the inside, or by the use of a jamming device. Of the two, I'd go for the second option. An extra man means more chance of discovery, particularly as they'd know we were bound to check out everyone at the security firm. Added to which an extra man means less of a share for the others.'

'All right, I accept that, but why didn't our patrol cars see anything?'

'Because I think they were looking in the wrong place.' Nash noticed the others looking at one another, obviously mystified. He pointed to a junction halfway along Bishopton Road. 'Call it luck if you want, but I know that area quite well. Last summer I took Daniel on a few outings around there, when we were getting to know one another. I wanted to show him some of our lovely scenery. That fork leads to Wintersett village. However, if you follow that road, it eventually winds over Black Fell and down the other side to Bishop's Cross and ends up in Bishopton. It's a heck of a long way round, and nobody in their right mind would opt to go that way normally. However, if you had to get to Bishopton, and you had no other choice, you could use that road.'

'How would they convince the crew of the van to take that road, unless they were in on the robbery?' Clara asked.

'There is a way,' Nash told her. 'I'm guessing, but after the recent weather I think it's credible. All they would need is some form of diversion. As soon as the van took the Wintersett road, they come along and remove the evidence. By the time our officers went past, there would be nothing to suggest the van hadn't continued on the main road to Bishopton. Once they'd got the van where they wanted it, all they had to do was arrange something to get the van to stop. How they got the crew out is another matter, possibly they were in on the robbery, possibly they were threatened. Once the gang had access to the interior, it would be the work of minutes to disable the GPS tracker. I think we ought to search the Wintersett road. It's a bit late in the day now, but we might find something. If we can establish which way they went we might be able to discover where they've secreted the van, and what has happened to the crew.'

It was Mironova who told Nash about Vanda Dawson's suspected abduction. Nash listened in silence until she'd finished. 'So, in the space of a weekend, a woman's been kidnapped, her husband has vanished and a security van with two guards inside has gone missing,' he commented ruefully. 'I'm bloody glad I didn't go away for a fortnight.'

'Where do you plan to start?' O'Donnell asked.

'I think I'll go to the missing woman's house, have a look round there and then talk to her sister,' Nash said thoughtfully. 'We ought to continue trying to locate Dawson. If Tom finds he didn't go to Spain, we must assume he's still in this country.' He turned to Clara. 'Dr Grey told you he's an accountant. Does he work from home, or has he an office here, or in Netherdale?'

'I didn't think to ask,' Mironova confessed. Why hadn't she asked? It was the one question she'd missed, the first thing Nash had pinpointed.

'Find out, will you? And let Viv know.' Nash turned to Pearce. 'Viv, if Dawson does have an office, go and ask if anyone's seen him recently, or knows where he can be located. I'd also like to have a look at those files when they arrive. If this is a Cremator abduction, we all need to study them, see if we can spot anything that might help. Will you man the fort here, and I'll take Clara with me? I'll check the Wintersett road after I've been to Dawson's house.'

The chief nodded her approval and indicated to Nash she wished to speak to him in his office.

On his return, Nash and Clara headed for the car park. 'Do you want me to collect Dr Grey?' Clara asked.

Nash looked up in mild surprise. 'I suppose that would be best,' he replied after a moment's thought. 'To speak to her at the house, I mean, rather than in her hotel. Then you can drive her back. I want to see if I can find any evidence of this van hijack.'

'I've also had an idea,' Clara said. 'As you'll be on your own with Daniel away, I thought the flat might feel a bit lonely and cooking for one isn't much fun. So David and I wondered if you'd like to come round to our place this evening?'

'That's really considerate, Clara, but the way things have been happening round here, let's wait and see what develops during the course of the day.'

IN DAYLIGHT, MILL Cottage looked to be a truly impressive property. Not only the house itself, but the nearby mill and the extensive grounds added to what was a highly valuable residence. Nash looked at the white Tudor walls with their blackened timber crosspieces with admiration. He wondered if they were original, or a later replica. It didn't matter, certainly not to the onlooker. The cottage was a long, low building. He stared at it appreciatively. When the time came for him to settle down it was the sort of house he had always dreamed of owning. Now he had Daniel to consider, that prospect was even more appealing. Somewhere like this would be the ideal place for them. Here, he could ensure peace from the stresses of his job, and here Daniel could grow up in safe and peaceful surroundings.

Nash shook his head to rid himself of the daydream. He culled the description of the interior from his memory of Mironova's report. Having got his bearings, Nash's gaze shifted to the bank of mature woodland that covered the far side of the stream. There was a narrow walkway across the water, too narrow to be classed as a footbridge. He guessed that its principal purpose was to house a sluice gate that would regulate the flow of water entering the millrace. Could the missing woman have fallen in the stream? Nash wondered if that had been checked out, and made a mental note to ask Clara. He turned his attention to the mill itself, and his memory shifted back to his school days. One wet summer afternoon, when bad weather had caused the cancellation of all cricket. A substituted history lesson had been rescued from boredom when the master had arrived bearing a sliced loaf and a block of butter. Having doled out slices to the ever-hungry boys, he commenced teaching them about the workings of the corn mill and butter churn that had processed many of the ingredients of the food they were devouring with all the appetite and lack of social grace only a group of twelve-year-olds can muster. Nash smiled, wondering if Daniel would be as fortunate in the quality of his teachers.

He walked across the paved patio area in front of the cottage and climbed the four shallow steps that led up to the long front lawn. This was flanked on three sides by rustic fences to which the stems of roses, bare at this time of the year, were clinging. This would be a beautiful garden in summer, Nash thought. He turned to view the rest of the grounds. The different angle showed him how steeply the land fell towards the stream, a fact that wasn't apparent from the rear of the building. Ideal, Nash thought, remembering that history lesson, for the construction of a corn mill.

A flash of movement to the left of his peripheral vision announced the arrival of Mironova and Dr Grey. Nash strolled round the end of the house to meet them. He looked in appreciation at the doctor's attractive features and shapely figure, a fact that didn't escape his sergeant.

Clara introduced Nash to the missing woman's sister.

'This is a bad business,' Nash told her as they shook hands. 'Hardly the weekend you were hoping for, I'm afraid.'

'There's still no news, I take it? Sergeant Mironova said there hadn't been any developments.'

'That's true, but it isn't necessarily a bad thing.' Which wasn't accurate, because Nash knew that in cases such as this the first few hours were critical; and at least three days had passed without any activity.

'Have you managed to locate Brian yet?'

Nash shook his head. 'It would help if we had a mobile phone number for him. Do you know if he has one?'

'I'm sure he does, but I've no idea what the number is.' She smiled faintly. 'We were never that close. I told Sergeant Mironova he has an office, but it isn't in his own name.' Jo frowned, trying to remember. 'Vanda did tell me the name once. He took over an old-established practice, one that had a settled clientele and he thought it would be better if he kept the name, which was well known locally. It's somewhere on Helmsdale High Street, I think. I believe...' she frowned as she tried to remember, 'Vanda told me it was next door to a place where the owner got in some sort of trouble, but I can't remember what she said.'

Nash glanced at Mironova. 'I've already given Viv the directions,' Clara told him.

'Did anyone think to check the stream on Saturday?'

Clara nodded. 'Viv did it whilst he was waiting for forensics to finish. He walked a mile or so downstream, but couldn't find anything.'

'Have you got the keys? I want to take a look inside.'

As soon as he was inside the building, Nash walked through to the hall and picked up the morning's post.

Jo eyed the bundle of envelopes he was holding, her expression apprehensive. She had read the news reports, worked out the similarity between her sister's disappearance and other cases and knew the significance of the detective's action. 'Is there anything in those?' she asked fearfully.

'Nothing to interest us,' Nash reassured her.

There was nothing threatening, unless the council tax bill sent by Netherdale District Council could be construed as a threat. Apart from that, the mail was typical of a Monday morning delivery. Flyers from Good Buys supermarket, a leaflet advertising a satellite TV and broadband package, and a warning that a furniture company's sale was due to end soon. Nash sniffed in disbelief at that statement.

Nash's tour of inspection didn't take long. He withstood the parrot's shock greeting, and the phone imitation which immediately preceded it, having been forewarned about the bird by Mironova's report. He listened to the African Grey's repetitive questioning for a few moments. 'Who are you?' the bird asked, time after time.

'You've both heard that before,' Nash turned to Clara and Jo in turn. 'Notice anything about it?'

'Such as?' Clara asked.

'The bird doesn't understand the meaning of the words. All he can do is mimic sounds he's heard and stored in his memory.'

'What's your point, Mike?'

'The ringing phone stops abruptly, as if it's either been answered, or—'

'Or the line's been cut?'

'Exactly. And the way the bird says, "Who are you?" That sounds almost as if he's scared, but look at him.'

They stared at the African Grey, who was preening his feathers, whilst continuing the refrain.

'What you're saying is, whoever the bird picked that expression up from was afraid?'

'I think we need to check the phone theory out. Clara, will you get on to the phone company and find out if there was an incoming call to this number at about the time you guessed Mrs Dawson was abducted, a call that wasn't answered, because, I guess, the line was cut by the kidnapper.'

'I'll get on it as soon as we're back in Helmsdale.'

Before they left, Dr Grey fed the parrot and replenished its water bowl. Nash watched approvingly. 'I don't want our only potential witness to keel over from neglect.'

As Jo returned to the kitchen to replace the bird food, Nash told Clara, 'I'm going to see if I can find anything that might prove or disprove my theory about the van hijack. I'll meet you back at the office, unless I find anything interesting on the Wintersett road.'

As they stepped outside, they heard the sound of a vehicle engine accompanied by an audible reversing alarm. They hurried to the corner of the cottage where they were able to see the orange flashing beacons on the roof of the vehicle cab. It looked, Nash thought, like one of those dust-carts he remembered from his youth. As it drew closer, moving slowly down the narrow lane, he realized his guess had been accurate. The local authority had obviously opted for the style of wagon they had used in years gone by, with curved apertures to place the refuse in situated behind the cab. The light commercial would be ideal for a single operative, which would represent a cost saving to the local authority. Nash wondered briefly if that had been the deciding factor in their choice.

The sight of the council wagon gave Nash an idea. 'Make a list of all regular visitors to the house,' he told Clara. 'Start with the bin-man.'

'Any particular reason?'

'If this turns out to be an abduction, unless it was totally random we should work on the principle that who-ever's responsible knew Mrs Dawson. That could mean someone at the bank, a supermarket checkout operator or one of the students in her evening classes. It might be a member of the library staff or'—Nash pointed to the wagon driver, who had emerged from his cab—'someone with a valid reason for calling at Mill Cottage regularly, like this guy.'

'We don't know Vanda Dawson attended evening classes,' Mironova objected.

'Precisely my point. I was using it as an example. We don't know anything about Vanda Dawson's life, about her habits, her daily routines, anything. Obviously, the person who could fill in some of the gaps would be her husband. Which brings me back to the question, where the hell is Dawson?'

As he was speaking, Nash approached the driver. He was broad in stature with a mop of thinning fair hair and a ruddy complexion. More like a farmer than a council worker, Nash thought. He looked mildly surprised, no more, when Nash showed his warrant card.

'Is this your usual round?' Nash began.

The driver nodded. 'Has been for the last three years.'

'It must be hard graft on your own.'

The driver grinned. 'Tell my bosses that, will you.' He winked. 'At least I've nobody looking over my shoulder. As long as I get all my collections done in the allotted time, I'm in the clear. I know the area like the back of my hand now so it gives me a bit of leeway for an extended lunch break.'

Nash asked the man's name, and commented on the fact that he wasn't wearing an identity badge.

'My name's Potter. Vic Potter. We're not allowed to wear badges. Health and Safety regulations, would you believe? One of our men cut his finger when a bag he was tossing into the wagon snagged on his badge. It went septic and he lost the finger. He was off work for a long time and the council had to fork out a huge sum in compensation. The ink on the cheque hadn't dried before a directive banning badges came out. There's a photo ID badge in the cab somewhere, but everyone knows me by now so I'd only need it if someone new moved in. And that doesn't happen often, the sort of places I collect from.'

'Do you always collect here on Monday?'

'Only during the winter months. End of April on, when the summer schedule starts, then it's a Tuesday. My area extends over past Wintersett to Bishop's Cross and the villages around Bishopton. That includes those two big caravan parks the other side of Bishopton. It's no bobby's job in summer, I can tell you. No offence meant,' he added with a smile. 'What's this about, anyway? Has something happened? I hope nothing's happened to Mrs Dawson.'

'You know her, then?'

'Not very well. She's usually about when I collect, but I don't always see her. She makes a point of being in at Christmas though, and she's a very generous tipper. Is that it? Has something happened to her?'

'We're not sure. She's been reported missing, but there could be an innocent explanation. Have you noticed anything unusual on your round in the last few weeks? Around here, I mean. Any strange vehicles, anyone without an obvious reason to be here hanging around the place?'

Potter scratched his chin thoughtfully. 'Can't say that I have,' he said after a while.

'Have you ever seen anyone visiting the house? They'd have had to use a car to get here, it being so remote.'

Potter shook his head. 'Sorry, I haven't seen anyone.

And I'd have noticed a vehicle, because there isn't that much room to manoeuvre my wagon.'

'Thanks, I'll let you get on your way. One more thing, though. Don't collect the rubbish today. It might need checking by our forensic officers. Besides which, it won't come to any harm leaving it until next week the way the weather is.'

Jo WAITED FOR Mironova to lock up at the cottage. 'I've requested a local joiner be arranged to come out today to fix that broken pane in the door,' Clara told her. 'We would normally have had someone on watch, but with the weather problems there's been no one to spare; damned cutbacks! Until it's secure, and until there's someone inside the house, it's very vulnerable out here.'

'I was thinking about that earlier,' Jo agreed. 'I wonder if I ought to move in here for the time being? We've no indication when Brian might turn up, and as you say, the place is open to any sort of burglar or tramp unless someone's in residence.'

Jo fought shy of the implication that Vanda wouldn't be able to return. By now, all hope that her absence might have had an innocent explanation had gone.

'Are you sure you'd be OK with that? Given what's happened, a lot of women wouldn't come near the place.'

Jo didn't smile, but her expression lightened a little. 'I'm not claiming to be particularly brave,' she admitted. 'But the chances of anything untoward happening a second time are more remote even than this cottage.'

'In any case, with luck Dawson might turn up, and it might not be necessary,' Mironova pointed out.

NINE

In the High Street, Pearce followed Clara's directions. He saw the accountant's brass plate attached to the brickwork alongside a door that appeared to give access to the upper floor of the terraced property. The ground floor was occupied by a shop; the fascia covered with what appeared to be a brand new sign, TOP RANKING POSTERS. Below the name, in slightly smaller lettering, it declared, 'The Home of TENNIS GIRL and hundreds of other iconic images'.

The shop window contained a display that included the famous picture of the girl in the tennis dress, plus T-shirts, and on the base, an array of key rings, badges, fobs and other trinkets designed to lure the cash from the pockets of Helmsdale's stream of tourists.

He smiled at the mildly suggestive message conveyed by two T-shirts that were pinned side by side on a flannel-board. 'Want it now?' one asked. The second provided the explanation, 'On the spot printing at unbeatable prices.'

Pearce tried the accountant's door. Predictably, it was locked. He paused, irresolute. He wandered up and down the street a few times, before making his mind up. He was unaware that his presence had been noted and was being remarked upon.

Inside the shop, the proprietor watched Pearce walking to and fro. He glanced round. The only customers were a young couple browsing a catalogue of posters. As they turned to leave, he picked up the phone. 'Tony? It's Jerry, I have company; a bloke in a blue suit is outside. He seems to be taking an interest in us. Hang on; he's coming inside. I'll call you back.'

The shopkeeper smiled at the newcomer. 'Good morning. Can I help you?'

Pearce produced his warrant card.

'There's nothing wrong, I hope?' The proprietor looked suitably concerned.

Viv smiled reassuringly. It was a natural reaction, one he'd become accustomed to. The most innocent of citizens tended to think the worst when confronted by a detective. 'Nothing to worry about,' he told the man. 'I'm trying to locate Mr Dawson, that's all.'

The shopkeeper frowned. 'Mr...?'

'Dawson, Brian Dawson. He owns the accountancy firm. Their offices are upstairs, above the shop,' Pearce explained.

'Oh, I see. Sorry to appear so dim, but I only moved in here a few weeks back, and I'm still finding my feet, so to speak. I decided to invest my redundancy in a little business. I'd already been trading on the internet and doing mail order, so when this lease came up I took the plunge. Haven't made my fortune yet.' He grimaced.

'Anyway, I hardly know the neighbours thus far. I've seen the chap you mean, or at least I suppose it's him, but I've never spoken to him. Just noticed him going in and out, that's all.'

'Can you remember when it was you last saw him?'

The shopkeeper puffed out his cheeks in an effort to think. 'Early last week maybe; or the back end of the week before. Sorry to be so vague. Has he done something wrong?'

That was the other reaction Pearce had become used to. Once they got over their nervousness, people were intrigued, wanting to learn the latest gossip. A nation of scandalmongers, he thought. He smiled at the man. 'Not that I'm aware of. We're anxious to speak to him, that's all. We did hear he might have gone abroad, but his wife has missed an appointment and her sister's a little concerned. Nothing too scandalous. Anyway, if you do see him, would you ask him to call me?' He dug a card out of his wallet and passed it over the counter. 'Sorry, can I take your name, Mr. . . ?'

'Freeman, Jerry Freeman.' The shopkeeper took the card; fingered the corner. 'I'm thinking of starting to produce these, so if you or any of your colleagues want some printing, let me know. And if I do see Mr Dawson I'll be sure to give him your message.'

He watched Pearce leave the shop before strolling casually to the window. When he was certain the detective was out of sight, he returned to the counter and picked up the phone again. 'It was Dawson they were after,' he told the person on the other end of the line. 'No, not according to this guy'—he glanced down—'name's DC Pearce. Said something about Dawson's wife going AWOL, so on the face of it nothing to do with us. What do you want me to do?'

He listened for a few minutes. 'I agree, Tony, no point in panicking. I'll check things out upstairs, though.'

The shopkeeper put the phone down and returned to the front of the shop. After five minutes inspecting the High Street, he was satisfied. When he was sure such activity as there was held no threat, he took a bunch of keys from his pocket and went out in to the street. He looked to the left, then to the right, before opening the adjacent door; closed it behind him and sprinted upstairs. He wanted this task over with so he could get back in the shop unnoticed. He wasn't at all worried about leaving the shop unattended. The till had only a few pounds in it, and such display stock as there was didn't amount to much either. What he was after here, however, was worth a whole lot more.

ONLY A FEW miles from where Vanda Dawson was being held, Tony pondered the police activity. He stood up from his desk and walked across the small office he was using and opened the door. 'Get Dawson in here,' he told the man waiting outside.

When the accountant appeared a few minutes later, Dawson was surprised by the man's opening question.

'Why are the police at your office?'

Dawson blinked. 'What?'

'The police were at Jerry's shop a few minutes ago asking questions about you. Something to do with your wife, or at least that's what they said. What's going on?' As he spoke, Tony was watching Dawson closely and saw the colour drain from his face.

'I don't know. I've no idea. What did they say?'

Tony repeated what he'd been told. 'Has your wife buggered off? Or is it something worse?'

'I haven't a clue.'

'Did you make any excuses for why you'd be away?'

'I told her I was going to Spain on a golfing trip.'

'They obviously don't think you're there, otherwise they wouldn't be checking up on you at your office. I think you'd better get this sorted out. Have you an alternative cover story? One they'll believe?'

Dawson nodded. 'I've just about finished here anyway. All you have to do when I've tied the last few bits down is follow the instructions I leave.'

When the accountant had gone Tony turned to his colleague.

'What do you make of that?'

'I don't like the sound of it. Dawson's a shifty bastard.

I wouldn't trust him. Put pressure on him and he might spill the beans. It's a hell of a risk letting him out of our sight with the police noseying around.'

'On the other hand we don't want them to come looking for him. We could hide him all right, but his car's a real giveaway. And don't try telling me we've hidden a security van, there's no room for another vehicle in the bunker. Which reminds me, we'll have to move that soon.'

His colleague grinned. 'And there was me planning a vehicle hire business. I take your point, but I still think it's risky.'

'That's why I want Dawson followed and watched. When he leaves here, you go after him. Report back on his movements, any visitors he gets, anybody he talks to. I'll arrange with the others to relieve you, all right?'

'What if it looks as if the police are going to take him in for questioning?'

Tony slid his forefinger across his throat. 'I take it you can manage that?'

His colleague smiled. 'I think I'll be able to cope.'

THE ACCOUNTANT'S WHEREABOUTS were uppermost in Nash's mind as he drove towards Wintersett. Had they leapt to the wrong conclusion about Vanda Dawson's disappearance? The circumstances surrounding it were so much like those in the Cremator cases that it was natural to assume this was another attack by the notorious serial killer.

On the other hand, perhaps that was what they had been expected to think. Wouldn't it have been natural, if Dawson had intended to harm his wife, to design her disappearance to look like the work of the Cremator? Police forces in the areas where the maniac had struck were stretched almost to breaking point owing to their total lack of progress. To add to their problems, the media had latched on to the case with a kind of hysterical feeding frenzy.

Nash had to assume that Dawson was an intelligent man who would know that unless he was able to come up with a convincing cover story and alibi for the period since his wife's disappearance, he would automatically become their prime suspect. With the passage of time, the odds were that Vanda Dawson had come to harm. And Nash knew from experience that after four days, the chances of finding her alive had diminished almost to zero. Sadly, no other explanation fitted the facts. But, if Dawson wasn't involved where had he vanished to? And, if he wasn't involved in his wife's abduction…? That was a road Nash wasn't prepared to go down: not at this stage. Yet it seemed as if he might be forced along it. It was an odd outcome, that the key to discovering what had happened to Vanda Dawson might lie with her husband's disappearance.

Nash travelled along Bishopton Road until he reached the turning that was signposted for Wintersett. He pulled the Range Rover on to the verge just before the junction and got out. He inspected the road surface before examining the verges. As far as he could judge, there appeared to be nothing out of the ordinary. If anything had happened here, the evidence had been removed without a trace.

He got back in the car and started towards Wintersett. From the elevated driving position of the Range Rover he was just able to see one or two of the roofs of the houses in the village. However, his attention was fixed for the most part on the view closer to hand. He was driving so slowly he would have collected a following of irate drivers had he been on a more popular route. The country lane was too narrow to allow for overtaking except in one or two places, but fortunately it was so little frequented that his only spectators were a posse of heavily pregnant ewes.

The heavy rain of the previous week had left the grass verges very soft. Nash had travelled almost half the distance from the junction towards the village when he noticed a spot on the opposite side of the road where the grass had been chewed up, obviously by the wheels of a heavy vehicle. This might have been caused by two large vehicles, say a van and a tractor, meeting at that point and striving to avoid contact. However, there was a designated passing place only a few yards away. Under normal circumstances, Nash might have dismissed the sight as evidence of no more than two drivers either too impatient to wait or too lazy to reverse, but with nothing else by way of evidence to back up his theory as to what had happened, he felt this merited a closer look.

The weather had improved and it was now a bright, sunny day, although one that promised frost later. The low winter sun came to Nash's assistance as he climbed out of the car. Almost immediately, he noticed that the rays had picked up something that sparkled, reflecting the brightness. It looked as if the reflection was being caused by a small piece of glass or plastic that was lying in the mud at the edge of the road on the nearside of his car. Nash walked over and peered at the spot.

Sure enough, the sun was catching a small piece of broken glass, one of several strewn there. Obviously, they had not been there long, certainly not before the rain, which would have covered them in mud reducing their brightness. Nash took a pen from his pocket. Uttering a silent plea for forgiveness to the Sheaffer pen company, he used it to turn the largest piece of glass over. It was just big enough for him to see the pattern on the reverse. Obviously, what he was looking at was a broken lens from a vehicle headlight or spotlight. Nash wondered if the chunk was enough for the forensic people to identify the type of vehicle that had shed it.

From his stooping position, he was able to get a better view of the road surface than would have been possible from standing. As he looked along the lane, he could see a faint discolouration in the grey tarmac and what looked like scratch marks. Whether he would have noticed these had he been upright, he wasn't sure. He moved closer and was able to confirm his first impression. Something had either slid or been pulled along the road surface, something heavy and solid enough to scratch the surface and leave what looked to be red paint.

These two scraps of evidence might have absolutely nothing to do with the hijacking of the security van, but as Nash looked further along the road, he saw another, larger stain. This had dried to a dark brown. With his experience in such matters, Nash had a fair idea what substance had been spilt at this point. Blood.

Here again, this might have been caused by nothing more sinister than road-kill, or a fox dragging his supper towards his lair. However, the hungriest carrion would have left fur, feather or bones, as would even the most voracious fox. Putting all three together, Nash reckoned he had come across the most likely position for the van to be ambushed. He looked round at the surrounding countryside. It was almost perfect for the purpose. He had been on the road for over twenty-five minutes. It was early afternoon. During that time, he hadn't seen another vehicle coming from either direction. In addition, the road here dipped into a hollow concealing whatever might have happened from anyone except those close to the action. There were no houses, not even a farmhouse, within sight. Even the highest roofs of Wintersett village were no longer visible.

He might be summoning a forensic officer to a wild goose chase, but Nash couldn't afford to do otherwise. At least, he thought with a smile as he returned to the car to retrieve his mobile, they were in the right sort of terrain for such a chase. He phoned Helmsdale station and explained to Mironova what he wanted.

She rang back a few minutes later to tell him an officer was en route; then passed him over to Pearce. Viv related his lack of success at Dawson's office before ending the call. Nash looked at the dashboard clock. He reckoned it would be at least half an hour before the officer arrived. He leaned back in the driver's seat and pondered the two cases that had hit their tiny force over the weekend, striving to find something he could use as a starting point for his investigation. With the abduction, the answer might be with the missing woman's husband. As far as the security van robbery was concerned, all they had was the possible evidence on the road in front of him. Where the van and its crew had vanished to remained a mystery. Although this road was little used, the gang who hijacked it couldn't have been sure they wouldn't be spotted. How had they prepared for that? What had they planned to ensure the security van disappeared?

His daydream ended when he saw a vehicle approaching him from the direction of Helmsdale. It proved to be the forensic officer, the telltale blue, yellow and white livery of the CSI van being distinguishable even at a long distance. Nash smiled, remembering someone describing it as looking like an explosion in a paint factory. He got out to greet his colleague and explained the situation. He pointed out the various scraps of possible evidence and waited as the man retrieved his kit from the back of the van.

As he did so, Nash heard the sound of another vehicle approaching, this time from the direction of Wintersett.

He watched with increasing concern as a Range Rover similar to his own hurtled over the brow of the hill. The car was being driven with all the determination, but none of the skill, of a Formula 1 competitor.

As the vehicle neared them, Nash noticed that his colleague had stopped what he was doing and was watching with even more apprehension. That would be because he was nearer. At that moment, the vehicle's brakes were applied with such ferocity that the car rocked on its axles. Despite its weight, Nash was worried it might go over. Seconds later, it juddered to a halt, emitting clouds of smoke from under the wheel arches. The vehicle had barely stopped its forward motion and was still shivering to a standstill when the driver emerged. For a second, Nash wondered if the car had been fitted with a James Bond style ejector seat. As he darted forward, Nash saw that the driver was in late middle age, and that his face was a shade best described as apoplectic purple.

'You're the police?'

Nash nodded, uncertain whether this was a question or a statement.

'Good! Saved me a journey! Want to report a crime! Serious one! Bloody vandals! What name?'

It appeared as if the man spoke much as he drove. Nash pieced the fractured sentences together and responded. 'Detective Inspector Nash. What's the problem?'

'Problem! More than a problem! Bloody outrage! Some bastard's wrecked one of my wagons! Joyriders, I expect! Damned scoundrels! Should be horsewhipped!'

Nash was intrigued. He had some difficulty in masking a smile. He hadn't heard the words 'scoundrel' or 'horse-whipped' for a long time. 'Sorry,' he said, his tone placating, 'what's your name?'

'What? Oh, yes. Cryer. Archie Cryer. I farm over there.'

Cryer waved a hand in a gesture that appeared to include a large chunk of the county plus substantial bits of Lancashire and Cumbria. 'I also transport livestock.'

'Right, when you say someone vandalized one of your wagons, exactly what have they done to it?'

'We've been away. Only time of the year to take a break. Had nobody wanting beasts moved so we slipped off to Spain for a week. Got back first thing this morning. Noticed immediately the wagon had been moved. Opened it up and looked inside. The buggers only dismantled all the partitions. Why the hell they've done that, can't begin to imagine.'

'You're certain the vehicle was moved?'

'Damned right I am. Left it parked in the corner of the yard. Always do. Thing was ten feet at least from where I left it.'

'How did they get it started?'

The farmer's expression changed from outrage to mild embarrassment. 'Ah, well, thing is,' he cleared his throat. 'We always leave the keys hanging in the porch. Farm's so remote we've never had any bother. Until now, that is.'

'Have you any idea when this happened?'

'No, they could have done it anytime after we left. So that gave them eight days. Thing is, it would have taken more than one person. Those units are bloody strong. Have to be to cope with the beasts we carry.'

'Who knew you'd be away?'

'Half the ruddy county, I expect. There was a big article about me in the *Netherdale Gazette* a few weeks back. It mentioned that we were going away. What you going to do about it, eh?'

'As soon as we've finished here, I'll bring our forensic man along and we'll give your wagon a good once-over. Please don't touch anything until we've checked it out.'

Nash watched the farmer reverse into a nearby gateway before returning towards Wintersett. The short conversation seemed to have calmed his fury, judging by the less violent style of driving. Although Nash hadn't told Cryer so, he had a shrewd idea why the vandals had damaged the wagon. The accuracy of his guess would be confirmed once he saw the vehicle.

As he waited for the forensic man to complete his work, Nash pondered the way the robbery of the security van had been conducted. The cash element intrigued him. It was a large amount, large enough to be conspicuous. Many of the thieves who had stolen large sums in the past had been caught. Not by any clues left at the scene or identification by eyewitnesses, most of them had been given up by informers tempted by the large rewards offered by insurance companies, or by conspicuous changes in their spending habits.

Much was made about the activities of money-laundering rings, who were experts at disguising the source of the money they handled. However, their services didn't come cheap, and Nash didn't believe the gang would use them. The robbery had been such a professional operation that he felt sure they would have the means of disposing of the money already worked out. Either, they already had their own way of cleansing the money or they intended to sit on it and release it slowly. He shook himself mentally. He was getting ahead of himself. No point in thinking about money-laundering until they had some clue as to who had committed the crime.

Nash's deliberations were interrupted by his colleague. 'That patch in the middle of the road is definitely blood,' he confirmed. 'We'll have to wait for the test results from the lab to see if it's human or not.'

Nash couldn't resist the chance of teasing the expert. 'I watch CSI on TV regularly. They can tell immediately.'

The officer sighed with weary patience. 'My name's Robson, not Grissom. And shows like CSI make my job much harder.'

Nash sighed. 'It seems such a waste having to wait a week only to find we've been testing the result of a Charlie dragging his dinner home.'

'Unlikely that it'll take so long. A couple of days, more like. I think you can discount Charlie Fox as the culprit, though, there's nothing tidy about the way a fox kills his prey. Like a lot of murder scenes, it's usually a bloody mess, literally.'

TEN

ALTHOUGH CRYER HADN'T given them directions to the farm, they found it easily enough. The large sign outside the gate advertising Cryer Transport was sufficient to guide them. Cryer was waiting in the yard. Nash looked at the vehicle. It was a large Scania rigid. A few years old but still in excellent condition—on the outside at least.

It needed Nash's restraining hand to stop the farmer climbing inside to demonstrate the extent of the damage. After Nash explained about possible contamination of evidence, Cryer obeyed with reluctance and departed for the house muttering something about coffee. Nash could have murdered some, but he doubted if either he or his colleague were included in the round. 'Check out the cab first and let me know if you find anything of interest. I want to have a look inside the animal compartment.'

Despite the brightness of the day, the interior of the wagon was quite gloomy. Nash reached for the torch he kept in the glove compartment of the car. He shone the beam on the floor and was immediately rewarded. There was a large, irregular stain in the middle of the wooden boards. He reached over and banged his fist on the bulkhead separating the box from the cab to summon his colleague. 'What do you reckon that is?' He directed the beam towards the stain once more.

'Given the usual occupants of this place, I dread to think,' the man replied.

Nash grinned. 'Normally, I'd agree, but in this case I

think we'd both be wrong. Pass me a glove.' He bent down and rubbed the middle of the patch with one finger. It wasn't wet, only moist, and slightly greasy. He looked at his stained glove before sniffing tentatively at it.

'I thought so. I don't think whatever produced this had the sort of horsepower you were suggesting. Not unless someone feeds their animals on engine oil.'

'Where's that come from?'

'At a guess, I'd say it came out of the leaking sump of the engine of a security van that vanished so mysteriously, wouldn't you? That's the reason the partitions were removed, to create a large enough space to fit the van inside. All they had to do was drive the van up the ramp, disable the GPS tracker, and the vehicle disappears. Anyone who saw the wagon would have assumed it contained nothing more sinister than a few dozen sheep. Valuable, I agree, given the price of lamb these days, but hardly comparable to over six-hundred-thousand pounds in cash.'

'The only flaw in your reasoning that I can see is the strength of the tailboard of the wagon,' the officer pointed out. 'Would it stand the weight? Those vans weigh a hell of a lot, that's why they use so much fuel.'

'True, but the tailboard is designed to cope with heavy weights.'

Nash called to Cryer, who was now loitering near the back of the vehicle. 'How much do the beasts you carry weigh?'

'Anything up to five-hundred kilos each.'

The forensic officer whistled. 'Blimey, that's a hell of a lot of steak.'

'Just out of curiosity, would your wagon be capable of taking the weight of something like a Transit van?'

'I'm sure it would. I've had a digger in that one.' He pointed to where the officers were standing. 'Had to lower the bucket of course, but a Transit wouldn't be a problem. Why do you ask? Is that what they did with it?'

'Can you tell if the wagon has been taken out of your yard whilst you were away?'

Cryer thought for a moment. 'Depends how far it was driven. We get our diesel on account at a garage in Helmsdale. They always record the mileage. Then there's the tachograph. Bloody things,' he added sourly. 'Unless they disabled it.'

'I'm going to need more help with this,' the forensic officer said.

'I'll radio-in, tell control what's going on.'

Before setting off back to Helmsdale Nash spoke briefly to Mironova, to report his discoveries. 'We need to find the crew, there's no sign of them here.'

'I can answer that, Mike. I've just taken a call from Lancashire Constabulary. Someone walking along Morecambe promenade this morning went in to the public toilet. They heard noises coming from one of the cubicles and found two men, bound and gagged, wearing the livery of Guardwell Transport. They reckon the men have been there a while because they're in quite a state. By the sound of it, they might be suffering from hypothermia. They're being checked over at the local hospital, following which, the local CID are waiting to interview them. They've promised to report back as soon as they know anything, and arrange for them to be brought home.'

'When they've been interviewed, get the Lancashire lads to fax the report. Those men have been through enough by the sound of it. We can always pay them a visit if their story doesn't stand up. One thing though, all this proves not only that our hijackers are highly professional, but that whoever's in charge has a sense of humour.'

'I'm sorry, I seem to have missed the joke,' Clara said.

'Oh, come on, you have to admit it has its funny side,' Nash said. 'They've had us scuttling around for forty-eight hours, looking in all the wrong places, convinced the crewmen were involved, and all the time the poor blokes were locked in a public loo on the other side of the country. Even now we've found them, there's very little more we can do until we hear their version of events. I'm going to make a call before I get back. When I do, I want us to have a look through those Cremator files, if they've arrived.'

'The last of them was delivered about ten minutes ago.'

VANDA DAWSON WAS back in the room where she was first held captive. The difference was she was no longer on the bed but tied to an armchair. When she came round from the effects of the drug, she found a small bottle of water had been placed on the table alongside her, close enough for her to reach and with only a small effort, raise to her lips. Further consideration was shown with a television set having been placed directly opposite the chair. The remote control for this was also by her side, as was a small hand-bell. If it wasn't for the fact that she was tied up in a darkened room she might have been a guest in an hotel, such was her treatment.

She was confused. When she was in the barn, she'd expected to be raped. When her abductor had straddled her she was convinced that was about to happen. But although he'd simulated the act at no time had he attempted to penetrate her. Tied up as she was, there would have been no way of resisting such an assault, but it hadn't materialised. Vanda wondered if that had been due to impotence.

She'd read somewhere that many sex-killers suffer from an inability to have intercourse, or to become aroused, and that they channel their rage and hate into violence. That didn't fit with her experience though. As he'd simulated the act, as his naked body was on top of hers, Vanda had ample evidence of his capacity for arousal. That being the case, what had prevented him slaking his obvious desire? And what had been the point of the charade?

Another thought struck her via her devotion to forensic detective shows on television. Had he refrained because he was afraid of leaving DNA that would be traceable to him? But she was expecting to be killed; her body burned as the Cremator did to all his victims—surely the fire would take care of such evidence? But instead of pouring petrol over her and lighting a match, he'd given her a drink of water. Drugged, as she later realized.

Meals began to arrive at regular intervals; other requirements answered whenever she rang the bell. Within minutes of sounding it, her abductor would appear, to take her to the toilet, or to replenish the water bottle. At night, she was told to undress and secured to the bed before the light was switched off. Her gaoler's last act was to move the bell from the table to the bedside cabinet.

All of his instructions were conducted in mime. From the moment she first woke up in this strange place, he had uttered no more than half a dozen words, all delivered singly. Nor had he removed the mask that obscured his face.

This was another layer to her increasing bewilderment. If he intended to kill her, what need was there to disguise his identity? The only physical characteristic she was certain of was that he was tall.

To begin with, Vanda was able to keep track of time via the programmes being shown on the television. However, her perception of reality soon became blurred as her captivity continued. She could no longer recall with complete certainty which nights her favourite TV programmes were broadcast.

Unknown to Vanda, her body was adjusting both to her

reduced physical activity and the mild sedative contained in every meal she ate, diluted in each bottle of water she drank. Occasionally, she thought about Brian. Had he returned from Spain? Did the police know she was missing? Was there a search being undertaken for her? What would Brian think had happened? Things between her and Brian were bad enough, without all the suspicion and accusations her absence would arouse.

She had remembered with something of a shock that Jo had been coming to visit her. Why hadn't she thought of that, recalled that before now? Jo would have been sure to have contacted the police. She couldn't quite recall how many days it was since her abduction. Was it Wednesday or Thursday she'd been taken? And what day was it now?

Even if Jo hadn't made it to Yorkshire, Brian would be back home. And he would miss her. Wouldn't he? Or wouldn't he care? Might he actually be glad she wasn't there? Tears came to her eyes at the thought of Brian, at the decline in their marriage. Sometimes she'd felt sure he'd be glad to be rid of her. Then, unbidden and unwelcome, a dreadful thought came to her. Was he behind all this? Was this some twisted horrible plan Brian had dreamed up? Was the man holding her in Brian's pay? A hired killer?

If it hadn't been for the man's size she might almost have thought it was actually Brian who was imprisoning her. But it couldn't be. All right, the mask could have been because her kidnapper was her husband, as could the fact that he didn't speak, but this man was taller.

Her long period of concentration was tiring her out. As her eyelids began to droop, Vanda's mind filled with images of her husband donning a mask and putting on shoes that would make him taller. But something in those images was wrong. Something Vanda hadn't accounted for. Something that proved it wasn't Brian that was holding her captive. She tried to think, but the effort was too much, and she was already so tired....

READING THE FILES on the Cremator cases was hard going. Even without looking at the photographic evidence, the contents of the dossiers made it a harrowing experience. 'God, this bloke's sick,' Clara muttered.

'You can say that again,' Nash agreed. 'What have you noticed about these cases? I mean apart from the obvious.'

Mironova knew Nash well enough to realize that behind the question was the inference that he had spotted something that merited discussion and wondered if she had seen it as well. She pored over the files for a few minutes before admitting defeat. 'All right, Mastermind, what have I missed?'

'A couple of things sprang to mind. I'm not saying you missed them. They may be significant, or they may be completely irrelevant when it comes to tracking this maniac. For the first point, we have to take victim number one out of the equation. That was back in 2004.'

'Is that because we don't know her identity?'

'That's part of it. Because we don't know her identity we know nothing about her personal circumstances. There are a lot of other differences. For one, her age, and the disposal of the body for another. But if we consider the other victims, they're all of a type. All of them were either married or in a settled domestic relationship.'

'I grant you that, but surely the fact that no one has come forward who might have known the first victim suggests that she wasn't missed, which blows your theory out of the water.'

'I think it's a bit of an exaggeration to call it a theory. But because we know absolutely nothing about the first victim, I think it would be unwise to rule anything out.'

'All right, let's beg to differ on that one. What's your second point?'

'I'm puzzled by the victims themselves. If you examine the most notorious sexually motivated serial killers, you'll find their selection of victims falls into three categories. Either they were picked completely at random, as in absolute psychopaths, or they were prostitutes, or were much younger, in their late teens or early twenties. I'm excluding paedophiles and the like, and I know it's a generalisation, but I think if you were to study the victim profile of a lot of such killers, those would be the types they went for.

'In this case, the first victim may have been under thirty, but not by very much, according to the pathologist at the time. He put her age range as mid-to-late twenties. All the other victims were over thirty, two of them were nearly forty. Three of them were mothers, the other two, including our mystery woman, had never given birth.'

'Where's this leading?'

'I'm not sure, to be honest, but one thing occurs to me, and it isn't a very pleasant thought. If we are looking at a Cremator case, then Vanda Dawson fits right into his victim profile. If the Cremator has abducted Vanda Dawson, then he's remaining true to type.'

'You really do think this might be significant, don't you?'

'I think it may be, but until we have a suspect in our sights it's impossible to tell.'

'I've just remembered something. After you left us this morning, Dr Grey and I were talking about Mill Cottage. In particular, she doesn't think the place should be left unattended. She wondered about going to stay there until either Vanda or Brian Dawson reappear. I said I'd check with you and get back to her, what do you think?'

Nash stared at his sergeant in amazement. 'You're joking, aren't you? Please tell me you're joking? Don't you think we've enough problems without going out of our way to create more? No way will I sanction any woman being allowed to stay in that remote cottage alone overnight given what we suspect has happened there. I wouldn't even allow one of my male officers to stay there alone.'

'I take it that's a no then? Will you tell her, or shall I?'

The door opened before Nash had chance to reply. 'Yes, Tom, what is it? Have you located Dawson yet?'

'Sorry, Mike, I haven't, but one thing I can tell you. Wherever he is, he is not playing golf in Spain. In fact, according to the airports and ferry terminals he's not in Spain at all.'

'Oh great! Just what I needed. Another mysterious disappearance.'

Pratt blinked. 'You don't think he's been abducted as well?'

'No, but it's fairly suspicious that he's unaccountably absent at the time his wife disappears. The only thing that stops me believing he might be responsible is that he knew Jo was coming to visit, and that Vanda would be missed immediately. Nash turned to Clara. 'In answer to your question, I'll go and see Dr Grey. I think I ought to talk to her anyway. One thing still bugs me, and that's the whereabouts of Dawson. I'd like to find out more about the state of the marriage, and about the man himself.'

'What about tomorrow?'

'I'm going out to Mill Cottage to be there in time for the postman arriving. Will you join me there? Better take two cars because the way things are happening at the moment we don't know where we'll be from one minute to the next.'

ELEVEN

BRIAN DAWSON TURNED off the lane into the long, winding driveway leading to Mill Cottage. He could see by the lack of light from the front windows that the house was in darkness. He took the left fork, the narrow path leading to the old mill. The double doors were closed. He hoped they were also locked. That was what he expected as per his instructions. He got out of the car, unlocked and opened the doors and drove inside. He parked alongside Vanda's car. After getting out, he closed and locked the mill doors from the inside. Nobody was allowed to see into the old mill. Those were the orders he had given. It was mildly comforting to know they had been obeyed in his absence.

He turned and stared briefly at his wife's car. Wherever she'd gone, she hadn't needed to take it. Possibly her fancy man had collected her. He felt sure that would prove to be the explanation. He dismissed her from his mind. His interest in her and what she was up to was minimal at best; except when it involved his comfort.

Further up the drive, a figure crouched in the bushes, watching through night vision binoculars that were trained, first on the mill doors; then on Dawson, and finally on the cottage.

Half an hour after Dawson entered the house the watcher reached into his pocket and took out his mobile. 'Tony, it's me,' he announced. 'Dawson drove straight home. He put his car in the garage then stayed in there a while. I've no idea what he was up to, I couldn't get near without risking discovery. Then he went across to his house. He's been inside ever since; looks as if he's there for the night because he shut and locked the garage doors behind him.

What do you want me to do now?'

'Stay where you are. I'll send one of the others to relieve you. I reckon they'll be glad of some fresh air.'

'They'll get that all right. Better warn them to put thermals on, bring a flask of coffee and something to sit on. Maybe a rug to wrap round them as well, it's bloody parky out here.'

After he rang off, Tony selected a number from his own mobile and pressed it. 'Jerry?'

'Yes, boss. Everything all right?'

'I need one of our shopkeepers for the night. It'll mean a cold, lonely, boring job. Very cold, very boring,' he stressed. 'Who do you suggest?'

'Any of them would probably welcome the change. Harry's probably the best bet. He won't worry about the boredom; so long as he can stick his iPod on and listen to some of that stuff he imagines is music.'

'All right, send him along to me. I'll give him instructions and directions. How's the work going?'

'A couple of days and we should be ready.'

'Excellent.'

THE PHONE WAS ringing when Nash opened his front door. Without waiting to close it, he hurried over to the table and snatched up the receiver. 'Papa,' Daniel's voice sounded excited. 'Papa, I have a bicycle.'

'What?'

'Tante Mirabelle has bought me a bicycle to ride whenever we come here. She says it will save having to carry one back and forward every time. Isn't that kind of her?'

'Very kind. I hope you said thank you?'

'Of course, Papa. She also bought me a helmet to wear. Like the ones the riders in the Tour de France have. Also knee pads, in case I fall off.'

'You will be careful, won't you? Don't go riding it on busy roads, please.'

'Yes, Papa. The bike has stabilizers. Do you know what stabilizers are, Papa? I have to use them until I have practiced riding it, tante Mirabelle says.'

Nash breathed a sigh of relief. 'I'm glad about that. Please be careful, son. Remember, cars and trucks are very dangerous. Keep on the pavement when you can. Promise me that.'

'Yes, Papa.'

'It sounds as if you're enjoying your holiday.'

'Yes, Papa, but I wish you were here. Are you all right, Papa?'

'I'm OK. Missing you of course, and busy at work. I love you, Daniel.'

'I love you too, Papa. Here is tante Mirabelle.'

Nash reassured Mirabelle that he was happy with her buying the bike, and that it was a kind thought.

'Daniel needs something to occupy himself with. I get too tired too easily for a young boy.'

Nash smiled as he rang off. He understood what Mirabelle meant. Until Daniel came on the scene, he'd found it difficult to comprehend parents' complaints about how tiring their kids were. Now, he found it easy to empathise with them. It wasn't only looking after an energetic six-year-old that was tiring either. After the long drive to France and back over the weekend, followed by a stressful day at work, Nash felt exhausted, barely able to contemplate cooking an evening meal. He still had to interview

Dr Grey, and decided he would get something to eat while he was out.

Nash reached the hotel and asked at reception for Dr Grey. The receptionist called her room, and told Nash she would be down immediately. When she arrived, Nash indicated the small lounge area to one side of reception. It was deserted, such guests as were in the hotel probably still dining.

'Have you made any progress?' she asked when they were seated.

Nash shook his head. 'Nothing positive, I'm afraid,' he told her. 'It might help if we could find your brother-in-law, and see what he has to say on the matter.'

Jo frowned. 'Do you think he might be responsible? Surely not? I admit Brian isn't my favourite person, he's made Vanda's life a misery over the past few years, but I don't think he's capable of....'

'How do you know? You told us you rarely see him. Do you know exactly how bad things are between them? Given what little you told us, it sounds as if the marriage was all but over, and were it not for the fact that he must have been aware you were coming to visit your sister, he'd be right at the top of our suspects list.'

'But he did know. Vanda had to ask him before she could confirm the arrangement. I agree that says a lot for their marriage, but surely it rules him out as a suspect.'

'What is he like as a person? You've made no attempt to disguise the fact that you detest him. Is that purely because of the way he treats your sister, or is there something else?'

There was a long silence before she answered. 'It was a long time ago. Just before they got married. I was alone in the house. Vanda had gone to the shops and my parents were away. He called unexpectedly, or so I thought.

Later, I found out that he knew Vanda was out. He tried to force himself on me.'

'He tried to rape you?'

She nodded, her eyes reliving the horror. I was lucky. I managed to get away and locked myself in the toilet. Short of smashing the door down, he couldn't get at me. I stayed there until Vanda got home. By that time he'd gone, but I was too scared to come out.'

'Did you tell her?'

Dr Grey's expression was sombre. 'I did, but she refused to believe me. Wouldn't have me at the wedding, wouldn't speak to me for a long time afterwards. Even my parents thought I'd got it all wrong and was exaggerating things.' She smiled ruefully. 'It's only as their relationship has got worse that Vanda and I have patched things up.'

'That reminds me, your names, Johana and Vanda, where do they originate from?'

'Our mother,' she told him. 'She was Czech. She came here with her family after the Prague Spring. Do you know about that?'

'I've read about it. An uprising against the Communists, wasn't it?'

'That pretty much covers it. Anyway, my mother's family weren't exactly flavour of the month once it was over, so they managed to get out and came to Britain as political refugees. They were granted asylum and stayed on.'

'Going back to your sister's disappearance, do you believe Dawson would be capable of harming her?'

'I don't honestly know. I've asked myself that lots of times since it happened. Tried to come up with reasons he wouldn't harm her, but can't find any. I take it from what you've said that you don't believe he's in Spain on a golfing holiday?'

Her perception was acute, uncomfortably so. 'We can

find no evidence of him going there, by air or sea,' he admitted.

'But you still haven't found him. That's why you're asking all these questions about him, isn't it? Because if Brian hasn't anything to do with Vanda's disappearance, who has? Are there any names on your suspect list apart from Brian's?'

Nash hesitated, and even as he answered, realized that hesitation had given the game away. 'Almost none,' he admitted.

'Almost none?' Her tone changed again, the pent-up stress returning undiluted. 'Apart from one name perhaps? Or is it a nickname? And is that nickname one I would recognize immediately?' She saw Nash's face change, saw the frown and the hard set of his jaw. 'The Cremator; that's what you think, isn't it?'

'It's a possibility, but no more than that,' Nash agreed reluctantly.

'And if that's true, it means I've to prepare myself for the worst. Because if Vanda's one of his victims there's no chance for her. You've no idea who he is, no idea where he's going to strike. All you can do is sit and wait for a body to turn up. That's what you're really saying, isn't it? I hoped you'd come here to offer me some comfort, some hope that Vanda might be all right. Fat chance of that. You're useless, simply useless, and what's really appalling is that you've more or less admitted it.'

She rose from the sofa and walked across to the reception area without a backward glance. Nash watched her go, prey to mixed emotions. If circumstances had been different, she would have been just the sort of woman whose company he'd have enjoyed. As she'd said, fat chance of that. Not least because it seemed the rules had changed, without him even noticing. Once, he'd treated a woman's companionship as a sort of game. Having Daniel was a permanent reminder that the only way to play was for keeps. Nash remained seated long after she left. She had a point, he thought ruefully. He'd read the Cremator's case files, and had felt a degree of sympathy for the investigating officers. If the circumstantial evidence proved reliable, Nash was beginning to feel the same helplessness and frustration his colleagues in other forces had experienced.

VANDA DAWSON WAS tired. Not physically so. Not as she had been for the last few days. She was tired of feeling afraid. Tired of being submissive. Tired of fearing to upset other people's feelings, which, when she thought about it, summed up the whole of her miserable life. A life of total non-achievement. Trapped in a loveless marriage to a husband who regarded her as nothing more than a cook and housekeeper. Except that he had other uses for her. Uses, such as someone to vent his cold anger and meanness on, someone to boss about and belittle because she was nothing. Less than nothing, someone who didn't do anything for fear she'd get it wrong.

The realization of all this came suddenly. Along with it came the knowledge that whatever the outcome she could never go back. She knew it, and on the first possible occasion, she'd tell him it. The marriage was over. That would be the message. He could find someone else to cook and clean, to wash and iron. Tasks she'd have undertaken cheerfully if he'd only repaid her with a little kindness, tenderness or physical love.

That thought came as a second shock. That all those years of repressed emotion added up to the frustrations of a highly sexed woman going without the joys of physical intimacy. Brian hadn't touched her that way for years. Hadn't shown the slightest wish—not even an admiring glance at her body. She needed it. From almost out of nowhere she felt this surge, this appetite for a man to make love to her. Like a bitch in season, this unquench-able flame of desire came over her.

All these things were immaterial. She'd never have a chance to express her feelings, whether to Brian or any man she met. Because next time her kidnapper came through that door, it might all be over.

She was lying, tethered to the bed and she was hun-gry. The winter sunlight was filtering round the edge of the heavy curtain and she guessed it must be near lunch-time. She frowned; there was something odd about her abductor's routine. He always woke her for breakfast, then he never reappeared until the next meal. Although she couldn't be sure, she thought he might leave the house after he'd fed her. She'd thought on more than one occasion that she'd heard a door close, after which there was a long period of silence. Silence that lasted for hours, until she was convinced she'd heard a car engine, then the sound of doors again. Why was that? Where did he go every day? Was he going to work? Trying to maintain some form of routine: showing respectability to the outside world? If so, where was he now?

Almost as if she'd given voice to her thoughts, he en-tered the room. For a second the old Vanda tried to re-turn, and she felt herself quail internally. Then her anger and frustration took over. 'What are you going to do?' she demanded.

He stopped, head on one side. Something in her tone of voice was new.

'I'm fed up with you coming and going, feeding me, fiddling about, pretending to be scary with that ridiculous mask. If you're going to kill me, why bother? Does it mat-ter if I know who you are, or what you look like if you're planning to burn me alive? Or is that not it? Could it be you don't want me to see you because you're too hideous to show your face?'

He shook his head. Her aggression seemed to have unnerved him.

'For Christ's sake do something, say something. Do whatever it is you've been planning. Set fire to me. Rape me. I don't care anymore. Or is it that you can't? Of course, that's it, isn't it? You tried once and failed miserably, now you're scared to try again. If that's the case, then I reckon it'll have to be plan B. So make your mind up. Either fuck me or go for the petrol can. Just don't drag this pathetic charade out any longer.' She paused, panting slightly. Was that from the emotion of her delivery, or was she a mite scared after all. She watched as he slowly digested what she'd said. Then again, the new Vanda Dawson took over. Where once she would have been too timid, now she was aggressive, demanding even. After all, what had she to lose?

'So what's next on the agenda? A spot of rough sex or straight to the funeral pyre? Why do you do that? Is it like the papers reckon, part of some weird Satanic ritual? Or simply covering the evidence of your other crimes? Burning off the DNA? And another thing, for fuck's sake ditch that stupid mask. Take it off and stop wandering around the place like *The Phantom of the Opera*.'

He turned and stared at her. Was that surprise behind the mask? As she returned his gaze, her eyes on his, unwavering, she moved one leg, slightly, invitingly, taunting him with her sexuality. As if to say, do your worst. I know what you've got, and it don't scare me. He loosened her bonds and turned away. She could see the skin on the back of his neck redden: a small victory for Vanda.

'Get dressed.' His voice was so quiet she'd to ask him to repeat what he'd said. 'Get dressed, please.'

This time she was sure there was guilt in his voice. And something else. A slightly familiar quality; something in his tone. Did she know him, or was she imagining it? Whereas previously when she'd dressed in front of him she'd been embarrassed, attempting to hide her shame and cover her modesty, the new Vanda Dawson wouldn't behave like that.

She stretched, long and languorously, all the time watching him with half-closed eyes. He was no longer turned away; he was all attention. Still on the bed, she rose to a kneeling position, leaning forward. Hands balancing her, breasts framed by her upper arms. Displaying her wares. 'Would you pass my bra and pants, please?'

She just stopped herself from adding, darling. That would have been pushing her luck too far. She slipped the bra cups over her breasts before turning her back on him. 'This is how you do it,' she called over her shoulder. 'Watch carefully, it'll come in handy, if you can manage to do what you keep threatening.'

She made a burlesque act out of the everyday routine of putting her pants on. A routine where she made sure he got a further prolonged display of all she had to offer. And it was having its effect too. She saw him move as if to mop his forehead, forgetting he was still wearing that mask. Instead, he rubbed the back of his neck. Another tiny victory. Once the show was over, she slipped her top and jeans on quickly, pushed her feet into her trainers and stood in front of him, hands forward. 'What now? Back to the chair and tied up for hours on end? Or off to the altar ready for burning?'

He didn't speak, merely grasped her upper arm and guided her to the door. He opened it and gently pushed

her in front of him, then guided her downstairs, through
the hall and into a farmhouse kitchen. She paid attention
to her surroundings. Her eyes wandered from the old,
but serviceable-looking Aga in the recessed fireplace to
the range of kitchen units, and the large picture window
over the double drainer sink. Outside, the view consisted
of rolling fields, grassland, dotted with cows. She was
on a farm.

'Please, sit down.'

She obeyed, although there was nothing in his tone to
suggest a command.

'Would you like a cup of tea?'

'What? You expect me to sit here calmly drinking tea
after what you've done to me? This isn't some vicarage tea
party, you know. We're talking kidnapping, false imprisonment, attempted rape and any number of other sexual
assaults. That's so far. God knows what else there is to
come. How the hell do you expect me to react? Sit here
calmly and say yes please, milk and one sugar.'

'You don't take sugar.' The words were out before he
could stop them.

'And how the fuck do you know that?' Vanda reckoned
she could count on the fingers of one hand the times she'd
used the word fuck during the years she'd been married
to Brian. Now she'd used it about four times in the last
twenty minutes. She should be ashamed of herself. No
she shouldn't, the new Vanda told her. If you want to say
it, say it, girl, and don't give a fuck.

The other interesting thing was that she was already
thinking of her marriage to Brian as a thing of the past.

'Come on, tell me. How do you know I don't take
sugar? You've never given me tea since you brought me
here. It's either been fizzy pop or water. Neither have had
sugar in, just sedatives to keep me quiet. And they've worn

off, by the way. So come on, spit it out. You've kidnapped me, stripped me naked, tried to rape me and failed; don't you think an introduction's in order?'

Vanda wondered briefly if confronting her abductor in this way would make things better or worse. What the hell, she thought, if her guess was right she didn't have long to live anyway. From what she'd read of the other Cremator cases, the attack was so brutal it would all be over quickly. No human constitution could withstand the level of pain this man inflicted for long, she was certain. She'd be dead and gone soon, almost unnoticed, almost unmourned, apart from Jo. She forced herself not to think of her sister. Once they'd been less than friends, now Jo was the only person Vanda was anywhere near close to. That came as a shock, as she realized how lonely her existence had been. That wasn't always the case. Before her marriage she'd had plenty of friends, of both sexes. She'd enjoyed her social life, but gradually, after she'd got married, her friends had dropped out of her life, or she'd dropped out of theirs. Why? And why had she never stopped to think of it before? It was hardly because her marriage was so happy, or that she was fulfilled by a meaningful career, or bringing up a family.

As she stared at the man in front of her, she wondered when the attack would start. Was he gearing himself up? Did he need to prepare himself? The rape would be horrid, but somehow that didn't seem as important as it would have done once. And hopefully it would be over with quickly.

No, she thought, that's the wrong way to look at it. Once he'd raped her, he'd move on to the torture and the burning. So perhaps the rape was the lesser of two evils. It would certainly pale into insignificance once he started on the rest of his vile tricks. She felt slightly comforted that she'd faced the inevitable; thought her way through what she felt sure was going to happen. By confronting her fears, she felt she was prepared for what was to come.

In the event, Vanda's wildest nightmares couldn't match the horror of what happened next.

TWELVE

NASH DROVE TOWARDS Wintersett next morning, the memory of yesterday evening's encounter still fresh in his mind. Dr Grey's implied criticism rankled, but he could understand the emotional stress that had provoked her outburst. His distraction could have proved dangerous, but there was little traffic on the road. His lack of concentration almost caused him to overshoot the entrance to the driveway of Mill Cottage. If he hadn't caught the peripheral flash of metal from the tail end of Mironova's car as she turned in to the drive, he might have ended up out in the countryside beyond the village. He shook his head, making the mental gear change into work mode.

The first thing Nash noticed as he got out of his car was the blinds at the kitchen window. He waited for Mironova to join him.

'When we left here yesterday, weren't those blinds drawn?'

She looked across the gravel pathway. 'Yes, they were. I closed them myself. I thought it better, with the house being unoccupied. Do you think someone might have broken in? It wouldn't have been very difficult, especially if they found that broken pane of glass in the back door.'

'I thought you were organizing someone to fix it?'

'I thought so too, but they're all up to their eyes in emergency repair work following last week's storms. A little thing like a replacement windowpane is very low on their priorities. Added to which, they all wanted to charge an arm and a leg just to come out here. If they'd been attending a big job, it wouldn't have been so bad, but the call-out fee for this was a hundred pounds on average. All for a piece of glass that you could buy at a DIY place for about two pounds and another fifty-pence for the putty.'

'Right, well you'd better stay here. If it is an intruder, they might be dangerous. Have your mobile ready to call for back up if needs be.'

Clara saw movement over Nash's shoulder. 'I don't think that'll be necessary.' She nodded. 'That's Dawson, isn't it?'

Nash swivelled round, sending a cascade of tiny pebbles scattering across the pathway. A man in his late thirties or early forties was standing in the doorway of the house. He wasn't so much watching them as glaring at them.

'Who are you?' the man demanded. 'And what the hell do you think you're doing on my property?'

Nash walked over to him, dragging his warrant card from his pocket on the way. 'Detective Inspector Nash, Helmsdale CID,' he told the irate householder. 'This is my colleague, Detective Sergeant Mironova. I assume you must be Brian Dawson?'

'That's correct. What's this all about? Where is my wife? Has there been some sort of an accident?'

'We don't know where your wife is. May we step inside?' Dawson moved reluctantly to let them pass.

Nash began to explain. 'When her sister came to visit her on Friday night, she found the house deserted and in darkness. It appeared as if the kitchen door had been forced. You may have noticed there's a pane of glass missing. Despite extensive searching and enquiries in the neighbourhood, there appears to be no trace of your wife. I have to say her disappearance took place in very suspicious and alarming circumstances. We're very concerned for her welfare and safety. Our one remaining hope is that you might be able to shed some light on to where she might be, and that there might be an innocent explanation.'

Dawson shook his head, less in denial than in sheer disbelief. 'I don't understand. Her car's still here, in the garage. Where do you think she might have gone? And what do you mean precisely by "suspicious and alarming circumstances".'

'The fact that she didn't take her car simply adds to our concern. Given the weather at the time of her disappearance, it's hardly likely that she simply put her coat on and walked out in the middle of a raging storm. In addition to the broken pane of glass the officers found when Dr Grey called them, there's a red wine stain on the lounge carpet, where a glass had been knocked over. That might have an innocent explanation, of course. What is far less easily explained away is why someone wiped all the surfaces in the lounge, hall and kitchen so that they were clear of fingerprints. Wiped them, may I add, with sanitized wipes. What is particularly disturbing is that we found no trace of any such cloths in the house, not even empty containers in the bin.'

'What you infer is that you think my wife has been abducted; is that it? Has there been some sort of ransom demand?'

Nash shook his head. He was irritated by Dawson's manner and couldn't quite work out why. Perhaps it was the man's coldness. Although he'd undoubtedly been surprised by Nash's statement, he didn't seem particularly distressed about the news that his wife had possibly been kidnapped. The other reason for Nash's dislike of Dawson was the way he kept referring to Vanda as 'my wife' instead of using her name. Dawson's aloof and distant arrogance struck him as particularly unfeeling. He decided shock tactics might ruffle the man's unnatural calm.

'We don't believe that money was the motive. I'm afraid we suspect that there might be a far more sinister motive behind her abduction.' Nash waited to see if his assertion provoked any noticeable reaction. When he failed to see one, he continued, 'Our strongest theory is that this might be the work of a man who has kidnapped several women in the past, in very similar circumstances. All the indications are that your wife's abduction fits that profile—almost perfectly.'

Once more, there was surprise, and this time something else. Nash wasn't sure, but it almost sounded like nervousness. If it was, what had Dawson to be apprehensive about? If he was upset by the news that his wife might be in the hands of a homicidal maniac, then Nash failed to see any evidence of it.

'The Cremator? Is that what you believe? That's impossible. You can't surely think this is the work of the Cremator?'

'I'm afraid that is exactly what we believe, Mr Dawson.'

Dawson opened his mouth as if to say something, but then changed his mind. He merely shook his head in denial. Nash continued as if he hadn't noticed the gesture. 'We've been trying to locate you since early on Saturday. Our enquiries revealed that you obviously didn't go to Spain on a golfing holiday, which is what I understand you told your wife you were doing. So would you mind telling me exactly where you have been and what you've been doing, Mr Dawson? You must understand that if your wife hasn't been abducted, your unexplained absence at the time of her disappearance could be seen as highly suspicious.'

'Don't be absurd.' Dawson's tone was arrogant, dismissive. 'You can't possibly think I had anything to do with this. In fact, it seems as if you have very little evidence whatsoever. That doesn't seem to have stopped you stringing together a couple of fairly preposterous theories. The fact that you seem uncertain whether it's me or this Cremator character you ought to be pursuing tends to reinforce the fact that you know absolutely nothing. For all you know, she might have gone swanning off with a new boyfriend or something equally innocuous.'

'Is that a likely scenario? Given that she was expecting her sister to arrive for the weekend,' Nash asked, with a quiet calm he was far from feeling. 'You must be aware that when a woman goes missing like this, the majority of such incidents later prove to have been sparked by some form of domestic dispute. So, I will ask you once more, Mr Dawson, would you please account for your movements over the past week?'

'I've been visiting clients.'

'I'll need the names and addresses of those clients.'

'I'm afraid that information is confidential.'

'Not any more, it isn't. I'll give you a chance to contact them, to warn them we'll be in touch, but I need those details.'

For a moment, Nash thought the accountant was going to argue the point but eventually he nodded. 'Very well, I'll write the contact names and phone numbers down. Is there anything else?'

'Yes, there is. I'm afraid we're going to remain here until after the postman arrives with this morning's mail.'

'Why on earth do you want to do that?'

'Because if this is a Cremator incident, part of his modus operandi is to send photographs of his victims to their relatives and I want to make sure that you don't get such a delivery.'

'In that case, I can write those details down whilst you're waiting.'

When Mironova had first entered the kitchen her automatic act was to look round. She noticed that Dawson had eaten breakfast—that much was obvious from the cereal bowl and coffee mug that were soaking in the sink. Apart from them, the room looked exactly as it had when she left it. The careful placing of the breakfast pots tallied with Jo Grey's description of Dawson's obsessive neatness. Although Nash was very observant, Mironova wondered how much of this he'd noticed.

'Stay there; I'll get those details for you.' Dawson went out into the hall.

Clara looked across at Nash. He shrugged, as if he was struggling to understand Dawson's mind-set, but Mironova could sense the speculation in his eyes. Whatever she thought about Dawson it was obvious Nash was forming his own opinion about the accountant. Clara would be interested to learn what that was.

Before either of them had a chance to speak, Dawson returned. He handed Mironova a slip of paper with a series of names and phone numbers scrawled on it. She nodded acknowledgment, and before the silence became oppressive, they heard the sound of an approaching vehicle. Dawson glanced at the kitchen clock on the wall above the range cooker. 'That'll probably be the postman.'

They followed Dawson through into the hall where Nash signalled to him to open the front door. Nash stepped outside in time to prevent the postman from thrusting the bundle of mail through the letterbox. As he reached for it, Clara noticed Nash was wearing latex gloves. She wondered when he had put them on, as she got closer to see what the mail comprised.

Nash singled out an A5 envelope from the rest and

passed the others to Dawson. He turned the one he'd retained over so it was address side up. The size and colour were not the most common, Clara thought. The name and address was printed on a label of the type produced for printers attached to personal computers. That in itself didn't suggest any sinister motive. Far more chilling however was the second, smaller label fixed in the top left hand corner of the envelope. It too had been printed, with a message that she could read as clearly as if Nash had spoken it: 'Photographs—please do not bend'.

She looked up to see Nash's expression conveyed the same foreboding that gripped her. He took his penknife from his pocket and passed it to Clara, asking her to open one of the blades. She passed it back and Nash began to work the envelope flap free, taking care to avoid the gummed section.

When he had loosened the flap, Nash inverted the envelope and shook it gently to release the contents. A trio of photos slid into his hand, all measuring about six inches by four. He turned the first of these over and as he scrutinised the subject, Clara saw his face wearing an expression of unparalleled grimness. Clara looked over his shoulder and saw with mounting horror that it depicted a woman lying naked on a bed, her wrists and ankles secured to the frame.

Nash tucked this to the back and looked at the second print. In this, the same woman had been moved to an oblong, altar-like table covered in some form of purple material. She was naked and tied up as in the first photo, and the altar was surrounded by a number of symbols that were only partly visible owing to the angle of the shot. Closer to the centre of the photo was an object Clara recognized only too well: a petrol can.

Nash turned to the final print. In this, a man had

climbed on to the woman. He too was naked, apart from the mask that obscured his head and the top of his neck. There was absolutely no doubt in Clara's mind that this photo had captured the woman being raped. No doubt in her mind, that the woman in all three photos was Vanda Dawson. No doubt, that the man who had abducted and raped her was the serial killer known as the Cremator.

Nash turned to Dawson and held up the first photo. 'Is that your wife?' he demanded.

Dawson's glance was cursory, no more. 'Yes, it is.'

'And this one? And this?' Nash held the second and third photos up in turn, giving Dawson ample opportunity to examine them.

Dawson looked from one photo to the other. His expression interested Clara. It changed from surprise to absolute astonishment, but at no time did she see the slightest flicker of distress. His voice was steady as he replied. 'Yes, those are all photographs of my wife.'

'Then I think you will have to brace yourself for some bad news. I mean really bad news,' Nash reinforced the point. 'Because it seems obvious that the man who has abducted your wife is the Cremator. Furthermore, having read the files on his other victims only yesterday, I think you should be aware that by the time photos such as these are sent out, the victim is either dead or within hours of it. We can't be certain on the timing, but I think you should prepare yourself for the news that your wife has already been murdered.'

Clara stared at her boss in astonishment. It was totally out of character for Nash to behave in such an unfeeling manner. Apart from this, his statement was surely against regulations.

Nash was watching Dawson even more closely than Clara was watching Nash. She switched her gaze to the

accountant. There could be no doubting his utter bewilderment on being confronted by the awful evidence of
the ordeal his wife had suffered. On the other hand, Clara
couldn't see anything to suggest that Dawson was in the
slightest worried by his wife's fate.

Despite several attempts by Nash to persuade Dawson
to accept the presence of a police family support officer
to stay with him at the house until, as Nash put it, the situation was resolved, the accountant steadfastly refused.
When Nash suggested the alternative of asking Jo Grey
to come over to the house, Dawson rejected the idea ve-
hemently.

Although Mironova was aware that the two of them
didn't get on, the force of Dawson's refusal surprised her.
Clara was left with the feeling that Dawson was either dis-
interested, or that he was bottling up his feelings. How
else could you explain his apparently calm acceptance
of the knowledge that she was in the power of a ruthless
and evil serial killer. She could tell from Nash's expression that he was equally baffled.

When they eventually left the house, Nash turned to
her as soon as they were out of Dawson's hearing. 'I don't
know what the hell to make of that bloke. He seems to
have no feelings whatsoever. Certainly not for his wife.
Although there is something he's not happy about. Did
you notice? What did you make of him?'

'I just thought he was unfeeling. He's so cold he made
me shiver. I had to remind myself he was the closest person to the victim. For all the interest he took, he might
have been reading about something that had happened to
a complete stranger as reported in a newspaper. What do
you make of those photos? Fairly conclusive, don't you
agree?'

Nash's reply surprised her. 'Actually, I'm not sure what

to make of them. I want you to get them across to the forensic guys in Netherdale for testing, together with the envelope. Leave the evidence with them, but bring me a photocopy of all three. I want to examine them and compare them with the others we have on file.'

'Are you doubting that they show Vanda Dawson is being held by the Cremator?'

'That's certainly how it appears on the face of it. But maybe that's what we're intended to believe.'

'You think this might be a copycat? Christ, Mike, it was bad enough with one Cremator roaming the country. Two would make it a nightmare.'

'I agree. That's why I want those copies as soon as you can possibly get them to me. Think of it as more urgent than urgent.'

Nash placed the photos and envelope into an evidence bag from his kit in the back of the Range Rover. He sealed and signed it before passing it to Clara, then waited until she had cleared the drive before he drove off. As he was turning the car round, he caught a glimpse of Dawson watching him from the kitchen window. The accountant's face registered absolutely no emotion.

As he drove slowly up the drive, Nash's thoughts were all on the missing woman, and the shocking content of the photos. No matter how their examination of the files might have prepared them, the sight of those images was devastating. And if he and Clara had been so affected by them, how had Dawson managed to view them so calmly? It was almost as if the man was incapable of any emotion. Was that something to do with the state of the marriage? Perhaps even the cause of the decline in the relationship.

Nash was far too deep in thought to notice that his progress along the lane was being observed. Even had he been on the lookout, he would have struggled to spot the watcher concealed in the dense undergrowth close to the entrance to the drive, for the man had plenty of experience in the art of concealment. He waited until Nash's car was out of sight before pulling his mobile from his pocket.

'Dawson's had two visitors this morning, apart from the postman, that is. They've just left. One was a bloke who looked to be in his late thirties, early forties at the most, medium height, fair hair. The other was a woman, late twenties, stunning figure, blonde hair and from what I could see, a nice pair of tits. The bloke was driving a Range Rover, the woman was in an Astra.'

'Why the detailed description? Is there something else about them I should know?'

The watcher grinned to himself; Tony wasn't slow on the uptake. 'I thought you'd be interested, or that you might recognize them from the descriptions. Added to the fact that the spotlight lenses on the Astra were blue.'

'A police car?'

'Yes, and judging by their appearance I'd say CID, but what would they want with Dawson? Is that why we're keeping an eye on him?'

'I don't think it has anything to do with us at this stage. Jerry said the copper who came to the shop was talking about Dawson's wife having gone missing. Let's hope that's all it is. Nevertheless it shows how important it is to keep our eye on Dawson.'

'Is there anything else you want me to do?'

His boss knew exactly what the man was suggesting. 'Not at this stage. I'll report what's happened up the line and see what reaction I get. I don't suppose you happen to have a camera with a telephoto lens on you?'

'Not in my pocket, but there's one in the car.'

'Good, keep it handy. I want photos of any visitors.'

Shortly after he'd ended the conversation and returned

from retrieving the camera from his car, the watcher saw Dawson leave the cottage. He cursed, thinking he'd have to make a hurried half-mile dash to his car, assuming that Dawson was going out. He watched closely as the accountant walked over to the old mill. Dawson cast glances to left and right, giving the procedure a furtive air. Once he'd unlocked the door, instead of opening both halves, he vanished inside. The watcher relaxed. Obviously Dawson wasn't intending to leave. He wasn't close enough to hear whether Dawson had locked the door and dared not risk discovery by attempting to find out. He settled back in his vantage point and waited.

He glanced at his watch as Dawson emerged. Twenty-five minutes had elapsed since he'd gone inside. He hadn't taken anything into the building, nor had he brought anything out. So, what had he been doing in there? The watcher scratched his head. It was a puzzle. Of course, Dawson might have been tinkering with his car, but somehow the man didn't seem the type. Besides which, the usual process was to run the engine when you'd finished, which would need the doors to be open. He reported the incident in another short phone call, but his boss could offer no explanation for Dawson's actions either.

THIRTEEN

NASH FOUND A fax on his desk from Lancashire Constabulary containing the statements of the security guards. Attached to it was a note commenting on their health and the state the men were in. The conclusion had been made that they were extremely unlikely to have been involved in the hijack. Nash filed the report and turned his attention to the Cremator photos.

He took them from the files and spread them out on the table in the CID room. When Mironova returned from Netherdale, he and Viv were studying them. She passed him the envelope she was carrying. 'These are copies. They dusted the originals for prints before I left. There were none.'

'I didn't expect any, to be honest. Our man's far too careful for that. Before we start, I have news for you.' Nash told them about the chief constable's conversation of the previous day, holding the name of their new boss back until the very end. When he eventually mentioned Jackie Fleming's name, Clara let out a long whistle. Nash eyed her suspiciously. 'What was that for?'

'I was just thinking that Jackie Fleming's done really well for herself. Reaching the rank she has, at such an early age. She's not exactly bad looking, either, as I remember. Do you think you'll be able to keep your mind on the job?'

Nash scowled furiously at her, his mood not helped by the sight of Viv trying unsuccessfully to hide a grin.

'Jackie Fleming was someone I, in fact *we,* worked with on one case, that's all.'

If Clara was intimidated by his tone or ferocious expression, it didn't show. 'I wonder if that will change, now you have to obey her every command.'

'On the subject of work, do you think you might be willing to do a spot? The chief constable's budget doesn't run to a gossip columnist, so I'm afraid you'll just have to stick to the job you were appointed to do. In case that's slipped your mind, it's called detective work. Now, if you're quite ready, let's see what we've got.'

Clara grinned unrepentantly and winked at Pearce.

Nash slid the new photos out of the envelope and set them down alongside the others. All three bent over the table, inspecting the images. 'They're different,' Clara and Viv exclaimed almost in unison.

'The man in the Vanda Dawson photo. He's wearing a mask but not a hood, like in the other photos,' Clara pointed out. 'And in the photo that shows him attacking her, he's naked. In the others, he's still clothed, even during the rape,' she added.

'Anything else?'

This time it was Viv who answered. 'The petrol can is different. It's not the same size or shape as the others.'

'I agree.' Nash smiled; listening to his team pooling ideas was something he enjoyed.

They scrutinized the images once more. 'The funnel!' Clara exclaimed triumphantly. 'All the old photos show a funnel alongside the petrol can. It's not there in the Vanda Dawson photo. Why is that, do you think?'

'Could be any number of reasons,' Viv suggested. 'He might simply have forgotten it. Or it could have been put down outside the camera shot. What puzzles me is why the need for a funnel?'

'You don't want to know, Viv,' Nash said quietly.

Pearce and Mironova stared at him in horror. 'You don't mean he pours petrol down their throats when he sets fire to them?' Viv asked.

Nash shook his head. 'Remember, part of the reason for the fire, in fact I'd suggest the main reason for it, is to cover up the evidence of the rape, because that would yield DNA which could trap him. If you check out the description of the bodies in those files'—Nash pointed to the stack on the corner of the table—'you'll see that the fire damage is worst around the groin area.

'This isn't only the most sadistic and perverted killer I've ever heard of, he's as cunning and careful, as he is cruel. He takes no chances whatsoever. That's part of the reason he's still at large. If it wasn't for the photographs he sends to his victims' relatives, we wouldn't even know for sure what ordeals he puts those poor women through.'

Clara heard Viv ask, 'Is there another reason you think the funnel might be missing, Mike?'

She replied before Nash had a chance. 'It might be because the photographer wasn't aware all the previous photos had a funnel in them.'

It was a few seconds before the significance of her words struck home. 'You don't think this is the same attacker? You think this is a copycat?'

Viv's question raised another in Clara's mind. 'If he's shown actually raping Vanda Dawson; that must mean someone else was present to take the photo.'

'Not necessarily.' Nash pointed to the photo in question. 'That could have been taken with a delay timer with the camera on a tripod. Alternatively, the photo could have been taken by a third party. Which would mean it isn't a copycat. It would mean the Cremator has an apprentice.

But there are a couple of other differences that tend to suggest Clara's copycat theory might be the right one.'

'I thought we'd got them all.' Viv stared at the photos again. 'Go on, tell us your thoughts.'

'First, the cloth covering what might be called the altar. It's a different colour to the one used in the other photos.' Nash pointed to the part of the photograph, 'Look, the shade is completely different, and the pattern too.'

'The room is different as well.' Clara was looking at the other photo. 'In fact this set of photos shows two different rooms. One's a bedroom, the other a sort of barn. In all the others, it's the same room in each, but much smaller, more like a cellar.'

'Good point, Clara.' Nash turned to Pearce. 'You didn't see it, but the envelope the Vanda Dawson photos came in was white. All the ones in those files are described as buff. Of course, you could argue the Cremator ran out of buff envelopes and had to switch to white, but somehow I don't believe that's the case. For one thing, he's too organized. Take it together with all the other differences and I think we might be talking about a different perpetrator. The final and most important difference is the evidence we don't have.'

'Sorry, I'm not with you.'

Nash looked at Pearce. 'If you exclude the first of the Cremator's victims, all the other women were known to be married. When the killer sent those gruesome photographs, he also included their wedding ring, sawn in two. This fact has never been made public. Only the victims' partners and the detectives involved in the investigation knew that. Which suggests that Vanda Dawson's abductor didn't know either.'

'All of which doesn't make our job any simpler, even if we're right,' Clara pointed out.

'And it doesn't make the chances of finding Vanda Dawson alive any better,' Nash added grimly. 'In fact, I'm afraid there's little else we can do at the moment, except to keep searching and hope we get lucky, or until we get a phone call from someone to report the finding of a body.' He reflected for a moment. 'I'll have to face Dr Grey and tell her about these'—he indicated the photos—'it's only fair she should know and be prepared for what might happen.'

'Do you want me to tell her?' Clara offered. 'I could pop into her hotel on my way home.'

'I think that would be best,' Nash said thoughtfully. 'I spoke to her last night, but at present she doesn't think much of me.'

Nash was about to leave, but remembered something. 'About tomorrow. One of us ought to go back to Mill Cottage first thing. Will you attend to that?'

EVEN AT NIGHT, even in solitary, there is always sound. Always the noise that accompanies human occupation of an enclosed space. There is always movement too, movement and light. Illumination is necessary at all times, to keep an eye on those under guard. This is particularly so for those prisoners regarded as posing a threat to others, or of being in danger themselves.

Thus, the prisoner's cell was constantly illuminated. He was a man the authorities felt merited close attention at all times. He was classified as the most dangerous inmate in a prison block filled with dangerous inmates. A man trained to kill, and one who had killed and killed again, whether directly, or by ordering executions carried out by others.

In this instance, the precautions put in place by those charged with guarding him actually worked in his favour.

His cell was lit both day and night. Had he been afraid of the dark, he would have been able to sleep soundly. The fact that he didn't sleep well had nothing to do with either the light or a guilty conscience. It was due to the ever-present pain from his leg, the one that had been smashed when he was arrested and had never mended properly. The benefit his disturbed sleep patterns gave him, arose from his ability to send and receive text messages on the smuggled mobile phone.

The text he received contained disturbing information. It read; 'potential problem with D. Blues are sniffing at his office. Wife disappeared. Have him under 24h ob. Blues turned up at house this am. Advise. T.'

His reply contained only two words, and was somewhat less than grammatically correct. 'What cops?'

It was only minutes later when his screen lit up again. If a prison officer had passed at that moment they would have wondered at the cause of the fury evident in his face as he read the contents. 'No name. Male, med height & build, fair, 40ish. Plus blonde female, well stacked, nice legs.'

The prisoner's breath hissed through his teeth. 'Nash!' he whispered. 'Nash and Mironova.'

It was several minutes before he trusted himself to reply. Even then, even when he felt calmer, he noticed that his hands were still trembling slightly. He began to type, slowly, carefully, glancing occasionally across the cell at the peephole in the door. 'Cop is Nash. V. Dangerous. His sidekick, Mironova. Also dangerous. Eliminate Nash if chance. If D poses a threat, take him out.'

He paused for a few seconds, considering the words, before adding, 'Deal with Mironova too.'

The recipient stared at the last text message. It was about what he'd expected. He picked up the phone. Although it was the early hours of the morning, he knew his team would be hard at work. 'Jerry, it's Tony. We need a meeting. I've had instructions.'

'When do you suggest?'

'As soon as possible. The situation is urgent, could become critical. Tomorrow is half-day closing; that would be ideal. Say three o'clock at my place?'

'I'll get on to it.'

HENRIETTA'S COSTUMES WAS in the centre of a terrace on the west of Helmsdale market place. The shop sold a wide range of chain store and mail order goods, mainly end of line items and some seconds. Offering these at a fraction of the original ticket price had established a niche market, attracting the thrifty, budget-conscious local residents and tourists alike.

The owner, whose name was Julie, not Henrietta, was always first to arrive in the morning, although her two assistants were never far behind. She parked in the small courtyard to the rear of the shop and lifted her briefcase from the car. It was heavy, carrying the floats she made up daily for the two tills. Julie was concentrating on the mental list of jobs she had to complete or delegate prior to her departure the following Monday on her buying trip for the shop's autumn collection.

Her attention was so distracted that she reached the back door and was fumbling with the shop keys before she noticed that all was not as it should be. The door had been forced, and none too professionally by the look of it. A long strip of bare splintered wood contrasted starkly with the dark green paint. 'Oh shit!' Julie breathed, language her customers would have been shocked to hear from her. She paused for a moment, listening intently, whilst trying to block out the sound of traffic on the road behind her.

The small room directly inside the back door was used purely for the storage of low value items necessary for the smooth running of the shop. Items such as mobile hanging rails, clothes hangers, display dummies and carrier bags in varying sizes, along with advertising signage. All were necessary, but of little intrinsic worth to anyone but those employed in the business.

As such, the room was the only part of the premises not covered by the alarm system. Thieves might not necessarily be aware of the fact. After several minutes without hearing the strident tones of the alarm, Julie relaxed slightly. What had happened looked like an inconvenience rather than a disaster. Her stock level fluctuated, and could be worth anything from thirty- to fifty-thousand pounds dependent on the time of year.

The loss of stock would have reclassified the incident as a disaster, with the inevitable knock-on effect on her insurance premiums. Margins in the business were tight enough, without having to cope with avoidable increases in overheads. Nevertheless, dealing with this was an unwelcome addition to the list of jobs she had been compiling. Instead of opening the door, Julie took out her mobile and dialled 999, something she had never done before.

DC PEARCE WASN'T particularly happy. This was an unusual state of affairs, for Viv was usually easy-going and relaxed about life. His dissatisfaction was partly because he felt he had been marginalized in the current enquiries. He wasn't sure why, or whom to blame, which made his sense of injustice difficult to cope with. Lacking the opportunity to clear the air, his grievance festered.

This morning had seemed like the last straw. With the probability of a sadistic serial killer on the loose, he had been handed the task of investigating a break-in at a clothes shop where the informant had already indicated that nothing of value had been taken. The trivial nature of the crime stoked the fire of dissatisfaction within him; he wondered why a uniformed officer had not been detailed to attend. He turned and walked out of the CID suite without a word to Nash. Mironova was on her way into the suite, having been to Mill Cottage to intercept the post. As Pearce brushed past her, Clara's cheerful greeting got no response.

She looked across at Nash, who was watching the DC stride briskly down the corridor, his gait reflecting the anger within him. 'What's Viv seen his arse about?' she asked.

Nash shook his head. 'I think he regards the job I've just given him as beneath his dignity. I'll have a word with him later and explain that we don't investigate the crimes we want to, we investigate those we have to.'

'Viv knows that well enough, Mike.' Clara grinned. 'He should do because you're always banging on about it. It could be that all isn't running smoothly on the domestic front.'

'Domestic front? What domestic front?'

'Mike, you're supposed to be a detective. Didn't you know? Viv's got a girlfriend. She's a nurse at Netherdale hospital. Her name's Lianne. Maybe they've had a lover's tiff.'

'I didn't know any of that. I was right, you are turning into a gossip columnist.'

Clara raised her eyebrows and laughed. 'Well you're no use to me on the gossip front these days. I have to get my fun elsewhere. Anyway, I've just come from Mill Cottage. There was nothing but junk mail for Dawson today. He was as charming and warmhearted as yesterday. He seems to think we're panicking over nothing, can't understand what all the fuss is about. What's our plan for the rest of this morning?'

'I want to go over those files yet again. Also, I'd like you to get in touch with forensics. They should have analysed those photos by now. Get on to them first, whilst I make coffee. Oh, and whilst you're talking to them, ask them if they've got any news about the blood on the road near the hijack. I don't think we'll find it to be human, given the security men's statements, but best to be sure.'

Nash returned with two mugs and sat down at his desk. 'What did they say?'

'You were right, the blood wasn't human. They're still looking at the photos and we should have the report tomorrow.'

'OK, then. Let's start on these files again.'

They had been reading for over an hour, occasionally one of them would comment on the contents of a statement or other information, when Clara sat bolt upright. 'Mike, I've got it. It has to be a copycat.'

'Why, what have you found?'

'There was no note.'

'Where?'

'With the photos. I was looking over your shoulder. Not only was there no wedding ring, but there wasn't a note. It says it here'—she pointed to the page—'read that.'

Nash took the file from her and read aloud, '"What others created, I cremated." I'll check all the files, see if there was a note in every case. You phone forensics, maybe it's caught in the envelope.'

A few minutes later, Clara put the phone down. 'It wasn't.'

PEARCE'S MOOD WASN'T helped by the news imparted by the shop owner. 'A dummy?' He stared at her in amazement. 'You've dialed 999 to report the theft of a tailor's dummy?'

'I told you, it's a mannequin. A tailor's dummy is quite different.'

Pearce sighed. 'Would you care to explain the difference? So I can circulate a description.'

The sarcasm wasn't lost on Julie. She decided to ignore it. 'A tailor's dummy consists only of the torso, mounted on a pedestal. It can be used for displaying blouses or jumpers, but can also be handy to drape material over when the tailor has to apply tacking stitches. Whereas, a mannequin is the sort of model you see in shop windows, a full-length replica of the human frame. Is that clear enough? Or would you like me to ask my staff if they can remember the mannequin's eye colouring or bust measurement?'

'I don't think that will be necessary. Now, are you certain that was the only item stolen? If so, why would anyone risk breaking into the shop simply to steal a dummy, sorry, a mannequin?'

Julie looked at him witheringly. Under different circumstances, she might have found his dark good looks attractive. His attitude rather spoilt that. 'I'm sorry,' she retorted, sarcasm crackling in her voice. 'I thought you were supposed to be the detective. I didn't realize I had to solve the crime myself. As to why I called you, I'm beginning to wonder why I bothered. You see, my insurers are incredibly picky. And if I decide to put in a claim for the damage done as well as the loss of the mannequin, they will insist that I have a police incident number to go along with the claim.'

Pearce realized he had allowed his personal feelings to get the better of him. 'I apologize, I didn't mean it to sound as if I wasn't interested. It's just that I find it hard to understand why someone should go to all that trouble simply to steal something of so little value, and of such limited use.'

He smiled, which Julie thought made him seem suddenly far more attractive. 'Perhaps I should go round your competitors and question them.'

'That'll take about five minutes in a town the size of Helmsdale,' Julie pointed out. 'I've a better idea. It's about the time I make a cuppa for the workers. If you like, I can make you one while you take down a statement or whatever it is you do.'

'That's very kind, especially as I wasn't very helpful earlier.'

Julie smiled at him. 'You're forgiven. Come upstairs into the stockroom. It doubles as the staffroom and my office. You'll be more comfortable there and you'll have a desk to write on.'

TONY CLEARED HIS throat. 'Sorry to drag you all away from your gainful labours. I'm sure you'd all prefer to be counting takings and arranging your shop windows. We have a potential emergency. Our operation might be in danger of being leaked.'

Tony held up his hand to quell any protest. 'I'm not referring to anyone in this room. I know you all far too well for that.' Tony glanced round the small group. All men he could trust with his own life. Had already done so in fact, more than once. 'Dawson's the problem. He was an asset, now he's a liability. What's more he's a dangerous liability. He knows everything about us. He knows what we've already done, what we're planning to do and how we dispose of our proceeds. Worst of all he knows who we are.

'Dawson's become the focus of police attention, allegedly in connection with his wife's disappearance. I'm not sure if anything's happened to her or whether she's simply buggered off with another bloke. Apart from that, even if there is something sinister behind her vanishing act I don't know whether Dawson's involved. All that's immaterial. What is critical as far as we're concerned is that if the police put pressure on Dawson he may talk. And if that happens, I wouldn't bet against him spilling the lot about our operations.'

'I wouldn't put anything past him,' Nick intervened. 'He's a cold, shifty bastard who makes my skin crawl. I'd guess he's definitely behind whatever's happened to his wife.'

'That's my point. If that threat becomes reality we will be forced to take drastic action. I've already had to borrow three of you for extra duties; essentially, a surveillance operation. In the meantime I want you all to be extra vigilant and keep an eye out for any unwelcome interest. In particular, I refer to two people I'm about to describe, and a third who Jerry will describe.'

He passed on descriptions of Nash and Mironova with photos obtained via the internet. They listened to Jerry describe Pearce.

One man asked, 'What do we do if they start getting inquisitive?'

Tony looked straight at him. 'My instructions are that they must be removed. If they pay you a call, you must act immediately. Is everybody clear on that? Right—back to it. Jerry, you got everything you need now?'

FOURTEEN

VANDA DAWSON'S PLIGHT was desperate. She was lying on a large slab of rock, around which her abductor had arranged a series of cards, each with weird symbols on. She was naked, apart from the broad bands of tape securing her wrists and ankles.

Her abductor was standing alongside her—a large petrol can in his right hand. He paused, holding the pose for a moment or two. 'Get on with it. Get it over with,' Vanda muttered angrily. 'Do your worst, otherwise I'll freeze to death waiting.'

He unscrewed the cap and held the can high. Then he tilted it and began to pour. Vanda squirmed as she watched the bright stream of liquid cascading down towards her, then gasped at the shock as it hit her skin. She opened her mouth to scream, but he was too quick for her. He pushed a handkerchief into her mouth to prevent any sound escaping. Mute, helpless but undaunted, Vanda glared at him balefully as he continued to pour, across her head, her breasts, her lower limbs. He moved away, leaving a short trail of the liquid on the ground. When the can was finally empty, he removed the gag and stepped back. He saw his captive's lips move, but couldn't make out what she said. He stepped closer. 'Get on with it, you sadistic bastard,' she muttered.

He walked away, a happy smile on his face. He reached the far side of the small clearing and set the can down. He checked the photos on the digital camera mounted on its tripod near the can. He smiled with satisfaction. They would do perfectly.

He lit the match. He watched it flare up for a moment, then tossed it in to the line of petrol. He stood in silence, watching the figure burn, ever brighter. He reached back, plucked the camera from the tripod and began firing off shot after shot. Only when he was satisfied that the damage he'd inflicted was sufficient did he collect the items he'd brought and thrust them into a black refuse sack. He glanced around the clearing to make sure there was nothing left to incriminate him. Satisfied on that score, he strode back towards the place where he'd left his car. He didn't glance back at the scene that in a couple of days' time would be the focus of so much police attention. As far as he was concerned, that was all over and done with. He had all but dismissed the smouldering body from his mind and was concentrating on what he had to do next. The burning had been fun, and all that went with it. What was to follow promised to be even more exciting.

IT WAS LATE morning when Pearce returned from the clothes shop. He'd hardly got through the door when Nash called him through into his office and closed the door behind them. Mironova smiled at this, knowing that Nash would confide in her later. The purpose of the closed door would be to allow Viv to sound off without inhibition.

'OK, Viv. Tell me about your morning.'

Pearce explained what he'd discovered at the clothes shop. He pointed out the triviality of the offence. Nash looked at him thoughtfully. 'Doesn't that make you curious?' he asked.

The DC shrugged. 'I just think it's pathetic. A worthless bit of junk. Who'd want that, and why?'

Nash leaned forward in his chair. 'That's precisely my

point, Viv. And that's the whole purpose of our job. To find out why. Look at it this way. Unless the burglar is a complete nutcase with a fetish for women who can't answer back, there has to be a reason for this theft. Our job is to work out what that reason is, and from that we might know who the thief is.'

'Sorry, Mike, I hadn't looked at it that way.'

'No, you've taken the theft in isolation, not unnatural. The interesting part of this incident is what use the person who nicked the model might have for it. Sometimes it's necessary to think beyond the facts themselves and look for the implications. So tell me, what's the real problem? Clara tells me you've got a new girlfriend. Have you had a row or something?'

Pearce paused and took a deep breath. 'Lianne missed her period last month, and she's late again this month.'

'Pregnant? How do you feel about that?'

'I don't know, I mean I don't know if I'm ready for that.'

'I'm sure it will sort itself out. For the record, I think you're more than ready for it. And if you have any other worries, come and talk to me about it, don't bottle it up, right?'

'I will.'

'Now go and make some coffee before Lucrezia Borgia out there gets near the kettle.'

It wasn't the best joke Nash had ever cracked, but the fact that it made Pearce smile was sufficient.

LATER THAT AFTERNOON, Nash, Mironova and Pearce awaited their new superintendent. Under different circumstances they might have been apprehensive about what changes would result from the appointment. Having worked with Jackie Fleming before removed most of those fears.

They had opted to meet in the main room of the CID suite rather than Nash's office. Apart from them, the room was empty, Tom Pratt having already vacated his workstation in the corner. Mironova glanced at the clock and repressed a smile as Jackie Fleming entered. It was exactly the time she'd mentioned in her phone call. Punctuality had always been one of her strong points. Nor, Clara thought as she looked at the superintendent, had the years made much difference to her appearance. Clara felt mildly envious that Fleming didn't appear any older than when they'd last met. Her slender figure and delicate, fine-boned features helped of course. She smiled at their new leader. 'Would you like a cup of coffee, ma'am?'

'It may say superintendent on my badge, but if I catch any of you calling me that, or ma'am again, I'll be seriously pissed off. I was Jackie then, and I'm Jackie now. As for the coffee, Mike, has Clara's coffee-making improved?'

'Not that I've noticed.'

'Then I will have one, but on condition Viv makes it. I'll make the next one.' She smiled. 'I haven't forgotten how the system works, or where the kitchen is. I'm happy to take my turn with the rest, but I'll need a settling-in period before I subject my system to Clara's brew. When we've got our drinks, perhaps you'll bring me up to speed with developments. I understand there have been some photos?'

The meeting lasted over an hour and a half before Jackie Fleming left to return to her base at Netherdale. Later, Mironova paused for a word with Nash. 'I forgot to mention earlier that when I was at Mill Cottage this morning the postman told me the mail train is an hour and a half earlier on Thursday, so they start deliveries that much sooner.'

'I want to go there first thing anyway,' Nash told her. 'I want a word with that milkman, what's his name?'

'McKenzie, Lindsay McKenzie. Any particular reason for wanting to talk to him? Have I missed something?'

'I'm not sure until I talk to him.' He saw Clara's puzzled expression and explained. 'It depends on McKenzie's routine. A lot of milkmen call each week to collect their money. Most of them do it in an evening, when they can be sure of catching people at home. If I had to guess, I'd say their favourite day would be Friday, but until I talk to McKenzie I won't know.'

'I see. I didn't think to ask him that. How come you worked it out?'

'You could put it down to my detective genius,' Nash paused, 'or you could say it was down to the fact that my milkman calls on Fridays.'

'Mike, you're a dreadful fraud sometimes.'

THE PHOTOGRAPHS WERE all he could have hoped for, and more. There was one he was particularly proud of. It portrayed Vanda Dawson, as he liked to remember her. The cold February air had caused her nipples to become erect. On her face was an expression of abject terror as he'd paused at the edge of the shot, poised, about to strike the match. He looked at her face, had he really inspired that look?

'Perfect,' he breathed. He considered printing an extra copy off, but decided against it. Not at this stage. Later perhaps, when his memories of the moment began to fade. That thought saddened him briefly. He turned his attention back to selecting the photos, to distract himself. He was mildly surprised that he was capable of such emotion.

The next photo he selected was equally dramatic. It depicted him holding the petrol can high over her head.

Examining it carefully, he could just see the liquid emerging from the spout. That would do, he felt sure Dawson would like that one.

His final choice was a shot taken when the flames were at their fiercest. When the heat's ferocity had distorted the image. The longer he looked at all three, the more he thought that final one was his greatest achievement. He gave them one final inspection before sliding them into the envelope he had prepared.

'One good thing,' he muttered as he looked down at them, 'at least I don't have to wear that bloody mask now.' He picked up his car keys. 'Must get these into the box before the last collection,' he muttered again. 'And then I can ditch these gloves as well. After that, I'm going to make something nice for tea. There's nothing like a good cremation for giving a man a hearty appetite.'

As he walked out of the house, he began to whistle, the notes echoing down the long hallway. He felt sure Vanda Dawson would have approved his choice of tune. *Come On Baby, Light My Fire.*

LINDSAY MCKENZIE WAS more than a little surprised when he swung his pickup round the end of Mill Cottage. He didn't recognize the cars parked on the gravel sweep that covered the area from the rear of the building to the edge of the stream. He certainly wouldn't have guessed the Range Rover was a police car until after he'd got out of his cab and was approached by the car's driver. Even then, it was the sight of the detective sergeant who'd interviewed him on Saturday that gave him his first clue, rather than the warrant card the male detective was in the process of producing from his pocket.

'Mr McKenzie? I'm Detective Inspector Nash, Helmsdale CID. I believe you've already met DS Mironova?'

McKenzie nodded. 'Have you found Mrs Dawson? I heard it on the news that she's missing.' There was undoubted eagerness in his voice. 'Is she all right?'

'I'm afraid there hasn't been any development there. Mrs Dawson is still missing. What I need to do is ask you one or two more questions, if you don't mind?'

'Not at all, Mr Nash. Although I don't know there's anything more I can tell you. Not much goes on at this time of the morning.'

'I understand that, but it's not this time of the morning I'm keen to ask you about. I understand when you spoke to my sergeant on Saturday, you told her the last time you saw Mrs Dawson was when you delivered the milk on Thursday, is that right?'

'Yes, just a brief glimpse. She was in the kitchen as I delivered, and I caught sight of her as she opened the blinds. She waved, and I waved back.'

'When did you last speak to her?'

'The last time I saw her to speak to? That would be on Tuesday morning.'

'And how did she seem?'

'She seemed OK to me.'

'Now, when does she pay you? Does she leave the money out in an envelope or something like that, or do you call specially for it?'

'No, I make a point of calling on all my customers. That way, they can tell me about holidays or if there are any variations in their order. And I'm sure to get my money. A year or so back, one of my customers claimed they'd left the money in an envelope, but I never found it. The lady said someone must have stolen it, but I had my doubts. I didn't say anything because her husband had left her and I think she was struggling to make ends meet. It was only a few pounds, so what the heck.'

'Did you collect Mrs Dawson's money last week?'

'No, I tried to, but there was nobody in. I collect from half my customers on Thursday evening, and do the rest on Friday night. At least that was the plan, but the weather on Friday was so rotten I decided to leave it a week.'

'Is Mill Cottage on your Thursday list, then?'

'That's right, it's my last call. I always finish up here on Thursday night.'

'What sort of time would that be? Last Thursday for instance?'

McKenzie thought about it for a few minutes. 'At a guess I'd say it was a touch before eight o'clock.'

'And you say there was nobody in?'

'That's what I assumed. It was raining heavily by then and the wind was already getting up, so I didn't get out of the car because the house was all in darkness, so I thought she must have gone out.'

'Had Mrs Dawson ever been out when you called for the money previously?'

'Not that I can remember.'

'Thank you, Mr McKenzie, that'll be all for now. I believe DS Mironova has your details if I need to ask you any more questions.' Nash looked across at Clara, who nodded.

The detectives watched the milkman collect the empty and place a single pint in the crate, guided by the small wheel indicator on the wire basket.

As McKenzie reversed the pickup, Clara asked, 'What do you make of that? Interesting that the house was in darkness.'

'I find it more interesting that he failed to mention his Thursday night call when you questioned him on Saturday.'

'Do you think he might be involved?'

'I'm just saying it seems curious. There may be nothing to it, but I think it might be worth checking Mr McKenzie out.'

'Tom's got him on his list of regular visitors already. Do you think it's urgent?'

'Not really, McKenzie doesn't seem the type, and besides…'

'Besides what?'

'I'm still not convinced this is a Cremator case. It doesn't feel right, somehow.'

'Is this your sixth sense working overtime again?' She was about to continue when she saw movement beyond Nash's right shoulder. 'Looks as if Dawson's up and about early.'

FIFTEEN

DESPITE THE HOUR, the accountant was already fully dressed for the office. Nash took in the dark suit, the crisp white shirt, the highly polished shoes and the sober tie bearing the emblem of some sports club. Nash wondered briefly if it was of his golf club, given the spurious alibi he'd given his wife for his absence the previous week. That reminded him of something.

'Clara, did we get confirmation from Dawson's clients?'

'Viv's following it up this morning.'

Nash watched Dawson approach. 'What are you doing here at this hour?' the accountant demanded. He sounded less than pleased by their presence.

'We needed to speak to the milkman and we were told the post arrives earlier than usual this morning, so we decided to combine the two.'

'Right, well, I don't suppose I can stop you.' Dawson turned on his heel, collected the milk from the crate and went back inside. The door slammed behind him.

'Bloody charming!' Clara muttered. 'He could at least have offered us a coffee. I'm gagging.'

'Me too,' Nash agreed. 'I'd even settle for one of yours, which shows how desperate I am.'

They hadn't long to wait for the postman who walked straight towards them rather than heading for the letterbox. 'Still intercepting the post?' the man asked.

'Yes, I'm afraid so.' Nash donned gloves and accepted

the proffered pile. He waited until the postman had driven away before sifting through the bundle. The top items were bulky, a newsletter from the county council and a host of the usual assorted junk mail. For a moment he relaxed, then saw a familiar envelope. Nash's heart sank. Following the trend of previous incidents, this could only mean one thing. The Cremator was announcing that he had tortured and murdered Vanda Dawson. He felt rather than saw Mironova close behind him, before she spoke.'

'Dear God, no! The sick bastard. I don't believe anyone can be so cruel.'

'He's had plenty of practice,' Nash observed grimly. As he was speaking, the door of the cottage opened.

Dawson looked from Nash to the envelope the detective was holding. 'Is that what I think it is?' His voice might just have held a note of concern, but if it did, it was minimal, Clara thought. If he was concerned, it was only echoed in his voice, for his face betrayed no emotion whatsoever. A few seconds ago, she had wondered how the killer could be so cruel, now she couldn't believe that Dawson could remain so calm.

'Yes, it is,' Nash replied. 'But once again you must allow me to open it. If there are fingerprints or DNA on either the envelope or contents, I can't risk them being contaminated. Also, in view of what the contents might be, I suggest you don't look at them.'

Dawson's expression was evident now, it was one of arrogance. 'Allow me to be the judge of that. I will see what is in that envelope. You can't stop me. You don't have a warrant, and you're interfering with my mail without one, which is against the law. However, I will allow you to take the envelope and contents away, but only on condition that I see what's inside first.'

Nash hesitated, looking at the accountant for a few

moments before giving a reluctant nod. 'Very well, but I ought to warn you that I've seen the other files, and these photos could be extremely distressing.'

He got no response, so he gently slit the end of the envelope and retrieved the contents. He looked at the first photo, hearing Clara's gasp of horror as she peered over his shoulder.

'Let me see,' Dawson insisted.

Nash held it up, his eyes fixed on the accountant's face as the man stared at the image of his wife, bound hand and foot, stark naked, on an improvised altar. The background was woodland, and the photo taken to give no view of the terrain beyond the immediate vicinity of the woman's body. She was obviously alive at that point—the look of terror on her face showed that—her expression also demonstrated that she knew exactly what was about to happen to her. If there was anything other than surprise on Dawson's face, Nash couldn't detect it.

The second image reinforced the Cremator's intentions; he was on the point of dousing his victim with petrol. Nash showed it to Dawson without comment. At last, there was a reaction, albeit a small one, from the victim's husband. He recoiled slightly, and muttered, 'I don't believe this. It's all wrong.'

The final photo was by far the worst. The flames licking round the body were horribly graphic. The shimmering air that distorted the camera's focus was a clear indication of the intense heat. There was no doubt in Nash's mind that Vanda Dawson had perished, and little doubt that the poor woman had died in the most dreadful agony.

He looked round at Mironova. She was pale and looked as if she was about to be sick. He turned back and with the utmost reluctance held the photo up for Dawson to see.

Once again, the accountant shook his head in plain denial of what was too graphically obvious to the detectives.

'No,' Dawson said after a moment. 'No, this isn't right. I don't believe this, any of it.'

Nash knew such rejection of the most terrible news was not uncommon, but there seemed more than that in Dawson's attitude. Despite his obvious shock, the man had his emotions well under control. 'Mr Nash, you will find out who did this, won't you? You will find out who is behind this sick practical joke. And find out what has really happened to my wife. I will leave it to you. Please inform me when you have something definite to report.'

To Nash's complete astonishment, Dawson turned as if to re-enter the cottage. Nash detained him with a hand on his arm. He pleaded with Dawson to allow him to call for a family liaison officer to come and stay with him, but in vain.

'I just want to be left in peace, can't you understand that,' was the nearest Nash got to eliciting some emotion from him.

The detectives walked back to their cars, both deep in thought. Nash placed the envelope and photos in an evidence bag. 'I want you to send Viv straight to Netherdale to deliver these. Whilst he's waiting he can tell Jackie what's happened.'

'What are you going to do?'

'One of the hardest jobs I've ever had to do,' Nash said grimly. 'I thought telling Dawson was going to be bad, but he's so cold it didn't seem real. However, I must tell Dr Grey what's happened to her sister.'

Clara's reaction surprised him. 'Why don't I speak to her? It would come better from a woman. Remember, I spoke to her last night and she does seem to react well to me.'

'Would you? You might think this is cowardice, and

I'm sure she will, but I think that's a good idea. I'm going to get in my car and drive out towards Wintersett. I need to think through everything that's happened without interruption. I'll be back in Helmsdale around lunchtime.'

While they were discussing what had taken place, they were unaware that Dawson was watching them from within the house. All trace of emotion had vanished from his face. The evidence they had shown him seemed to point to his wife being a victim, either of the Cremator or an acolyte. The belief held by the police that the notorious sadist might be responsible for what had happened to her had caused a momentary flicker of reaction in the accountant's eyes, but what emotion it was, even the keenest observer wouldn't have been able to guess.

It appeared that he was now alone. That Vanda would not be returning. And that the local police would be searching high and low for the Cremator. Surely, this was the worst possible time to carry out the plan he had in mind. Or was it? He watched the cars leaving; then began making his preparations, with meticulous attention to detail. Now, an observer would have been able to detect some form of emotion. A kind of repressed excitement. Making sense of what it signalled would have been far more difficult.

On the journey back to Helmsdale, Mironova tried contacting Pearce, who was on the phone chasing up Dawson's alibi. Viv rang back to tell her the officer who'd investigated Dawson's alibi would be on duty later that day, and his report would be forthcoming then. 'It hardly seems relevant now,' she told him, explaining what they'd discovered at Mill Cottage.

THE WATCHER WAS about to call Tony to report on yet another police visit to Dawson's cottage when his eye caught a movement in the woodland at the other side of the stream. He trained his binoculars on the area, expecting to see a pheasant, perhaps, or, if he was really lucky, a deer. He searched for some time, moving the glasses and adjusting the focus for longer distance before he identified the figure of a man. He fine-tuned the focus, and as the object of his attention became clear, the watcher raised his eyebrows in surprise. 'Well, well, well,' he muttered. 'What's this about, then?'

He waited a few minutes more, until he was sure what the man's motives were. When there was no doubt in his mind that he too was watching the cottage and its occupant, he pulled his mobile from his pocket.

'Tony? Sorry to drag you from your pit.'

'Don't worry, you didn't. What's the score?'

'I thought you might be interested to know that there's been quite a lot of early morning activity here. First off, CID landed. After they'd been here a few minutes, the milkman arrived. He was a bit longer than usual, that was because Nash looked to be asking him a load of questions. After he left, Dawson came out and had a word with them. He didn't seem at all pleased to find them camped on his doorstep.'

'I wonder why not? And I wonder why Nash would be questioning the milkman? Is that the size of it, then?'

'Oh, no, I've only just got started: Dawson went back indoors and they waited outside until the postie arrived. As soon as he saw the van, Nash scuttled towards him. It turns out Nash was interested in one envelope. He took charge of it and examined what looked like some photos. Dawson came out. Nash showed him the photos as well. Dawson didn't seem upset by them, but the woman cop, turned distinctly green. I thought she was going to throw up. Anyway, after a bit more chat, Nash and Mironova went back to his car, but get this, before they got in, Nash stuffed the envelope and doings into an evidence bag. No idea what it's about, but it didn't look good from our point of view.'

'I take your point. I'm going to have to think about this and decide what we should do.'

'Hang on, Tony, I haven't finished yet. I was just about to ring you to tell you all this, when I noticed something else. There's another bloke watching the house.'

'What?'

'I know; I didn't believe it myself. Not for a few minutes. I thought it might have been someone doing a bit of poaching, or something like that, but he's definitely watching the place. Got himself a good vantage point as well, for an amateur.'

'How do you mean, "for an amateur"? Who do you think he is? Another of Nash's lot?'

'I don't think so. Not unless one of them is moonlighting as a milkman.'

'A milkman?'

'Yes, the guy who delivered the milk has come back, installed himself on the far bank of the stream and is watching the house. Probably been there since he dropped the pint off. I was concentrating on the action at the house and damn near missed him. What do you want me to do?'

'Nothing for the moment, just keep watching. I'll have to sort out a team to go in and do what's necessary.'

Tony replaced the receiver and looked across at Jerry. 'The time has come for us to pull out,' he told his second in command. 'Get the lads busy. I want all the premises stripped and cleaned by tonight. Only your window display must remain. That has to look normal. Once the shop's been emptied, I want you to clear Dawson's of-

fices out. I want nothing left that could possibly be traced
back to us.'

'Everything?'

Tony nodded. 'Everything, down to the last paper clip.
Tell the lads to go round all the surfaces in their shops
using medicated wet wipes: that should fetch all the fingerprints off. Not that anyone has a record, but it's better to play safe. We'll all meet up later today for a final
briefing.'

'Nick said to tell you the new accounts have been activated and tested.'

'Good, that means Dawson's now a disposable asset.
Tell Nick to start the transfer process. Once we've hit our
targets we'll assume the new identities we've got set up.
As far as anyone trying to find out what's happened is
concerned, we'll have vanished as if we never existed.'
He paused and smiled. 'Which of course is true.'

NASH PARKED THE Range Rover on the north side of Wintersett village. Through the driver's open window, he could
hear the distant bleating of sheep. Lambing season was in
full swing, but although the sound registered, his thoughts
were elsewhere. Throughout his career, Nash had always
had the rare ability to put himself in the place of the criminal. By doing that he could visualize how the crimes were
committed. This in turn often led him straight to the identity of the perpetrator. If not, it showed him the route his
investigation should take.

The problem was that Nash was unable to get even a
hint of how the abduction had taken place, or of what the
kidnapper was thinking. Despite Clara's conviction that
the disappearance of Vanda Dawson was the work of the
Cremator or a copycat, Nash was becoming more and
more convinced this was not so. That puzzled him, but

he was aware that there were a whole series of anomalies connected with the abduction.

He remained motionless in the driving seat of his car, staring at the harsh beauty of Black Fell and the bare, leafless woodland that covered the lower slopes of the hillside. He stared at the scene, but took in little detail as he tried to make sense of what few facts they had.

Remembering the files they had read, Nash listed the differences between this current case and the first that had been reported; comparing it to other known Cremator incidents. There was still doubt as to whether the first unfortunate woman had fallen prey to that sadistic monster, or whether it was a lone incident, from which the Cremator gained inspiration. That first victim had been younger than the others, and there was no evidence to suggest that she had been married. And, whereas all the other victims had been reported missing soon after they vanished, nobody had come forward to question her disappearance. More than that, despite huge publicity and the passage of time, she had still not been identified.

There were other differences too in the case of the first victim. There'd been no sending of photographs to the victims' partner, nor the gruesome addition of the sawnup wedding ring. That all suggested the woman was single and unattached—unlike the others. From thereon, the killer had maintained a pattern—until this latest incident, which itself had failed to match the others. Despite his best efforts, Nash couldn't come up with any solid reason for this. Like so many aspects of the case, it simply didn't make sense.

Nash turned his attention to consideration of the security van hijacking, and how they might be able to identify those responsible. There was a way, or there might be. As he started the car and swung back on to the road for Helmsdale, Nash felt marginally less depressed than he had since the abduction photos arrived.

THE FIRST THING Nash did on reaching Helmsdale was to find Tom Pratt. 'Tom, I've a bit of work for you,' Nash began, 'quite a lot in fact. Here's what we need to look at.'

He'd just finished giving Pratt the details when Mironova walked in. Nash glanced up, she looked subdued, no doubt as a result of the meeting with Dr Grey. There were few worse jobs than having to break bad news to relatives. He wondered briefly if they'd been precipitate. Should they have waited until they recovered the body before revealing details to either the missing woman's husband or her sister?

'I don't think I need to ask how it went.'

Clara shook her head. 'She was in a terrible state, even before I broke the news. As I was doing it I had this awful thought. What if one day there's a knock on my door and someone stands there telling me about David?'

'His service time is nearly up, isn't it?'

'On paper, yes, but the lot he's with don't operate by normal rules. Mike, I don't think I could stand it if that happened.'

'Well, it hasn't happened. What you must do is tell David how you feel. It might affect decisions he makes about his career.' Nash smiled. 'In the past, he's only had to think of himself. A bit like me, I suppose. Maybe now that I've got Daniel to think about, I'm looking at things differently.'

'I'll tell him tonight.'

'WE NEED TO move. Jerry has passed on my instructions, I hope you've all managed to comply. As for our friend, Dawson, I'm not going to take any chances. We need to take him out before he can drop us in it. He's already been interviewed by the police twice. I'm not prepared to wait for a third. I want him dealing with. Speaking of the police brings me to a second problem. My instructions are that Nash represents an even bigger threat than Dawson and, therefore, he's also to be disposed of. That will be down to me. I think I can dream up something spectacular, and what's more, something we can use to our advantage. What I need to know is how we're progressing? When do you think we'll be ready to go ahead?'

'We could go now,' Jerry assured him. 'Although we might need a bit of a distraction.'

Tony smiled, 'I think I can provide one. Let me tell you what I have in mind. We'll start with Nash.'

'How are you planning to do it?'

Tony explained, adding, 'It won't seem suspicious until it's too late. Too late for Nash, certainly.'

'How much time will you need?'

'A couple of hours should be ample. Then I'll have to wait there until I know Nash is on his way home.'

Jerry frowned. 'Why do you need to know that?'

As Tony explained, Jerry gasped. 'That's brilliant. Where did you learn that?'

'The basic idea came from something I saw in Bosnia. I simply added the refinement.'

'Well, we're all set to go. When do you want us to do it?'

'As soon as I can arrange the diversion. I've been watching Nash. The problem is his movements are unpredictable.'

'I suppose you've to wait for him to go out before you can set it up.'

'That's right, but from what I've seen so far, I could be waiting a while.'

Their conversation was interrupted when Tony's mobile rang. 'Our man watching Dawson,' he told Jerry. Tony listened. 'You've lost him? Where?' He waited, then said, 'If he went in that direction, he obviously isn't going to the police. Go back to his place and pray he returns.'

SIXTEEN

WITH JACK BINNS at Netherdale, Helmsdale police station reception desk was manned by a young constable not long out of training college. He glanced up as the phone rang, glad to switch his attention from the pensioner he'd been dealing with. He knew the procedure for dealing with the call, although as yet the steps hadn't become a reflex. He had to log the time and duration of every call manually, plus noting the incoming number and establishing the caller's identity. Helmsdale was one of the few stations that, as yet, hadn't been supplied with a computer to assist in his task.

As he recited his opening message, the constable scribbled the number shown on the phone's display on the telephone log sheet and pressed the record button on the phone so there would be a permanent record. 'North Yorkshire police, Helmsdale station, how can I help you?'

The signal on the mobile was poor; the caller must be in a bad reception area the constable thought as he struggled to interpret what the man was saying. Within the first couple of phrases, his attention was total; his biro scribbling furiously as he noted down the details.

'Can I have your name, sir?'

The request was refused, but the explanation sounded reasonable even if the constable disapproved of the reason. Certainly, it was plausible enough for him not to press the caller on the identity issue. But then the constable was extremely inexperienced. He put the phone down and tore the message off the pad. Ignoring the renewed demands of the pensioner standing in front of the desk, who seemed aggrieved that his complaint about his neighbour's cat fouling his flowerbeds wasn't receiving the attention he believed it merited; the constable headed straight for the stairs leading to the CID suite.

The trio of detectives listened in horror to the young officer's words. No matter how much they might have expected it, the news that confirmed their worst fears was no less shocking. They watched the constable depart, their silence a mixture of sorrow and stirring anger. Nash glanced out of the window. The short winter afternoon was already drawing to a close. 'We'd better get out there straightaway. Even if we get lucky, we'll not be able to do much more than identify the site today.'

'Can't we organize some men to search the area?'

Nash considered Viv's question. 'The final decision on that isn't down to me. Only Jackie has the authority to pull enough men in to search that sort of terrain. The other problem with doing that is we risk contaminating the evidence if half a dozen brawny coppers go trampling around the site of the body. Forensics wouldn't be happy, and they'd let us know about it. We'll get off and hope for the best. You two go ahead. I'll meet you there. I'd better warn Jackie what's happened.'

'Where shall we meet?'

'Park up in that old workings, Lady Luck Quarry. That's the car park all the hikers and ramblers use. If this couple were taking a romantic stroll, I reckon the body will have to be within striking distance of that car park.'

As Clara and Viv headed for the door, Nash went to pick up his phone, but was forestalled when it rang. 'Mike? It's Tom. I've been checking those names like you asked me to.'

'The tradesmen who call at Mill Cottage regularly?'

'That's right. I thought it was going to be a dead end, but then I spotted something familiar and checked our files. There's a name on one of them, and it's far too strong a connection to be coincidence, I reckon.'

'Oh yes?'

'Chris Willis.'

'Remind me.'

'Works for Good Buys, does their delivery service. Did two years for assault: on his wife.'

'Now that is interesting. See if you can turn anything else up, will you?'

'I already have, wait until you hear this.'

IT WAS FIFTEEN minutes later before Nash started out for Black Fell. He'd intended setting off earlier, but his talk with Tom Pratt had detained him, after which he had spoken to Jackie Fleming. As he drove, Nash reflected that he couldn't remember the last time he'd been so wrong. He'd been wrong to suggest this wasn't a Cremator crime. Wrong to believe that no crime had been committed, or that Vanda Dawson might have contrived her disappearance. Why would any woman conspire at her own murder? Worst of all, he'd been wrong in his assessment of one of the men he'd met, a man who now seemed likely to be the worst serial killer in Nash's memory.

By the time he reached the car park at Lady Luck Quarry, dusk was a recent memory and Black Fell was living up to its name. Clara had left a visiting card tucked under her wiper blade. On it, she had drawn an arrow. Nash smiled faintly and followed the direction indicated.

The path was overgrown with brambles and bracken. There were few ramblers at this time of year to combat the overgrowth and maintenance of such footpaths was a haphazard affair at best. It would have been a tricky walk even in broad daylight. With the night blackened further by the surrounding trees and only the beam from his Maglite to help him, Nash found it slow going.

Eventually, he caught up with Mironova and Pearce. Without his noticing it, the path had been rising gradually. The reason he had gained on the other two was that they had stopped. As he joined them, Nash looked round and saw the reason why. The rising path had brought them clear of the woods on to the bare, steep side of Black Fell. Either they hadn't been able to spot the site of the body due to the density of the undergrowth, or the call had been a hoax. Nash remembered the young constable's words. 'The caller said the body is in the woods, near the path up Black Fell. It looks like someone's set fire to it.'

'We've missed it.' Clara voiced all their thoughts.

'Yes, and the chances are, if we miss it again going back the other way we'll not find it until daylight. Either the body's farther from the path than that caller suggested, or he was having us on.'

'Why would he do that?'

Nash shrugged. 'Why does anyone make false alarm calls? The news that Mrs Dawson is missing has been on the news and in the papers. That sort of headline attracts all sorts of cranks. We'll have to leave it until morning. We've something more urgent to contend with.'

'What's that?'

'I asked Tom to check on all regular visitors to the Dawson house. As a result of what he discovered, I think we've identified the Cremator.'

'How? Who is it?' Clara and Viv's questions clashed.

'One of them used to live in a small village only two miles from Covermere.'

'Covermere?' Clara asked. 'Isn't that where the first of

the Cremator's victims was found, the one who's never been identified?'

'That's correct, and the victim's body was discovered less than a mile from the house occupied at the time by Lindsay McKenzie. Lindsay McKenzie, who now delivers milk to Mill Cottage every day. And who, by his own admission, was the last person to see Mrs Dawson before she disappeared.'

Although all three had torches and shone these along both sides of the path as they returned slowly towards the car park, they failed to spot the slightest indication of where the body, if it existed, might be lying. When they reached their vehicles, Nash told the other two to head back. 'I promised Jackie I'd call her as soon as we'd finished here. She's coming over to discuss how we proceed against McKenzie.'

Although the signal from his mobile was less than brilliant, Nash managed to convey the news that they had been unsuccessful and that he was heading back to Helmsdale.

'I'll meet you there,' Fleming said.

THEIR MEETING DIDN'T last long. 'I've arranged for a search warrant for McKenzie's farm,' Jackie began. 'It should be ready for signature in the morning. DC Andrews will be back on duty, she can bring it through to you. I'm ordering an ARU as backup. There's no saying what might happen if he's cornered. In the meantime, I think we should keep the place under surveillance. I don't want McKenzie to slip from our grasp. Capturing the Cremator will mean the eyes of the world's media will be on us.'

'Surveillance should be easy,' Clara responded. 'I know the location quite well. There's a farm track leading to some fields alongside woodland on the north side of McKenzie's place. It overlooks the whole of the property.

Anyone parked at the end of the track will be able to see not only the house and its doors, but the outbuildings and the lane leading on to the property.'

Nash eyed his sergeant with interest. 'How come you know this track so well? Is that where you and David go when you fancy a spot of alfresco nooky?'

Clara's cheeks were scarlet. 'Don't judge everyone by yourself,' she answered weakly.

Nash smiled triumphantly, having in one sentence repaid years of taunts from Clara about his sex life.

'I think you should split the night shift between you,' Fleming intervened hastily. 'And to be on the safe side, I think we should have a couple of uniforms standing by. Tomorrow, Mike and Clara will lead the team searching McKenzie's place, along with Andrews. That leaves Viv free to locate this body on Black Fell. I'll assign some uniforms to help you,' she told the DC. 'I'm off to report developments to God. She was in a meeting earlier, but I know she's keen for an update.' The trio of detectives smiled at Fleming's use of Chief Constable O'Donnell's nickname.

'Will you take the first shift, Clara?' Nash asked when the superintendent had gone. 'If Viv takes over from you at 10 o'clock, and I relieve him at 2 a.m., that means I can follow McKenzie on his milk round.'

They nodded in agreement.

'Oh, and, Clara, pop in at my place on your way home tonight and let me know what's happened. By the time McKenzie's finished deliveries, Lisa should be through from Netherdale with the warrant, and as soon as the ARU team are in place we can start work.

'That takes care of McKenzie.' Nash turned to Pearce. 'You assemble your uniforms at Lady Luck Quarry at first light. Take the other path to begin with and stick rigidly to it. If you manage to catch sight of the body from there, don't go near it. Get some uniforms to stand guard until forensics and Mexican Pete arrive. SOCO might be kept fairly busy tomorrow.'

'Can I nip home for a sandwich and another sweater before I set off for McKenzie's place?' Clara asked.

'Of course. I'll go and locate this track of yours and wait there until you arrive.'

There was a knock at the door and the desk constable entered.

'Excuse me, sir,' he said hesitantly. 'I've been tying off loose ends before the station closes for the night and I think you should take a look at the mobile number that call came in on.'

Nash looked at the number. 'Is this whose I think it is?'

The constable nodded. 'Yes, sir, Sergeant Binns left a note of it on the pad, but I've only just compared the two.'

'I think that dismisses the idea of a hoax call,' he told the others. 'The report of the body being found was made from Vanda Dawson's missing mobile.'

LATER WHEN NASH reached the flat, the building was in darkness. He considered the idea of cooking dinner, but after inspecting the contents of the freezer and glancing at the time, decided against it. As he closed the freezer door, he noticed that he'd forgotten to switch off the coffee machine that morning. Luckily, the device was fitted with an automatic cut-out. He helped himself to a mug of coffee, which he reheated in the microwave. He sipped the hot liquid, pondering the day's developments. It looked as if they were close to solving the Vanda Dawson case, and bringing the Cremator to book. Once they had McKenzie in a cell, he could concentrate on the security van robbery. Before that, he was going to have a curtailed night's sleep.

Better get moving and have something to eat. He opted for La Giaconda. At this time of the year, the restaurant would be quiet and Gino would ensure he'd get served quickly. That would leave him time for a few hours kip before he went on surveillance.

CRAIG WAS AWAY from Monday to Friday each week. Normally, that didn't worry Janet in the slightest. Tonight, however, although she didn't know why, she was jumpy. The slightest sound was enough to have her on edge. And there were plenty of those in this big old house. Hinges squeaked, floorboards creaked, even when there was no one near them.

Familiarity, they say, breeds contempt. Janet had dismissed her fears as irrational, just as she had dismissed the sensation she'd had once or twice recently that someone was watching her. Over-active imagination, she thought, nothing more.

When she heard the floorboard creak as she left the sitting room, Janet did no more than glance idly down the corridor. Purely a reflex action. Then, in a heart-stopping moment, she glimpsed the figure. Silhouetted in the pale moonlight through the window behind him. That was when she screamed. The first of many screams.

THE PHONE CALL was brief. 'Nash has left his flat. He's on foot. I'm following him.'

'Let me know where he's going. If he's just out for a stroll, that won't give me enough time.'

Tony put his mobile back on the table and pulled his rucksack towards him. He checked that all the tools he would need were inside. It was the third time he'd done that, but he wasn't prepared to leave anything to chance.

When he was satisfied he had everything he needed, he waited, pacing slowly round the small room.

It seemed an age before his phone rang again. 'He's gone into that Italian restaurant in the market place. I can see him through the window, sitting at a table in clear view. He's studying the menu.'

'Good; that'll give me ample time. Let me know when he calls for the bill, or if you can't do that, ring me the minute he leaves. How long did it take him to get there?'

'No more than ten minutes.'

Tony placed the phone in one of the zip pockets of his leathers and slid the straps of the rucksack over his shoulders. He put his helmet on, picked up the bike's ignition key and set off. He reached Nash's flat a few minutes later and parked the bike round the corner of the street. It took only minutes to enter the flat, following which he headed for the kitchen. He inspected the gas cooker and smiled. This should be easy. Before he started work, he moved the coffee machine on to the table. He placed the grids and hot plates from the hob on the space where the coffee machine had stood, and set about removing the oven top. The securing screws had obviously not been moved for a long time. It took considerable effort to get them all out. The last one proved very obstinate, and he was on the point of sawing through it when he felt it move. He exerted a little more pressure, taking care to avoid stripping the thread on the screw head. Eventually, he worked it clear and was able to look down into the oven cavity and the space behind it. The inlet pipe was in a very inaccessible spot. This was not going to be as easy as he'd expected.

Before he started work on the pipe, he opened the double-glazed oven door. He sealed the gap at the bottom with sellotape before filling the cavity with the contents of a bag he'd removed from his rucksack. The purchase had been made at the local ironmongery a couple of days previously. The shrapnel effect of a large quantity of three-inch nails at high velocity would be lethal. Added to the blast itself, nobody inside that room, or the flat itself, would stand much chance of survival.

Having filled the cavity, Tony closed the oven door. All he had to do now was introduce a controlled leak into the gas pipe leading to the oven. Then, as soon as he knew Nash was on his way back to the flat, he would set the automatic timer on the oven. When the oven switched itself on, the flame would ignite the gas. When that happened, Nash would be history.

The next part was the trickiest. The inaccessible position of the inlet pipe didn't help. Tony worked slowly, taking great care. The slightest spark at this stage would result in him becoming the victim of his own device. He glanced at his watch. The work had taken longer than he anticipated, but eventually it was done, and not a moment too soon. As he was replacing all the screws, his mobile rang. 'Nash is just paying the bill,' the watcher told him.

Tony checked his watch. Only ten minutes left. Working quickly now, he replaced the rings and grids on the hob and stuffed his tools back in his rucksack. He checked his watch again; six minutes. He made sure the clock on the oven was working and switched the automatic timer to ignite in ten minutes time. That should be ample, he thought. He switched the kitchen light off, exited the flat and shut the front door behind him. He'd taken no more than a dozen strides when he remembered the coffee machine was still on the kitchen table. He checked his watch, no time to go back.

NASH RETURNED HOME. Having drunk only one glass of wine with his meal, he refused Gino's offer of coffee, aware he still had half a pot in his machine. He had time for some before he relieved Viv, and headed straight for the kitchen. He knew something was wrong immediately. His gaze travelled from the coffee machine to the cooker. To the glowing red light, indicating the automatic timer was on. To the glass door that was obscured by something. As these facts jelled, Nash realized their significance.

He turned, at that precise second he heard a sound. For a sickening moment, he thought it was the oven timer. Then realized it was the front doorbell. He ran and opened it wide. 'Get out of the way!' Nash screamed as he lunged forward.

Clara opened her mouth to answer, then she heard a noise. It sounded like a huge sigh. At the same time, she felt a hot draught of wind rush past her, followed by a huge detonation. Her eardrums felt as if they were on the point of bursting.

Nash was almost out of the door, pushing her to one side, when the shock wave hit him. At the same time something struck his arm and the back of his head. He thought he could hear a buzzing sound in the distance. Then his vision went black as consciousness left him.

CLARA RAISED HERSELF, her face contorted with horror. Nash was lying across the threshold, half-in, half-out of the doorway. The shattered remnants of the heavy wooden door were lying across his upper body. Behind him, through the dust created by the blast, she could see flames already shooting upwards. She fought against panic. That wouldn't help. She scrabbled swiftly across to Nash. There was blood on the back of his head. She reached down, her fingers going instinctively to his neck for a pulse.

A phone. That was what she needed. She dragged her mobile from her pocket and dialled the control room. As she was pressing the keys, she heard the sound of a motorbike. She thought momentarily of trying to flag the rider down for help, then dismissed the idea as the emergency operator answered. She fought to remain calm. She knew not to move an injured person. No time to worry about that with fire already taking hold of the building. As soon as she ended the call, she began moving the debris from him, glancing up every few seconds to see how close the inferno was.

SEVENTEEN

DAVID SUTTON WAS relaxing in front of the TV. The phone rang as the news summary was ending. David reached over and plucked the handset from the cradle. He listened for a moment. 'I'll be right there,' he said.

He reached Nash's street in minutes, but the road was blocked by emergency vehicles. He abandoned his car rather than parking it. Ahead, he saw a couple of police cars, an ambulance and two fire engines, the crews deploying their hoses. The air was thick with smoke, flames licking from the windows. He noticed a motorbike pull away from the kerb at the far end of the street. I'd have been better with one of those, David thought fleetingly.

Two paramedics came into view, wheeling a stretcher. The blanket covering the victim only reached as far as his shoulders. Sutton heaved a sigh of relief. It was Nash; at least he was alive. As he watched, he saw a woman walking alongside the stretcher. Her face was covered in grime, with twin tracks down her cheeks where tears had flowed.

Despite the dirt, David had no difficulty recognising his fiancée. 'Clara,' he called out. She looked round, unsure where the sound had come from. 'Clara,' Sutton called again. She located him, and pointed to the ambulance. Sutton nodded and signalled that he would follow her. Sutton watched the lights recede into the distance, the sirens blaring their strident warning.

The fire crew began to tackle the blaze as the police officers moved onlookers away and cordoned the area. Inside the ambulance, Clara took out her phone and called Netherdale station. She told the officer in the control room to get Fleming on the phone and ask her to ring her back. The officer agreed. After Clara ended the call, the man wondered why the normally quietly spoken sergeant had been shouting.

Jackie Fleming had left her hotel details with the station control room. Within minutes, the superintendent rang Clara back from her room at the Golden Bear. Fleming reacted with predictable horror to Clara's news. Once she'd ascertained that Clara was unhurt, and that Nash's injuries didn't appear to be life-threatening, she told her, 'I'll meet you at the hospital. I'll let Pearce know what's happened, and warn him he's going to be on surveillance longer than planned. I'll let the chief know too, then I'd better head for the crime scene. Who's in charge of the fire crews?'

Clara had seen a familiar figure climbing out of a fire service car before she got into the ambulance. 'The CFO is Doug Curran. He'd just arrived when we left.'

TONY PARKED HIS bike round the corner from the end of Nash's street and walked back until he reached the high brick wall surrounding the garden of the last house. From there he could watch what was happening without being seen. He took out his mobile. 'Everything set?'

'Ready to go,' Jerry answered. 'We're just waiting for the word.'

'Start right now. The police are going to have their hands full here. The building's well alight. Nash has been carted off in an ambulance, but I couldn't get near enough to tell what condition he was in. By the look of the way the place is burning, they'll have to evacuate residents from the surrounding properties, so that should give you

ample time. I'll stay here a bit longer to make sure nobody
leaves in a hurry. You don't want to be rudely interrupted.'

AFTER THE AMBULANCE containing Nash and Mironova left,
Sergeant Binns arrived in the street outside Nash's flat.
He sought out Curran. 'Thank God you're here, Jack,'
the fire officer said. 'We're going to need help getting
everyone out of the rest of the terrace. How many men
have you got?'

Binns gestured to the quartet of uniformed officers
whose official task thus far had been to keep the street
clear of onlookers and vehicles that might block access.
'What you see is what you get.'

Curran grimaced. 'My men will have to concentrate
on the fire, I can't spare anyone. Will you get your chaps
working on getting residents out? We'll have to chance
blocking the road.'

Binns issued instructions and watched as the four
moved off in pairs to start work. He could tell they were
meeting with some success as a trickle of people in a
wide variety of garments began to appear on the pavement. Binns herded them clear of the fire engines to a
distance safe behind the cordon. As he was moving the
last of them, he saw Fleming striding down the street towards him. 'Any news from the hospital?'

'I've alerted the chief. She thought you'd need all the
help you can get so she told me to head here. She's gone
to check up on Nash. What's the situation?' She gestured
towards the burning building. 'They could be a long time
getting that under control.'

'Curran reckons it'll take until morning, at least. And
that's as long as the fire doesn't spread to other buildings.
Although the gas has been shut off at the mains, there's
all the residue in the pipes. Luckily, the rest of the build-

ing was holiday lets, so there was no one in them. Nash's flat was the only one occupied.'

'That's something, I suppose. I'll go and introduce my-self to Curran. The chief was going to organise backup but they're short-staffed at Netherdale, so we can't count on much help.'

Binns and Fleming were trying to calm the residents, most of whom were milling about at the end of the street, when the superintendent's mobile rang. She listened in si-lence as the control room officer passed her the message from his screen. 'Have you got any patrol cars free?' she asked. 'If so, raise the key-holder and get him to meet them there. It's probably frost in the mechanism, or something equally trivial. The chances of it being anything other than a false alarm are minimal.'

Although she had dismissed the alert, Fleming told Binns about the development. She had just passed on the information when she got another call, this time from the chief constable. Fleming put it on speaker so Binns could hear what she had to say.

'Nash is all right,' O'Donnell began. 'When I say that, I mean he isn't seriously hurt. He's got a broken arm, a cut to the back of his head and a load of scratches on his face, but he's conscious and fairly lucid. I only had a mo-ment to talk to him. They've stitched him up and wheeled him off to X-ray, that's where he is now. The doctor says their main concern is the possibility of concussion. From what Nash told me, there was some sort of a device rigged to make his gas cooker blow up. He was very lucky. The bomber was careless and Nash knew someone had been in the flat. He spotted the device, seconds before it blew. Clara's just a bit shaken up and has a couple of scratches and a bruise or two. At the moment she's being comforted by her fiancé.'

'I'm glad they're both all right; we've more than enough to contend with. On top of everything, we've just had a message from the control room. Apparently, the alarm has gone off at a bank here in Helmsdale. Probably a short circuit or something, but it's bad timing when we're already overstretched.'

'Bloody cutbacks,' the chief muttered. 'They wanted me to trim the establishment even further, but this will show the Authority we can't cut any more. I'll stay here to talk to Nash.'

O'Donnell had been about to ask how long it would be before Nash returned from X-ray, when her mobile rang. Ignoring the disapproving frown of the nurse at the reception desk, she answered it. As she was listening, she glanced across the waiting room. 'I'll be there ASAP,' she told the caller.

As O'Donnell looked around for someone to inform that she would have to leave, she saw a nurse heading towards her.

'Aren't you the chief constable?' the nurse asked. 'I'm Lianne Ford. I'm Viv's, I mean, DC Pearce's girlfriend. Viv phoned to tell me what had happened. I came straight down from the ward. I'm on nights this week,' she offered by way of explanation.

'I'm sorry Viv's stuck out there, he must feel out of it,' O'Donnell sympathized. 'But the job he's doing is very important.'

'I think he'd rather be out there and bored, than where Mr Nash is,' Lianne pointed out.

'Yes, I'm sure. And the way things are kicking off, we can't spare anyone to relieve him. I've to go back. Things are so desperate; even I'm having to lend a hand. Will you explain to DI Nash why I couldn't stay? Tell him thieves have broken into one of the banks in Helmsdale. They got in via the basement of the shop next door.'

'Good Heavens!' Lianne exclaimed. 'Is it the one below the accountants' offices?'

'Yes, do you know them?'

'I had a Saturday job in one of the shops downstairs before I left school,' Lianne told her.

As she was listening, O'Donnell glanced at the clock. 'How long does an X-ray take?'

'I'll nip down and find out how long they'll be,' Lianne offered. 'I know the staff.'

She returned within a couple of minutes. 'They had to raise a radiographer, which is why there's a delay. It should be done in half an hour or so.'

'I'd better go. Please be sure to pass on my message.'

Lianne had been hanging around for what seemed an age. She had just started across the tiled floor to return to the ward, when the doors to her right opened and an odd trio emerged. A man she assumed to be Nash, appeared in a wheelchair which was being pushed by a tall man, who looked to be the only one who wasn't the worse for wear. The man was also supporting a woman whom Lianne guessed to be Sergeant Mironova.

Nash's face looked as if he'd suffered a delayed attack of teenage acne. Close inspection revealed it to be a myriad of tiny cuts inflicted by the exploding granules of glass from the outer door of the building.

His companion was in better shape, as she had escaped the blast itself, protected by the outer wall of the building, the inner door and Nash's body. Nevertheless, her white blouse would never be white again, the combination of dust, soot and blood from Nash's injuries rendering it fit only for the waste bin. Her slacks were similarly stained. Her hair was tousled, her face besmirched with dust and her normally immaculate hands were blackened, the nails grimy as a gardener's.

'I wish you'd let me walk, there's nothing wrong with my legs,' Nash grumbled.

'No, it's your head that's the problem,' Clara retorted tartly, 'your brain in particular.'

Lianne hurried over. 'Are you Mr Nash?' She introduced herself.

'How are you?'

'He's got a broken arm, a possible broken collarbone, possible concussion and a terribly bad temper.' Clara smiled at her. 'I'm Clara. DS Mironova.'

'The chief constable was here,' Lianne told them. 'She asked me to tell you she had to go.'

'Has something else happened?' Nash asked.

'The bank in the High Street in Helmsdale has been broken into. The robbers got in via the basement of the place next door. You know, below where the accountants, Armstrong and Gill, have their offices.'

Nash nodded agreement, then wished he hadn't. 'I ought to get out of here. See if I can help.'

'You mustn't do that,' Lianne told him. 'Not if there's the chance of concussion.'

Before Nash could argue the point, which he showed every sign of doing, another nurse appeared and took firm hold of the wheelchair. She swung it none too gently round and marched Nash towards one of the cubicles. 'Doctor wants to examine you again now we've got the X-rays back,' she told him in that bright, no-nonsense tone that nurses adopt for patients who behave like unruly five-year-olds.

'I don't think there's much I can do here,' Lianne told him. 'Just do what you're told, Mr Nash.'

After a further ten minutes, a doctor appeared from

behind the curtain shielding the cubicle. He approached
Clara and Sutton. 'I've sedated Mr Nash,' he told them.
'He's going to be fairly doped-up for a few hours. The
good news is that there seems to be no trace of concussion. On the downside, his arm is broken, but it is a clean
break; his collarbone is also cracked, both of which are
causing him a lot of pain. The problem with collarbone
injuries is that too much movement creates pressure on
the bone, which causes even more discomfort. He won't
be able to drive for some time, I'm afraid, but apart from
that he seems fine, and we should be in a position to let
him go home after the ward round in the morning.' He
smiled brightly and turned away.

NASH WAS DREAMING. In his dream he was confronted by
two faceless men. Men he knew to be responsible for
all that had happened. They were the men behind Vanda
Dawson's abduction, behind the security van robbery, the
bomb that had destroyed his home and the break-in at
the bank.

The curious thing about his dream was that, although
he couldn't see their faces, he knew their names. He knew
them, because he'd recently been told them. Had he been
told? Or had he read it somewhere? He must concentrate…
He had been told it, he was sure, but why would he think
he'd read it? Read it where? On a poster? No, that was ridiculous. But he knew things about them. Where could he
have learned of them? Knew about their weird lifestyle.
Well, you'd have to call it weird, wouldn't you, living underground all the time.

He wanted to ask them about this, wanted to question
them about lots of things in fact, but whenever he tried
to, either he fell asleep or they vanished. He wished they
wouldn't do that, it was so disconcerting. It wouldn't have

been so bad if he'd any idea where they went to when
they disappeared. Did they go underground? Was that
where they were keeping Vanda Dawson? If so, he ought
to know where that underground place was. After all he'd
been told about it, hadn't he? Well, more than told about it.
He'd been made to learn it, hadn't he? All because cricket
was cancelled. Anyway, perhaps that wasn't where they
went to. Perhaps they went somewhere else. Somewhere
he didn't know about....

AFTER A BRIEF inspection of the crime scene, O'Donnell
called a meeting at Helmsdale police station.

Much to Sutton's annoyance, on leaving the hospital,
Clara had insisted on going back on duty. Having dropped
her at the station, he headed back to Netherdale General.
'If I can't persuade you otherwise, I suppose I'd better
make sure Nash is OK,' he grumbled. 'At least I can stop
him trying to do anything stupid.' He softened the anger
by kissing her gently. 'Just you take care. No heroics, understand?'

'That comes well from you, Major Sutton,' Clara remarked as she got out of the car. 'Honestly, I'm fine, now
that my hearing has come back.'

'That's good news, you've been deafening us all for the
last couple of hours.' Sutton smiled and waved goodbye
as he drove away.

If any local inhabitants had been passing the police
station they would have wondered why the place was lit
up at 4 a.m. Fortunately, few Helmsdale residents were
prone to wandering the streets at that hour. 'We can't examine the bank premises until a forensic team has been
in,' O'Donnell told the detectives, 'and they can't go in
until structural engineers have ensured the premises are
safe. Removal of a large chunk of the dividing wall means

that until they get jacks in position, the buildings could collapse at any time.'

The chief constable looked round at her colleagues. With Pearce still on surveillance duty, she had called in DC Andrews, who, although officially still on leave, had agreed to come in. The fact that the request came from the chief may have influenced her decision.

'We're hamstrung as far as the bank's concerned until later this afternoon, and as we appear to have ground to a halt with regard to the security van hijack, that leaves us with the abduction, and the fire at Nash's flat. What's the latest on that?'

'The fire brigade will be sending their forensic officers in to inspect the place once it's safe to do so,' Fleming reported. 'I'm liaising with CFO Curran. He knows this is to be treated as a suspicious incident, so he'll insist they give it priority.'

'What's the strength of our information about the cause of the fire?' the chief asked.

'According to what Mike told me,' Clara said. 'He returned to the flat after a meal and went into the kitchen for coffee. He saw the coffee machine had been moved and noticed the oven timer light was on. He could see a load of nails had been stuffed into the cavity between the glass doors, presumably to act as shrapnel. He was attempting to leave the flat as I arrived, that was when the explosion happened. I think he'd have been killed instantly had he been inside. We'll have to wait until he's fit to talk to us to find out if he knows more. At the moment he's sedated, so it'll be a while before that happens.'

'I think it's significant that the explosion happened at almost the exact time that the bank was being broken into,' Fleming commented.

'Designed to distract us, you mean? I'll buy that. If

we're right'—the chief grimaced ruefully—'it worked perfectly. Again, we'll have to wait on forensic reports.

'What I suggest,' O'Donnell continued after a few seconds' thought, 'is that we concentrate on wrapping up the abduction case. We're fairly sure Vanda Dawson's body is lying somewhere in those woods on Black Fell. Number one priority must be locating that and getting SOCO and Professor Ramirez to work. At the same time, continue with the plan to arrest McKenzie this morning. We're in line for a lot of flak from the media over the hijack and the bank robbery, so the PR benefit of being able to bring the Cremator to book will outweigh the negatives completely.

'Clara, if you feel up to it, I want you to take over from Pearce on the surveillance of McKenzie's farm. When he leaves on his milk round, I want you to follow him just as Nash had planned to. Pearce must head out to Black Fell in time for first light with the officers.'

She turned to DC Andrews. 'Lisa, I'd like you to go through to Netherdale and pick that search warrant up as soon as it's ready. Meet Clara back at McKenzie's place. Superintendent Fleming has already arranged to have an ARU on standby for the arrest. Apart from the fact that McKenzie's one of the most sadistic serial killers of all time, I don't want him topping himself once he knows the game's up. Either that, or harming any of my officers, so I want you all in vests, understand?' she added. 'He's capable of anything, by my reckoning. Not only the torture his victims have to suffer, but the anguish he puts their relatives through means he'll stop at nothing: so we take no chances.'

NASH REGAINED CONSCIOUSNESS. Although his eyes were closed, he was aware this wasn't his room, his flat. Then memory returned in a flood. Like flood water his rec-

ollection was a jumble of thoughts jostling one another
downstream. The bomb. That was the strongest current.
It dominated his thinking. He had been injured, but what
of Clara? He remembered she was OK. She'd taken care
of him, summoned help, stayed with him at the hospital.
He wondered where she'd gone after she came with him
to casualty.

He opened his eyes, blinking in the bright light. He
was in a small, sterile looking room, so obviously a hospital ward. His was the only bed, but he wasn't the room's
sole occupant. A man was bending over a chair sorting
through a small pile of clothes. Examining them and making notes on a small piece of paper. They were his clothes.
He recognized them and David Sutton in the same instant.

'David, what are you doing?'

Sutton looked up, his frown of concentration lifted.
'I need your clothes sizes. What you were wearing last
night'—he indicated the pile—'is ruined. All the rest of
your things went up in the fire. The hospital is planning to
release you this morning, all being well. I don't think February is the right time of year to be wandering the streets
in nothing but a hospital gown, do you? Apart from the
fact that you might scare old ladies. So I thought I'd go
to the shops as soon as they're open and buy you at least
one change of clothing to tide you over, and have it ready
for when you leave.'

'That'll be as soon as I can get out of this bed.' Nash
went to sit up; then winced as the pain in his arm and
shoulder went into hyperdrive. He gasped slightly before
trying to move again, this time more cautiously. He hoped
this would make the discomfort less. It didn't. As if summoned by some form of NHS telepathy, a nurse entered
carrying a small plastic cup. She smiled at Sutton as she
moved past him and stood looking at her patient.

'Good morning, Mr Nash, how do you feel?'

'Rotten,' he admitted, 'but I'll feel better when I get out of here.'

'You're due for discharge this morning once doctor has had a good look at you. How's your head? Any pain, blurred or double vision?'

'No, my head's fine. The pain is in my arm and shoulder.'

'Not surprising. You've a broken arm and cracked collarbone. These will help.'

She offered him the cup. Nash moved gingerly to take it, using his left hand. He was learning. As he was swallowing the tablets, she poured him some water from the jug on the bedside cabinet, filling the glass only halfway. Nash realized he was very thirsty. He drained the glass. As if expecting this, the nurse immediately refilled it. He drank more slowly this time. 'Doctor will probably be round to see you in a couple of hours or so. I'll be back shortly to take your temperature and blood pressure, then they'll bring you your breakfast.'

Once the nurse had gone, Sutton looked across at Nash. 'I've got all the details I need, so whilst you're being sorted out by the medics I'll nip to Good Buys and get you something to wear. It'll be nothing fancy, but it will tide you over until you can make more permanent arrangements.' Sutton's expression changed. 'I think, from what I've heard, you can kiss goodbye to anything that was in your flat. By all accounts it was completely gutted. Sorry, and all that, but the main point is you escaped without permanent damage.' He paused, before adding, 'The other thing you've to be thankful for is that Daniel was away at the time.'

Nash moistened his lips. 'Small mercies, but you're

right, David. There was very little in the flat that can't be replaced.'

'I don't know what you intend to do once you're out of here, but for the time being you can't drive. There are other things to consider. Fortunately, your wallet was in your trouser pocket, so I've got that safe, as well as your mobile phone.' Sutton patted his jacket pocket. 'For someone who professes to know nothing about computers, an Android phone is fairly sophisticated.'

Nash shrugged, then wished he hadn't bothered. 'It was a good offer in the shop, and I've promised myself I'll become more computer literate. Before my son outdoes me.'

'It'll be no good to you unless you get a replacement charger soon. That's another thing on the to-do-list. The main thing you have to consider is a place to stay until you can get sorted out. That isn't going to be easy with you being fairly immobile. Added to that there's the question of getting about. And then, as you said, there's Daniel to think about.'

'Oh Lord! I'm supposed to be driving to France next weekend to collect him.' Nash glanced down at his arm. 'That isn't going to happen.' His face clouded.

'What's wrong?' Sutton asked.

'I haven't got his aunt's phone number, it was in the flat. I never got round to putting it in my contacts list on the mobile.'

Sutton took Nash's phone from his jacket and Nash saw his fingers flying across the touch screen, far faster than he'd ever managed it. He read out a phone number, then looked up with a grin.

'How did you do that?' Nash asked.

'It was in your call log. You must have rung France on your mobile at some point.'

'That was clever, I'd never have thought of it,' Nash admitted.

'You would if you'd been thinking straight. Anyway, let's talk about the more immediate needs. How about if I book a room for you at the Square and Compass? You're going to need somewhere comfortable and with decent facilities until you've got some use in that arm again.'

'I don't like imposing,' Nash said meekly.

'Well, you'd better get used to it. Anyway, it isn't an imposition. Right, I'm off. Oh, and by the way, Clara and the chief constable asked me to pass a load of sentimental messages on to you. I don't do that, so make the best of the fact that I told you.' Sutton gave a cheery wave and departed.

Nash smiled and made to move, to sit up straight. The smile vanished immediately as the pain surged through his shoulder.

Sutton had only been gone a few minutes when the door opened. He half-recognized the good-looking young woman in nurses' uniform standing in the gap. After a second, he made the connection. 'It's Lianne, isn't it?'

'That's right. Good morning, Mr Nash, I wasn't sure if you'd remember. You were in a fairly grotty state last night.'

'I'm not exactly singing and dancing this morning,' he admitted. 'Are you here on duty, or is it a social visit?'

'I promised Viv and DS Mironova I'd keep an eye on you. And the chief constable,' she added. 'A lot of people are concerned about you.'

'Have you heard what's happening? Has anyone been in touch this morning?'

'Not yet, but I imagine they're being kept busy right now. Apart from the bomb at your flat, there's the robbery at the bank,' Lianne lowered her voice, 'and that surveillance that Viv's on. Between those, I doubt they've time for anything else.'

'You mentioned something about the bank raid last night.' Nash struggled to remember, but struggled in vain. 'I'm afraid I wasn't in a fit state to take it in properly. Tell me again, will you?'

Lianne eyed him doubtfully. 'I hope you're not thinking about work,' she told him severely. 'You're supposed to concentrate on getting better.'

'I'm OK. Go on, tell me again.'

'I don't know very much, just what I heard the chief constable say. Apparently it happened soon after your bomb went off. The thieves got into the bank vault by tunnelling through from the cellar of the shop next door. That interested me, because I used to work there on Saturdays when I was at school.'

'Which side of the bank was it?'

'On the left, on the ground floor of the building where the accountants, Armstrong and Gill, have their offices.'

'Armstrong and Gill,' Nash said thoughtfully, 'that name rings a bell, but I can't think why.'

'Don't worry about it. Concentrate on yourself for once. Leave the others to take care of work. When Viv rings, I'll tell him you're feeling better.'

Nash thought about what Lianne had told him for a long time after she left. Without distraction, he was able to puzzle over why the accountants' names were familiar. Despite his efforts, he failed to make the connection. In the end, he gave up the struggle. Apart from the frustration, the effort was giving him a headache.

EIGHTEEN

JACKIE FLEMING WAS less than amused. Her displeasure stemmed from the delay in getting the warrant for McKenzie's farm. DC Andrews conveyed the news, saying it would be early afternoon before the paperwork was available.

Fleming had only just ended the call when Pearce rang in. The news from Black Fell was no better. 'We've covered almost half the ground between the road and the end of the woods. So far, there's no sign. There are loads of paths and the undergrowth is so dense in places we've had to work round some areas. The only positive is that if we can't penetrate it, there won't be a body in there. From here though, the ground starts to level off in to the woods. It's going to take a fair while before we're through. I only hope it turns out to be worth the effort.'

Neither Pearce nor Fleming questioned the improbability of a couple being on such inhospitable terrain for a romantic stroll.

Jackie's irritation abated when Clara rang in to report. 'I hope you're not in a hurry,' she began. 'McKenzie's finished his milk round, but now he's gone into Helmsdale on what looks like a shopping expedition. So far, he's been to the chemist's, the butcher's and the greengrocer's. Judging by the carrier bags he's loaded into his van I'd say he's stocking up with a month's supplies. Either that or he's planning a barbecue,' she ended wickedly.

'I think you've been around Nash too long,' Fleming

told her. 'Your sense of humour's as sick as his. Where's McKenzie now?'

'In Good Buys supermarket. That's going to be another big purchase,' Clara suggested.

'How do you work that out?'

'Because he took one of their big trolleys instead of a basket. I'd hate to tell him it's all going to be wasted.'

'All right, keep your eye on him and let me know when he gets back home.'

'I will, but I can't risk getting too close. I don't want him to recognize me.'

It was an hour later, during which Fleming's tension level had risen appreciably, before things began to happen. First of all Clara rang in to update her on McKenzie. 'Would you believe it, after he'd finished at Good Buys he went for a haircut. Anyway, he's back home now. I've taken up position in the lane overlooking the farm. McKenzie unloaded his shopping and went inside. There's no movement to report.'

That was true. However, had Clara been in position a few minutes earlier, she would have seen signs of activity.

'We'll be on our way as soon as Lisa arrives with the warrant,' Fleming told her before she rang off. She had to wait no more than five minutes before Andrews called to say she was on her way. Fleming instructed the waiting team to assemble in the car park ready for the DC's arrival. As they were filing out of the door, Sergeant Binns called Fleming back to the reception desk. He held out the phone. 'Pearce is holding for you,' he said.

'Yes, Viv?' Fleming's voice quivered with anticipation.

'We've spotted something. The only problem is the location. It's impossible for us to get close enough to be positive from this side, but the site has all the trappings of a Cremator murder. The altar-like rock, some weird symbols that I can just make out. The undergrowth is really dense. I think we should have started from the other side of the woods. If we try to get any closer we risk contaminating the evidence.'

'But you think there's a body?'

'Sure of it,' Pearce said. 'Even from this range I can see a foot and the lower end of the leg sticking over the end of the rock. Or what's left of them.'

Fleming felt her stomach churn with nausea. 'All right, find the access route then leave one man by the roadside to guide SOCO and the pathologist to the dump site. As soon as you can, make your way to the surveillance spot overlooking McKenzie's place. We'll be setting off in a few minutes. If you get there before me, tell Clara to switch her mobile off, and you do the same. I want complete silence as we approach the house. I certainly don't want to chance McKenzie making his escape because he's heard the T-Mobile jingle.'

SUTTON RETURNED TO the hospital to find Nash sitting on the edge of the bed, his arm encased in a pot, and wearing a sling to prevent overuse of his shoulder. 'I've been given the all clear,' he announced. 'They're kicking me out this morning. They've prescribed me some strong painkillers and the doctor reckons there's no concussion, so I can leave as soon as I'm dressed.'

Sutton placed a couple of carriers on the bed. 'I got you a pair of jeans, a couple of loose-fitting shirts and a zip-up fleece. I thought they'd be easiest to manage. I also bought a pair of slip-on shoes, because I thought laces might be a bit of a struggle. Also underwear and socks similar to what you had on.'

'That's brilliant.' Nash watched as Sutton took the garments out of their bags.

'I've removed all the tags. I'll help you dress. It's going to be difficult enough.'

Nash soon realized that dressing is a task you take for granted until it becomes difficult. Even with Sutton's supporting arm, it took him ten minutes to complete what he would normally manage in two or three.

'Now, let's get out of here,' he said. 'I hate these places.'

'I'll get you to the A and E entrance, then go and fetch my car. You'll still be a bit wobbly on your legs, I'd guess.'

Nash frowned. 'Damn, I've just realized something. I think I left my car keys in the flat before I went out last night.'

'I shouldn't worry about it,' Sutton laughed. 'You're not going to be driving anywhere for a long time. The dealer will provide you with a duplicate set. Where do you want to head for when we leave here?'

'Will you take me to Helmsdale police station? I need to have a word with Tom Pratt. After that, the hotel, I suppose.'

On the journey to Helmsdale, Nash attempted to thank Sutton. 'I really appreciate this, David, but shouldn't you be on duty?'

'I'm on leave for another three weeks, and I've nothing better to do,' Sutton told him. 'I was planning to decorate Clara's living room, so this has come as a welcome distraction. I'm only glad I was on hand to help, with everything that's happened in the past few days.'

'So acting as my chauffeur is a better option than splashing emulsion around?'

'No contest.'

Nash smiled and was about to reply as Sutton swung the car on to Helmsdale High Street. He glanced across towards the bank, where forensic officers would still be working, noting that the shop alongside had a signboard that read 'Top Ranking Posters'. He frowned, something that Viv had told him rang a bell. He struggled with the elusive memory, only recalling it as Sutton pulled in at the station.

IT HAD BEEN a hectic morning at Helmsdale. Sergeant Binns had just brewed a cup of tea when the door opened. He looked up, surprised to see the newcomer. 'Mike, how are you? I thought you were still in hospital?'

'Apart from a broken arm and a cracked collarbone I'm fine. Put it this way, it could have been a lot worse.'

'You had a narrow escape by all accounts,' Binns agreed. 'Is it true what I've been hearing, that it was a bomb?'

'It was, but that'll have to wait. The reason I'm here is to talk to Tom. Where are Clara and Jackie?'

'I'm afraid you're out of luck as far as they're concerned,' Binns told him. 'Tom's here, but everyone else is out. They've gone to execute a warrant on Lindsay McKenzie's place. Apparently, Viv found the body on Black Fell and they're intent on nailing McKenzie. If they're right, I'll need to find a new milkman.'

'Damn, I wanted to talk to them about the van hijack and the bank robbery. I think I might have a lead.' Nash thought for a moment. 'I'll go and talk to Tom.'

Their conversation took several minutes, the first part of which was spent fielding more questions about his health. 'Tom, I want you to cast your mind back. Somewhere, sometime, I feel sure that accountancy firm, Armstrong and Gill, have been mentioned, or involved with one of our cases. I keep trying to remember where and when, but I can't.'

'Armstrong and Gill, yes, the name does ring a bell. Let me think.'

There was a long silence as both men struggled for re-call. After a few minutes or so, Pratt said, 'Got it!'

'Go on, Tom, put me out of my misery.'

'Armstrong and Gill were Simon Wardle's accountants.'

'Of course they were! Damn, why couldn't I remember that?'

'It was a long time ago, and you didn't have much to do with the paperwork, as I remember. Anyway, what's brought them to mind all of a sudden?'

'Because the bank robbers tunnelled through via the shop underneath the accountants' offices. Now, that might be pure coincidence, but—'

'You don't believe in coincidence,' Pratt finished for him. 'Where's this leading?'

'I'm not really sure, but by what little I heard, this gang sounds highly organized. As were the villains who hijacked the security van.'

'You think it might be the same crew?'

'I do, and I think there might be a way to identify one of them. All we need to do is get hold of some background information.'

'The last I heard, the chief constable was fuming be-cause we have no idea who they were. How come you've got a line on them? Is this the famous Nash intuition? Known to others less blessed, as good guesswork.'

Nash laughed. 'Hardly,' Nash's tone was dry, 'That seems to have deserted me altogether—if it ever existed. No, it was the attack on my flat that gave me the clue. That, added to something in the security guards' state-ments, and something you said.'

'Care to run it past me?'

'The gang who hijacked the van used motorbikes. You saw a gang of bikers in town the same afternoon. When I was being blown up, I think I heard a motorbike in the street outside. It might be worth checking with Clara to see if she heard or saw one. I reckon the main aim of the explosion at my place was to distract attention during the bank robbery.'

'I still don't see how that gives a clue to their identity.'

'I said diverting attention was the main reason, I didn't say it was the only one. That bomb was intended to kill me: nothing less. Not to injure me or purely to keep me occupied elsewhere. Therefore, we can assume a level of personal vindictiveness. Whoever bombed my flat hates me enough to want me dead.'

'There could be a long list of candidates for that role,' Pratt pointed out.

'I agree, but if you add the ability to plan criminal acts like a military operation, and the technical know-how to plant and detonate a device like that, the list shortens dramatically. To one person, in fact. Someone I deprived of their fortune and stuck behind bars for the best part of thirty-years. Simon Wardle, whose accountants happen to occupy part of the premises used to carry out the bank raid.'

'Yes, Mike, but that's the point. Wardle is behind bars.'

'True, and so is his sidekick. But if you think about it, they had a lot of other men working with them, men with the same background and training. And the fact that the ringleader is tucked up in a prison cell doesn't stop his brain from working. I reckon a good starting point would be a phone call to the prison. Find out what visitors our man has had in the last year. If any of them served in the same regiment, they must top our list of suspects. In fact, I'd be tempted to get the name of anyone who served with him.'

'How are we going to pick out which of those men

might be involved? The number could run into hundreds, thousands even.'

'That's the second part of the job. Run the names through DVLA. You're looking for any of them with a motorbike, not cars, so that should shorten the list.'

'Blimey, Mike, that's some task. I reckon your broken arm might have healed by the time I've finished.'

'I'm sure you'll get it done sooner than that,' Nash reassured him. 'Liaise with Jackie and Clara.' He was about to depart, when he stopped. 'When you get to talk to Viv, show him any photo ID driving licences you get. See if any of them matches the bloke from the poster shop. Also, that guy told Viv he'd been running the business online for a while. Ask Viv to check that statement out.'

After he left Pratt, Nash waited by the reception desk, thinking. Eventually, he made up his mind. He looked across at Binns, who was studying him with respect. 'Jack, I need someone to go to Mill Cottage and interview Dawson. As there's nobody else available, I shall have to do it myself.'

'Two problems with that, Mike. One, should you be working? And two, I've nobody to drive you, and you're in no fit state to drive yourself.'

"I can't sit at home doing nothing. For one thing, I've no home to sit in. As for a driver, I've already got one.'

'That wouldn't by any chance be Major Sutton, would it? Because he's waiting outside.' Binns pointed to the street.

'That's it. Right, I'm off.'

'If the others return with McKenzie or if they call in, do you want me to tell them where you've gone?'

'No, don't bother; it's only a hunch at present, and a pretty wild one at that.'

'I'VE BOOKED YOU a room at the Square and Compass,' Sutton told him as Nash opened the passenger door. 'Do you want to go straight there?'

'You'd do almost anything to get out of decorating, wouldn't you?'

'Pretty much,' Sutton admitted. 'Why, what have you in mind?'

Nash told him. When he'd finished, Sutton said, 'I can think of loads of reasons not to. Apart from anything else, Clara will probably kill me.'

'Don't underestimate yourself, David. I'm sure you'll manage to convince her it was for the best.' Nash told him, adding 'given time,' under his breath.

Nash settled back gingerly, grateful for the soft upholstery. As they travelled towards Wintersett, he explained why he wanted to talk to Dawson. Major David Sutton had been involved in the latter part of the Wardle case and listened with great interest. As they drove slowly down the drive towards the cottage, Nash glanced to his left. 'Hang on a minute, pull in, will you? The old mill. The doors are open. Let's take a closer look.'

Sutton slipped the car into reverse and moved gently back, his eyes watching the hedges on both sides via the wing mirrors. He shifted into forward gear and the car rolled slowly down the track towards the building.

They were still thirty or so yards from the entrance when he jammed his foot on the brake. Nash ignored the pain caused by the sudden jolt. 'Oh Dear God!' he exclaimed.

Through the open doorway, they could see the lower half of a body, the legs dangling in mid-air. Nash fumbled to unfasten his seat belt, but David beat him to it. As Nash closed his door, he heard a corresponding click from the driver's side of the car. He looked across to see Sutton, his jaw set firmly, moving towards the mill. 'We'll have to stay outside,' Nash warned him. 'If this is what we think, we can't risk contaminating the evidence.'

They stopped in the doorway. 'Mike, I have to check whether he's still alive. You know that.'

Nash nodded, it was their duty to check for any sign of life, and he wasn't in a fit state to manhandle the body if the man was still breathing. 'Go ahead,' he agreed, 'don't touch anything but the body.'

As Sutton checked for a pulse, Nash thought he heard a faint sound. He looked at the major, who was staring intently, not at the body, but beyond.

'Did you hear that?' Sutton said in a low voice. 'I thought I heard a noise. What do you think it was?'

'I don't know.'

They waited, hardly daring to breathe, straining to hear a possible repeat. After a few seconds they heard it again. 'There!' they exclaimed in unison.

'What it is, and where it's coming from, I've no idea. Keep listening, will you. I need to organize Mexican Pete and a forensic team.'

Nash pressed a Short Code on his mobile and waited.

'Ramirez,' the pathologist sounded angry, 'is that you, Nash? I thought you were orbiting the sun?'

'I managed to escape before the rocket went off,' Nash replied. 'Are you still at Black Fell?'

He moved the phone away from his ear as the blast of sound came over the speaker. Once Ramirez had cooled off slightly, Nash asked him to repeat what he'd said. 'This time in English, Professor.'

He listened with growing astonishment. As the pathologist added a few trenchant comments, Nash had to bite his lip. 'Oh dear,' he responded when Ramirez eventually ran out of words, or breath. 'That is most unfortunate. However, as you're in the area perhaps you'd call in at Wintersett on your way back and bring the team.'

Nash explained the circumstances. 'I'm afraid this one is definitely not a hoax.'

He rejoined Sutton who was standing in the doorway listening intently. 'Anything?' he asked him.

Sutton shook his head. 'Whoever you were talking to didn't help. Even from here, I could hear their voice. Who was it?'

Nash explained the cause of the pathologist's anger. The humour of the situation, in stark contrast to their recent grim discovery, didn't escape Sutton. He laughed aloud as Nash repeated some of Ramirez' choicer phrases.

As he finished speaking, they heard the sound again. 'That's it,' Nash said instantly. 'But where's it coming from?'

They stared into the interior of the mill. Apart from the two cars, the corpse and a few odds and ends, the large open space was empty.

'I'll go and see,' Sutton said as he took a step forward.

'No, David, we've got to wait for the team. Let's have a look at the outside of the building. Clara searched it, but I haven't examined it,' Nash said, leading the way.

They walked round to the side of the mill. Dimly, Nash remembered that rainy Wednesday afternoon when all his school's cricket had been cancelled, and they had been forced to listen to their master explaining the workings of water-powered gristmills. After a few minutes, the answer came to him. 'Of course,' he breathed, 'the pit-wheel-housing. The pit-wheel and the wallower.'

'What?' Sutton was baffled.

'This is how a watermill works. As the water turns the wheel, it revolves an axle running from the centre of the waterwheel into the lowest level of the mill. At the other end of the axle is a large gearwheel called the pit-wheel. That is connected to a smaller gearwheel known as the wallower. This turns the vertical driveshaft that runs the height of the building and turns the grinding stones.'

'That's absolutely riveting, but apart from demonstrating the extent of your knowledge on the subject of corn mills, what's the point?'

Nash pointed. 'Look at the way the land here slopes down towards the mill stream. Imagine if the waterwheel was still in place. The top of the wheel would barely reach above where we're standing. Certainly no more than waist high. Therefore'—he gestured towards the building— 'that can't be the lowest level of the mill. There has to be a space underneath. Usually the pit-wheel room would be accessed via a flight of steps or a ladder, but I certainly saw no sign of one. The access has either been blocked off or concealed.'

'You think this pit-wheel room might be where the sound was coming from?'

'It could be.'

'Do you think the missing woman might be in there? A prisoner?'

'I've absolutely no idea.'

As they returned to the front of the building, they heard the crunching of gravel under tyres, signalling the arrival of the pathologist and the SOCO team. Ramirez looked at the detective.

'Should you be at work?' he asked. 'But I forgot your obsession. You wouldn't let a little matter like a few broken bones keep you away when there are cadavers to drool over. I'd love to DNA test you. I'm sure you'd prove to have Transylvanian ancestry.'

Nash explained the situation to the new arrivals. Once the forensic officers were kitted out in their protective clothing, the party moved to the interior of the mill. Sutton helped Nash into a suit before he stood and waited alongside the doorway.

'We'll move that vinyl sheet and see what's underneath,' the SOCO team leader said. 'If we slide it to the back of the building it won't cause any contamination.'

'Can you do that before you remove the body?' Nash asked.

The man smiled. 'He's not going anywhere,' he replied dryly.

Removal of the vinyl took only minutes. 'An inspection pit, by the look of it,' Nash said.

'You mean like in a garage?' Ramirez asked.

'Yes, a lot of people used to do their own car repairs, before all these modern computer-controlled vehicles,' Nash replied.

As they were speaking, the forensic men were removing some sleepers obscuring the pit. The space below was about eight-feet deep, Nash guessed. He moved inside the building, telling Sutton to remain outside. 'Can we have quiet for a second?' he asked.

All of them stopped and listened. The silence seemed to last for ages. Absolute silence. Nash signalled to two of the officers, who descended into the pit. After a few seconds, one of them called up.

'There's what looks like a door here. I'm not sure how to open it though.'

The two men inspected the far wall of the pit. After what seemed a long delay, one of them spotted a tiny hole in one side of the oblong shape. He took a multi-bladed knife from his pocket and slid one of the narrowest blades into the hole. The door sprang open with a click and the officer shone his torch inside. He took one look and called out, 'Inspector Nash, I think you'd better get down here, if you can manage it.'

Supported on either side by two forensics officers, Nash made the descent safely. As he stepped off the final rung, he wondered how he would fare on the return journey. Nash moved towards the opening. It smelt of damp. He peered through the gap, staring in disbelief at the scene inside the small, dank chamber, illuminated by the officer's torch.

It was over half an hour later when Nash asked to be excused from the scene at the old mill. As he was helped up the ladder, he paused. He stared across at the corner of the room, beyond where the dead man's corpse had been lowered on to the sheet spread out by the SOCO team. In the corner, he saw two objects he hadn't noticed before. Everyday objects, in no way out of place. Their significance here, however, caused Nash a fresh revulsion of horror. He completed his ascent and joined the pathologist.

'There's nothing more I can do here,' he told Ramirez. 'I assume you'll be presenting this as suicide?'

'It looks like it, on the face of things, but I'll need to complete the post-mortem first. I think it would be foolish to take anything on face value,' he said cynically.

'You've got a point,' Nash agreed with a wry smile. He climbed into the passenger seat of Sutton's car.

'Where to now?'

Nash stared at Clara's fiancé, noting the grim expression on Sutton's face, and wondering if it matched his own. 'If you don't mind, David, I'd like to go to McKenzie's farm,' Nash sighed. 'I want to hear what he has to say. Then I might get some idea of what the devil is going on.'

They were within half a mile of the farm when Nash shouted, 'David, stop the car.'

Sutton pulled to a halt. 'What is it? What's wrong?'

'Back up, will you. I've just seen something. You know the saying, "seeing is believing"? Well, I've seen it, but I don't believe it.'

NINETEEN

THE FARMHOUSE WAS a two-storey redbrick building typical of many in the area. Fleming guessed there would probably be three bedrooms on the first storey, whilst the ground floor would most likely comprise a lounge, a dining-room and a kitchen. As the team of detectives gathered at the surveillance spot, she issued instructions.

'We can't wait for Viv. I want Clara alongside me when the ARU have opened the door. Lisa, you stay further back. Don't forget, this man is the most dangerous, violent and sadistic killer in the country. We take no chances. This operation must be quick, clean and efficient. If we come away with McKenzie under arrest, it'll be our best day's work in a long time. Lisa, will you and one of the officers check the outbuildings? I want you to look particularly hard for the place where the rape was committed. You've seen the photos. Clara has a copy for comparison purposes.' She watched Mironova pass the photo across.

Silently they crept round to the farmyard. The ARU leader stepped up to the door, raising his ram as he did so. Before he could strike, the door opened. Looking over Fleming's shoulder, Clara stared at McKenzie. The man standing in the doorway appeared no different to when she had spoken to him earlier in the week. To all intents and purposes, the same well-mannered character she had interviewed outside the Dawson house.

'What's going on? What can I do for you?' McKenzie's gaze travelled beyond the officers. 'Sergeant Mironova?'

Fleming stepped forward, brandishing the search warrant. 'I'm Detective Superintendent Fleming. We have a warrant to search these premises in connection with the murder of Mrs Vanda Dawson.' She produced her warrant card.

McKenzie's smile widened if anything. He didn't look at either her credentials or the warrant. 'You can search to your heart's content. I think you'll have difficulty finding anything to link me to any murders, particularly Vanda's.'

Either they had got it badly wrong, Fleming thought in a moment of doubt, or McKenzie was a brilliant actor. She noted with interest the use of Mrs Dawson's Christian name. She pressed on, ignoring McKenzie's denial of guilt. As she was about to instruct McKenzie to allow them entry to the house, Fleming was further surprised to see that the milkman had already opened the door wide and was standing to one side, ready to usher them in. He's treating us like guests at a ruddy coffee morning, she thought. She stepped inside, motioning Clara to follow, sandwiching McKenzie between them.

The hall was bare of furniture, the carpet worn, but far from shabby. 'Take the first door on your left,' McKenzie told her. Fleming walked into the lounge, which was similarly lacking in furniture. There were two armchairs and a TV set, no cushions or personal touches to signify comfort. Mironova followed close on the milkman's heels, an armed officer behind her. Although she was still alert for signs of trouble, even her guard was lowered somewhat by his relaxed attitude to the incursion. Once inside the room, McKenzie turned to face the detectives. 'Now, what do you need to know?' He looked genuinely interested, seemingly trying to be helpful.

Fleming rounded on the milkman. 'Enough tricks,' she snarled.

'We've found Mrs Dawson's body. On Black Fell, where you took her after you raped her. On Black Fell, out in that wilderness where you burned her to death. Admit it why don't you, so I can charge you with her rape and murder, and the rape and murder of all your other victims.'

At that moment Andrews entered the lounge. 'Ma'am,' her voice quivered with excitement. 'We've found a barn that looks like the place where the rape was photographed. The one in the latest photos. But there was nowhere like the location in the earlier ones.'

'That seems conclusive.' Fleming turned back to McKenzie. 'I think once our forensic officers have been through the place, we'll have all the evidence we need to charge you. Other charges will probably follow.'

As Fleming was speaking, Clara, who was facing the door, saw Nash walking into the room. He was flanked by two people. Clara recognized her fiancé immediately. She did a double-take when she saw Nash's other companion.

'I think you'd find murder a bit difficult to prove,' Nash told Fleming gently.

As Fleming turned, she saw a slim, petite and attractive woman standing, framed by the doorway. She appeared well fed and content. She didn't look at all like the terrified rape victim portrayed in the photos, or the burnt-up corpse of a Cremator victim. But she did look remarkably like Vanda Dawson.

They all stared at the woman in open-mouthed astonishment. It was several seconds before Fleming spoke. 'Mrs Dawson! Are you all right? Have you been harmed? Has this man hurt you in any way? And could somebody please tell me where she came from, and exactly what is going on?'

'We were on our way here,' Nash said gently, 'when

we saw Mrs Dawson. She'd been for a walk. She was returning here.'

'Then whose body is on Black Fell? And why didn't anyone report any of this in to me?' Fleming demanded.

'We tried, but I think you'll find all the mobiles are switched off.'

Momentarily, Fleming looked nonplussed. 'Yes, they are. As per my instructions.'

'I'm sure Viv will explain his findings when he gets here,' Nash replied cryptically.

At that moment, Viv Pearce appeared breathlessly at the door. 'Sorry, ma'am. I couldn't get away any sooner.'

Nash wasn't sure if the scowl Jackie Fleming gave him was related to his timing or being called 'ma'am'.

'Why don't we go into the kitchen,' Vanda Dawson suggested. Her voice was calm and level, with no trace of the trauma they'd been led to believe she'd suffered. 'We'll be more comfortable there.'

She looked across and smiled at McKenzie. 'Lindsay hasn't done much in the way of furnishing this place, I'm afraid. But then, he's had other things on his mind, far more important things.'

'As long as someone gives us an explanation, I don't mind if I've to sit in the attic.' Fleming turned to the leader of the ARU. 'It doesn't look as though we'll be requiring your services after all.'

The kitchen, by comparison with the other parts of the house they'd seen, was lavishly furnished. Although DC Andrews and David Sutton had to lean against the worktops, the others sat at the large kitchen table. 'Right,' Nash told McKenzie when they were settled, 'time for some explanations, I think.'

McKenzie took a deep breath. 'It began with Ninette.

She was the first. The only one not to have been identified. The first of the Cremator's victims.'

Clara was struck by the curious use of words. McKenzie had said 'the Cremator's victims' not 'my victims'. Was that some strange schizophrenic way of looking at his crimes, ascribing them to another part of his personality?

McKenzie sat back in his chair, apparently at ease, showing no sign of remorse, or any other emotion. If Clara was puzzled by the man's opening words, what followed had her increasingly baffled.

'I met Ninette in Prague. That wasn't her home; where she came from originally I have no idea. She was on the run then, but from what I didn't find out until later. All she wanted was a lift. Well, more than that, someone to smuggle her across a couple of borders until she reached Western Europe. She told me she had no money, nothing to pay me. I would be doing it out of charity. I was driving an artic in those days. I'd no family, no home ties and the money was good.' McKenzie paused, unscrewed the cap from the bottle of water in the middle of the table and took a sip.

'I agreed. I knew what I was doing; what I was risking, but I didn't care. I was alone, a long way from home, and I suppose I thought I'd get my leg over, if nothing else. What I wasn't prepared for is what actually happened. We set off and as I drove, we talked. Her English was very good, and she had a lively mind. I suddenly realized how lonely my life was, how nice it was having a woman in the wagon alongside me. When the heater got the cab warmed up, I could smell her perfume and that musky woman's smell. She was as attractive as she was intelligent, and I knew before long that I didn't want to lose her. I suppose it was love at first sight, but I didn't know what that was, so I didn't recognise it. I offered her the chance to come all the way to England. She was worried about how she'd cope here, without money, papers or anywhere to live, so I offered her a job as my housekeeper.'

McKenzie smiled. 'Of course there was no such job. I made it up because I didn't want to lose her. I thought if she came to England without identification or money she'd be dependent on me and that way she'd have to stay. So that's what happened. I brought her here. And then I killed her.'

Fleming sat forward in her chair. McKenzie was about to confess. The milkman looked up and his eyes met those of the detectives. He smiled. 'That was what you wanted to hear, wasn't it? That's what you've been waiting for me to say?'

Jackie frowned. McKenzie's interpretation of her thoughts was uncanny. If what they'd heard before was unexpected, what followed was completely off the radar.

'I killed her because I brought her here within range of a perverted, evil bastard who raped, tortured and slaughtered her and then set fire to her poor abused body. He destroyed the only thing of beauty in my life. The man they so glibly refer to in the media as the Cremator. The man I've been trying for years to find. The man you're going to arrest and put away where he can't harm any more defenceless women. Because I'll tell you something, if you don't get the law to punish him, I'll have to take the law into my own hands. Then you really will have something to arrest me for. Because I shall take him and put him on an altar, same as he did to those poor women; then I shall set fire to the bastard and watch him burn. And I'll dance round listening to his screams and I'll feel good. For the first time in years, I'll feel happy.'

He saw Fleming and Mironova exchange puzzled glances and laughed. 'Not quite what you were expecting, I guess? Well, let me spell it out for you. Am I the Cremator? No. Do I know who the Cremator is? Yes. Can I prove it? Yes, at least to my own satisfaction. Probably not sufficiently to convince a court of law, not without your help. That's why I stage-managed everything that's happened recently; everything to do with the abduction of Vanda,' he glanced sideways.

She nodded, obviously aware of what was to come. 'And here's my proof.'

Nash, Fleming and Mironova stared at the object he tossed on to the table. Their bewilderment was complete. The object was a key ring. Attached to it was a fob in the shape of a tiny rugby ball. On the leather surface were five letters inscribed. NRUFC. 'Would you care to explain?' Nash asked.

'I was living near Covermere in those days. I had a cottage I inherited from my parents that I'd extended and modernised. It was out in the wilds, ideal for me and Ninette. She moved in with me, using the spare room. As she began to trust me, she told me bits and pieces about her former life. Of course, she offered herself to me, not once but several times. I refused; I didn't want her to sleep with me out of gratitude. That way I thought she'd resent me. I suppose I was scared of losing her. I told her if I'd wanted a prostitute I could go into the nearest town. That was how things stayed until Christmas. Ninette was so excited. She had no happy memories of Christmas in the past, but from the moment we bought the tree and decorated it she was like a five-year-old.

'We spent Christmas Day alone, content to be with one another. We did what most couples do. We cooked a meal, overate, drank too much wine, pulled crackers, fell asleep watching TV and went to bed early. Except this time, we went to bed together. It happened almost by accident. We were a bit wobbly from the wine and sleepy into the bargain, so we were holding on to one another as we went upstairs. Ninette started to kiss me. Then she told me she loved me and that was that. I had no control over what happened, no chance to object, even if I'd wanted to. So she made love to me. I can remember her voice in my ear as we were lying together. "I want us to make babies", she told me. "I want to hold your baby inside me". It was without doubt the most beautiful thing anyone has ever said to me.'

McKenzie stopped and this time took a longer drink of water from the bottle. Nash could tell McKenzie was reining in strong emotions by the way he screwed the top back on the bottle. Round and round his hand went, even after the cap was firmly in place.

'In the days and weeks that followed, Ninette told me more of her former life, and it wasn't pretty. Her father was an alcoholic, a wife-beater. She herself was married at eighteen to a man she discovered had two pastimes. One was consuming vodka by the bucketload, the other, using her as a punch-bag. Eventually, she decided enough was enough and when he started on her, she took a rolling pin to him and beat him unconscious.'

McKenzie smiled sadly. 'Ninette couldn't understand why I started to laugh. I had to explain the old music hall joke about the wife who takes a rolling pin to her errant husband, like Punch and Judy.' His smile faded. 'Then I'd to explain what a music hall was, and Punch and Judy.

'Everything had changed by then, and my employers weren't exactly happy because I'd stopped doing long-distance work, and certainly wasn't prepared to do any European trips. Not that I cared, I was too happy. But Ninette was bothered. We weren't short of money, but she was desperate to contribute. It's strange the way her attitude changed. She'd not been bothered until we became lovers, but after that she kept pestering me to find work she could do, no questions asked, so she could bring something into the house.

'How it happened, I can't quite remember, but she managed to get a job at the local rugby club. She had no experience of bar work, but she was a quick learner. The treasurer there was happy to pay her cash in hand; no doubt he was fiddling her hours. The man was a bit of a chancer, and I heard later that they'd given him the elbow because of his sticky fingers. Anyway, as the season was coming to an end they asked Ninette to work one extra Saturday afternoon. It was a special fixture against a representative side, some sort of club centenary, I think. She agreed because she wanted to buy herself some summer clothes. The match started early, so her plan was to do the bar work, then go shopping and catch the bus home afterwards. Normally I picked her up, but I needed to do some work on the car to get it through the MOT.

'When your head's stuck under the bonnet of a car you forget what time it is. By the time I'd finished and got the car running it was gone 9 p.m. There was still no sign of Ninette, so I rang the rugby club. There was no reply; they must have shut much earlier. So I set off to look for her. I hadn't gone far when I noticed the smell. I'd my car window open, and the breeze was wafting smoke through the gap. That made me look; and that was when I saw the fire. I stopped and went to see what it was.

'I found her jacket first. It had been discarded in the struggle, I guess. I knew then it was Ninette on that funeral pyre. The jacket was very distinctive. I picked it up without thinking. I still have it. As I got nearer, I could tell it was her. I could tell even after all the terrible things he'd done to her. Don't ask me how I knew. I just did. I

think I only just missed her killer. If I'd been a few minutes earlier, perhaps I'd have been in time to catch him,
to save Ninette even. And all those other poor women
would have been alive today. As I was turning away, because I couldn't bear to look any longer, I trod on something. Without thinking, I picked it up and put it in the
jacket pocket. Then I drove home. It's a good job there
wasn't much traffic, because I must have been all over,
like a drunk. I got home, shut the doors and locked them.
I went into the kitchen, took out a full bottle of whisky
and sat down. I didn't get up again until that bottle was
empty. Believe it or not, I was stone-cold sober. I drank
non-stop for weeks on end. I almost lost my job at the haul-
age company because of it. I thought if I drank enough I
might forget what I'd seen; forget her, but it didn't work.

'The drink blurred my memory of what had happened
at the scene of the fire. It was much later, when I was
deciding whether or not to throw her clothes away, that
I found that jacket in the bottom of the wardrobe. I'd
screwed it into a ball and tossed it there. That was when I
found that.' McKenzie gestured to the key ring. 'And that
was when I started my manhunt.'

'Why did it take so long to find him?' Nash wasn't convinced by McKenzie's story, but he was prepared to see
where he was going with it.

'By the time I got started, the trail had gone cold. Bear
in mind I'd none of your facilities to help me. Things you
find out in hours take private citizens weeks, months even.
Added to which I'd to work, to support myself and to fund
the enquiries. Also, I'd to be discreet. The last thing I
wanted was to alert the killer. And every lead I followed
could have done that.'

'Why did you abduct Mrs Dawson?'

McKenzie stared at Mironova as if she was dense. In-

stead of answering her question, he continued. 'The first
difficulty I had was identifying which rugby club that key
ring belonged to. There were players in that match from
all over. I'd had to choose between Neath, Northampton,
Nottingham and Netherdale. Unluckily, I chose the bigger clubs first. What complicated matters, was that each
club brought a handful of spectators with them. To begin
with, I couldn't be sure if these'—he pointed to the key
ring—'were on sale to all and sundry, which would have
made my task well nigh impossible. Luckily, they were
presentation gifts for the players.'

'Going back to Ninette, why wasn't her body identified? Why didn't you come forward and tell the police
what you knew?' Nash asked.

'I can't expect you to understand the effects of grief
such as that. For one thing I don't think I was sober
enough for long enough to reason it through rationally.
Certainly not until far too late. By the time I was able to
it would have looked highly suspicious. What would you
have thought? I'd smuggled an illegal immigrant into the
country, harboured her for over a year; kept her as my
mistress. You'd have thought either I'd tired of her and
wanted rid, or we'd had a lovers' quarrel. As to why her
body wasn't identified, who else was there to do it? It was
the last match of the season, by the time they re-started
in September they'd have forgotten she existed. Can you
remember the bar staff from somewhere you haven't been
for several months?'

'What about the treasurer?' Clara suggested.

McKenzie laughed. 'He had enough problems of his
own. He was already being investigated by the commit-
tee for embezzlement. No doubt, he was fiddling the staff
hours as well. He'd be the last person to tell the police.'

Fleming was still unconvinced. 'You're saying you

staged all this simply in order to bring the real killer to justice? You're claiming you're not the Cremator, in spite of the fact that your abduction of Mrs Dawson looked like one of the Cremator's cases? What made you pick her, anyway? There must be dozens of other women in the area who fit the profile just as well, better even.'

Nash already knew the reason. 'You think Brian Dawson is the Cremator? That's it, isn't it? That's why you abducted his wife?'

'I was angry with Vanda.' McKenzie turned and smiled at her.

'Because I couldn't believe any woman could live with a monster like that and not realize what was going on. Once I had her here, I found out how brave she really is. She wasn't going to give in. Even when she thought I was going to rape her, when I pretended to rape her for the sake of those photos, she wouldn't cry out for help, wouldn't show me she was afraid. All the time I was holding her she never showed me any fear, then, after she got over the shock of what had happened, she challenged me to do my worst. Even though she believed I was the monster who'd done all those horrible things. That takes a very special sort of courage. Even if I had been going to do all those things the Cremator did, I couldn't have touched her, not after her display of bravery.' McKenzie shrugged. 'But perhaps that's just the way a normal person thinks. Perhaps the Cremator would have seen that as some sort of challenge to his virility. Something to master, not admire.

'I guess it was simply bad luck on her part that she got hitched to a sadistic pervert. I explained to her what I'd discovered. She didn't believe me until I showed her the key ring, explained where I'd found it, told her about everything I'd done to discover the truth, and in the end, when I could bear to, I told her about Ninette and what happened to her.

'Dawson wasn't playing in that rugby match,' McKenzie explained. 'But I found out a long time later that he was one of the substitutes. One of the reasons I took Vanda prisoner, apart from wanting to put pressure on him, was in the hope that if you searched the property thoroughly looking for her, you'd find something incriminating, something to tie him in to the murders. But you didn't look hard enough. So I took it one step further. After I showed Vanda the evidence that proved her husband was the Cremator, we thought up the idea of providing him with a "real" body. I stole a shop dummy and set fire to it in the woods on Black Fell. Before that, Vanda posed as if she was the victim. I made sure the dummy didn't burn long enough to destroy the appearance. I sent the photos to Dawson, but even that didn't break the callous bastard. That was when I made the phone call to report the body.'

'From Vanda's mobile?' Nash suggested.

McKenzie nodded. 'I was desperate to stir some action up. Everything I'd tried was hitting a brick wall.'

'We'll have to check the information you've given us,' Fleming told McKenzie. 'Obviously there are still a lot of unanswered questions. However justified you might have considered your actions to be, taking the law into your own hands that way simply isn't on. By your own admission you've committed a string of very serious crimes, crimes that must be answered for, no matter what your motive. There's the kidnap and false imprisonment of Mrs Dawson for a start. Added to that there's the sexual assault. Although the rape may have been simulated, there is no mistaking the evidence that photo shows. You can throw in the breaking and entering charge, theft of a mannequin and wasting police time.'

If Jackie expected McKenzie to attempt to find excuses for his actions, she was surprised by Vanda Dawson's intervention, but then, it was turning into a day of surprises. 'I think you're clutching at straws. What's more, you're concentrating your efforts on the wrong target. Let me set you straight on a few points. First of all, the kidnapping and sexual assault nonsense. You can't prove that Lindsay kidnapped me. Not unless I give evidence against him, and I wouldn't hold your breath for that to happen.

'As for the sexual assault, you would only be able to prove that if you could show that I was unwilling.' Nash watched with fascination as she put her hand on McKenzie's and held it. 'If I still haven't convinced you, let me tell you this. I asked Lindsay to fuck me. Begged him to, in fact, because I wanted him as I haven't wanted a man in years. That's because Lindsay's a real man, not a sick, twisted pervert like that creep I am married to. Despite my pleading, Lindsay wouldn't do it. He wouldn't do it even though I'd tormented him to the limit, got him as aroused as a man can be. That's because he wouldn't take advantage of me because I was under his protection. I will tell you this though, the minute we're alone together, I'm going to do my very best to persuade him to change his mind.

'So, where does that leave your investigation? You've the break-in and theft of the model. I know the owner of Henrietta's quite well, and I'm sure she won't press charges if I offer to repay her for the loss and damage. Now we're down to wasting police time, but as Lindsay's put you on the trail of the most wanted serial killer in years, I don't see how you can hope to make that stick, at least without it looking as if the prosecution is purely vindictive.'

Clara was astounded. From what Dr Grey had told her, her sister was a cowed, timid woman, browbeaten into submissiveness by her husband. The doctor's account varied wildly from the spitfire confronting them, who rejected their accusations with the fury of a tigress defending her cubs. But there was also the far more serious matter of the accusation that McKenzie had made. His claim that Dawson was the Cremator could not be ignored or taken lightly. Perhaps there was going to be something worth salvaging from this wreckage of a day after all.

Jackie Fleming tried to take control of the situation. 'All right, let's be realistic about this. As you quite rightly pointed out, Mrs Dawson—'

'Please call me Vanda,' she interrupted. 'I'd like to dispense with any association with the name Dawson. That belongs in the past: to an unhappy time I'd rather forget.'

'Very well, Vanda it is, but I'm afraid it's in connection with that past that I need to ask some questions.' She indicated the key ring on the table. 'This is quite strong circumstantial evidence, but I'm afraid it's far from conclusive. Dawson could easily claim that he stopped at that point to relieve himself on the way back from the match and dropped the key ring then. An unlikely coincidence, I agree, but without more proof, we'd find it impossible to get a conviction. CPS wouldn't even bring the case to court.'

'I think we have that proof.'

Attention switched to Nash. Sutton, who had some idea what was coming, thought it was as if a leading actor had walked on-stage.

'First of all, Vanda, I have to tell you that your husband is dead. His body was discovered in the old mill this morning. Appearances tend to suggest that he took his own life.'

Nash paused to allow the shock of his announcement to sink in. Clara stared at him. Knowing Nash so well, she wondered if his phraseology was significant. 'I'm afraid that's not all we found there.' Nash's tone was grave. 'Did you know of the existence of a hidden room below where the cars were stored in the old mill?'

Vanda Dawson shook her head.

'We found it when we were trying to trace a sound. The room was where the wheel that drove the millstones was housed. It had been blocked up and turned into what was effectively a cellar. Inside we found a young woman named Janet Watts. She was naked, chained to the wall and in danger of dying from hypothermia. She was almost hysterical with fear. She managed to tell us she had been abducted from her home in Leeds yesterday. She had been raped and beaten by her kidnapper. As he was raping her, he took photographs.

'That was part of the reason for her terror. The other was what she could see around her. The walls are covered in photographs. I saw them. They are all photos of the Cremator's victims. Graphic photos taken in that room. We also found clothing and other effects, jewellery and so forth, which I'm sure will turn out to match those belonging to his earlier victims.' Nash paused as they absorbed the horror of what he'd told them. He then added an extra level. 'I believe the Cremator was about to increase the torture he inflicted on his victims. In the corner of the mill, I saw a fuel can identical to those shown on the photos.' He paused. 'Alongside it was a flame thrower.'

Nash turned to McKenzie. 'I can understand your actions even if I can't condone them. I'll leave it Superintendent Fleming to decide whether you have other charges to answer.'

His gaze switched to Vanda Dawson. 'And I'll leave you to make your peace with your sister. I think you owe her an enormous apology for the ordeal she's been through. Remember it was particularly bad for her, because she was aware from the media of what the Cremator did to his victims. Whether or not she accepts your apology is another matter.' Nash paused for a moment. 'One thing I must ask you. Apart from the cars and a few pieces of wood and an old engine, what else was in the old mill? Was there any rope?'

Vanda Dawson shook her head. 'Not as far as I know, but I only went in there to put my car away or get it out. I'm not sure I'd have noticed it if there was any.'

Nash stood up. 'I'm going home now. I shouldn't have been at work in the first place.' His face twisted with pain as he recalled his own situation. 'Or rather, I would do if I'd a home to go to. Instead I'm going to the hotel, whilst I think up how to tell my little boy we're homeless.'

TWENTY

As HE DROVE them back to Helmsdale, Sutton asked Nash if he was happy the way the case had unfolded. 'Not really,' he admitted. 'I'd rather have put Dawson on trial. Apart from that, I'll be curious to hear what the forensic boys and Mexican Pete have to say about the way he died.'

'But that was suicide, surely?'

'I don't think Dawson killed himself. In fact I'm almost sure he didn't.'

He was about to say more when his mobile rang. After a struggle, Nash got the phone from his pocket. He glanced at the screen. 'Yes, Professor?'

Glancing sideways, Sutton noticed Nash's expression change. He wondered what the pathologist was saying. 'That more or less confirms what I thought,' Nash said after a long time. 'Which only leaves the question of who was responsible. Will you inform Superintendent Fleming?'

He ended the call and looked across at Sutton. 'Ramirez has just told me that from his provisional findings Dawson was murdered. I thought as much, now it's official.'

'How come? I mean, what made you suspect it?'

'Whoever strung Dawson up, did so without placing anything there that would suggest he might have stepped off it. Of course he could have climbed on the roof of one of the cars, but if he'd done that, he'd have left marks. There weren't any. When Mexican Pete examined the body, he found bruising on the back of Dawson's neck in the shape of a thumb and some fingers. The spread of them suggests they were made by the right hand, and the thumb mark was on the left. Try as hard as you like, you can't bruise yourself that way unless you're a contortionist. Someone gripped Dawson by the neck, either to subdue him or whilst they were putting the rope in place. Apart from that, he found traces of adhesive on Dawson's wrists. Ramirez suggests they were from duct tape that was used to bind him.'

'That was why you asked about the rope. Because you didn't think Dawson committed suicide?'

'Yes, the rope looked new, as if it was bought specifically for the purpose. If Dawson didn't own any rope, it's another pointer to the fact he was murdered.'

'Do you think it was someone taking revenge? Someone like McKenzie, a relative of one of his victims? Or could McKenzie have done it?'

'Not McKenzie, that's for certain. Mexican Pete gave the time of death as somewhere in the early hours of this morning. I think at that time McKenzie had an excellent alibi. Apart from the fact that he was probably in bed with Vanda Dawson, his house was under surveillance by our officers.'

'You think he and Mrs Dawson are sleeping together? Despite what she said?'

'I'd bet on it.'

'So who did kill Dawson?'

'The idea that it might be a vengeful relative did cross my mind, but look how long it took for McKenzie to trace him, and he had some evidence. The chance of another relative tracking him down is too remote. One of the trademarks of the Cremator was that he was ultra-cautious and left nothing that could lead to his identity being discovered.'

'What other motive could there be?'

'I'm rather hoping Tom Pratt might find that out. With everything else that's happened I forgot that I'd asked for certain enquiries to be made. I'll have to follow up on them. If I had to guess, I'd say this is linked to the bank robbery.'

'Why would an accountant be involved with a gang of thieves?'

'Stealing the money is only part of it. Once you have it, you have to launder it. Who better than an accountant for that purpose? They would know we were talking to him about his wife's disappearance, it's been in the press for goodness sake. They must have been scared stiff he'd lose his nerve.'

He went to use his mobile, but Sutton warned him, 'Leave it until you get to the hotel, and use a landline. You've a lot of calls to make.'

Nash looked at him, puzzled.

'Don't you think you should be speaking to your insurers? And your mobile must be almost out of charge by now.'

Nash glanced at the screen, and sure enough, the indicator showed that the battery had little power left. 'I'll switch it off.'

Sutton thought for a moment before asking, 'Is it all over and done with? The Cremator case, I mean?'

Nash looked at him, his expression grave. 'Yes and no. It's all over in the sense that we can close the files on all the murders. It certainly isn't over for the other victims.'

Sutton frowned. 'I don't understand? What do you mean by "the other victims"?'

'The victims for whom it will never be over. The ones the media talks so glibly about, when they go on about getting closure. It's one of those phrases that sounds good, but when you think about it, is completely meaningless.'

'I still don't follow you.'

'I'm talking about all those people who were close to the women Brian Dawson slaughtered. There's no way they'll be able to forget. Every time some new incident comes up, the media will compare it to the Cremator, and there they are back at square one, reliving the distress.'

'How do you cope, knowing all that?'

'All I can do is think that with him out of the way there can't be any addition to the tally of grieving friends and relatives.'

'I suppose it's lucky this country doesn't suffer from as many serial killers as they seem to attract in America.'

'You think so?' Nash's smile was without humour. 'Ever since Jack the Ripper, and before that for all I know, there have been regular occurrences that can be put down as repeat offences by the same perpetrator. Not all of them hit the headlines because some of them remain no more than suspicion in the minds of investigating officers, but the well-documented ones are bad enough. You've only to think of the Moors Murderers, the Yorkshire Ripper, the Norfolk Strangler and Harold Shipman to quote the most notorious. I could add plenty more. And that's without going into the ones that never get caught.'

Sutton stared at him in astonishment. 'You mean there are people walking the streets, who have committed more than one murder and got away with it?'

'Of course there are. Bound to be. Examine crime statistics. We don't have a one hundred per cent record in solving other crimes, why should it be different in murder cases. I can think of three incidents we currently have under investigation that we've no idea who committed the crimes. The security van hijack, the bank theft and the bomb at my flat.'

'They weren't murders.'

'Agreed, but what I'm trying to point out is that it isn't like books or films. We don't always solve the case and bring the criminal to justice.'

IT WAS MID-AFTERNOON before the detectives returned to Helmsdale. As soon as they arrived, Tom Pratt buttonholed Fleming and Mironova. 'I've just got the details from Felling prison that Mike asked me for,' he told them.

Jackie frowned. 'What was that about?'

'After I remembered that Dawson had been Simon Wardle's accountant, Mike wondered if he might have been involved in organizing the robberies from his prison cell, so he asked me to check on what visitors Wardle has had recently. He thought some of Wardle's old cronies might have carried out the raids. That's why I'm trying to find out if any of them owns a motorbike.'

'Not Wardle again. We had enough trouble with him before. I thought I'd heard the last of him,' Jackie said. 'Has he had any visitors?'

'Not recently, but he had two last year, both interesting. One was Dawson, but you could explain that away as he was Wardle's accountant, I suppose. The other was from Wardle's supposed cousin. According to the visiting order, his name is Charles Grenfell.'

'You said "supposed cousin", have you any reason to doubt that?' Clara asked.

'Several reasons. First of all, I checked Wardle's background. He has no cousins, either male or female. Secondly, the address he gave on the visiting order, and the one on the driving licence he produced as proof of identity, is eighty-nine, High Street, Helmsdale.'

'Eighty-nine? Isn't that…?'

Pratt finished Fleming's sentence for her, 'The address of Armstrong and Gill.'

'We ought to try and trace this mysterious Grenfell character and have a word with him.'

'Ah, that's the biggest problem of them all.' Tom paused, 'The only Charles Grenfell I've managed to trace died in 1977.'

WHEN NASH REACHED the hotel, the first thing he did was to take a couple of painkillers. He had managed to sign in, which was a slightly farcical procedure given his inability to use his right hand, and prepared to go up to his room, when he was stopped by the receptionist. 'Mr Nash, there's a visitor for you in the resident's lounge. She asked if you would join her there.'

Nash thanked the woman and turned in the direction of the lounge. When he entered the room, the only occupant looked up and smiled. 'Mike, good to see you. How are you feeling?'

Nash nodded to the chief constable. 'I'm OK, apart from this'—he indicated his arm—'and a few bruises.'

'I understand you've been working this morning. That must stop. I want you to organize things here, get your personal affairs in order. I'm aware there will be things such as insurance to sort out. Once that's done, I want you to take a complete break,' she paused, 'sorry, bad pun. I'm sure you'll be able to get a sick note for two months or so.'

'It's not that simple, ma'am. I've to fetch Daniel home from France.'

'You can't do that if you're unable to drive,' O'Donnell pointed out. 'Can you get there by train?'

'I could do, but it would be a struggle.'

'In that case, leave it with me. I'll see if we can dream something up.'

She stood up and set off for the door, then stopped and turned. 'Oh, and I've got a message for you from Viv Pearce. He said you would understand. Two words: "she's not", whatever that means.'

Nash smiled. The stress that Viv had been under had eased, apparently, as Lianne wasn't pregnant.

After the chief constable left, Nash sat for a few moments, reflecting on the outcome of the case. It was ironic that they had hounded McKenzie because they thought he was the Cremator, and all the time he was trying to unmask the killer. They had thought of Vanda as a victim and yet she was nothing of the sort. They had sympathized with Dawson only to discover that he was a sadistic monster. The gang thought he was a danger, so they had him killed. That had helped confirm the police suspicion of him, and when they looked into his background, it pointed to his association with the criminals: which was the opposite of what they wanted. All along, everyone had been running around in circles, looking in the wrong directions. When McKenzie abducted Vanda, he could have had no idea as to the chain of events that would follow. The big remaining question was, would they catch the gang?

Nash wasn't sure. In any case, he had more immediate concerns to worry about. A home for himself and Daniel, the insurance company to fight with, getting someone to clear the debris from his flat, buying new clothing and a whole range of household items.

That evening, when Clara came to see him, along with David Sutton, she mentioned work only briefly. 'I thought you'd be interested in this. When the forensic team had finished in the bank vault and the poster shop, Jackie ordered them to open Dawson's offices. They were empty.'

'That's hardly surprising, with Dawson lying on Mexican Pete's table in the mortuary.'

'No, I mean totally empty. No computers, no filing cabinets, no desks, chairs, phones. Everything had gone, apart from the carpets and blinds.'

'So there's nothing left to tie them to Dawson,' Nash commented.

Later, the question of where he would live was raised. Nash, who by now had got used to avoiding shrugging, told them, 'I'm going to look for somewhere when we get back from France, not before. I want Daniel to be involved in the decision. I think it's time I bought somewhere. A nice cottage, or something like that, preferably in one of the villages.'

'That could be expensive,' Sutton pointed out.

'The money isn't a problem. When I was young, we had a big house in Ilkley. My sister emigrated to Australia and married a farmer whose place is about twice the size of Yorkshire. She hardly needed any extra, so my parents willed the house and contents to me. After they died, property prices had shot through the roof, and somewhere like theirs, in an area like that was worth a fortune. Added to that, my father collected antique furniture, and TV had just kick-started the craze for antiques. When my mother and father died, I was single, living and working in London. I didn't need much, so I sent the furniture for auction and put the house on the market. Even I had to blink twice when I got the cheques. I stuck the money in a couple of building societies and forgot about it. I haven't touched it since, until Daniel came along. Then I decided a motorbike wasn't ideal for carting a youngster on, so I bought the Range Rover.'

'That must have put a hole in your nest egg?'

'No, because the money's been sitting there so long, accruing interest, buying the car barely touched the capital.'

'Speaking of your car,' Mironova looked at her fiancé, who smiled encouragingly. 'We've got a proposition for you. I spoke to the chief early this afternoon and she mentioned your transport problems, and that she's banned you from work. David and I thought we could drive you to France, and leave you there. David would drive your car and I'll drive his. That way we get a few days' leave together as well. Then you can drive yourself and Daniel back when you're fit again.'

Nash stared at each of them in turn. 'That's a wonderful, thoughtful gesture, but are you sure?'

'Of course,' Clara continued as if she hadn't heard him, 'now that we know how loaded you are, we can get you to fork out for all the expenses.'

'I'm more than happy to do that.' Nash sat back, before remembering and moving to a more comfortable position. 'Tomorrow, I'll ring Daniel and tell him what's happened. I intended to do it earlier, but then the chief arrived and I got too weary. I don't think he'll be too worried about the flat and he took the *Gruffalo* with him.' He smiled at Sutton's puzzled expression. 'His favourite book. I bought it for him when he began to master reading English. He took it to show his aunt.'

'That's settled, then.'

'By the time we come back from his holiday, he'll probably be looking forward to the change, seeing it as a new adventure.'

THE TRAFFIC DIVISION of the local force had recently taken delivery of a new piece of equipment that they hoped would help crack down on vehicle theft, the evasion of excise duty and uninsured drivers. The kit was known by the acronym ANPR, which stood for automatic number plate recognition. The device was installed in an unmarked car and two of the area's most experienced traffic officers were charged with trialling it.

The ANPR had already proved valuable on their first day's patrol, bringing to book two vehicles that had no current tax disc, plus one driver whose insurance had lapsed. It was on the second day, though, that they really hit gold. As the officers were driving through the Carthill estate in Netherdale, the ANPR pinged a motorcycle as it turned into the drive of a house. Rather than alert the rider at this stage, the police driver cruised past whilst his colleague retrieved the information from the on-board computer.

The operator whistled as he read the details. 'I think we'd better park up and contact CID. I don't fancy tackling this bloke if the info on here is correct.'

He repeated the message to the driver. 'Quite right, let the suits deal with it.'

Fleming ordered the house to be put under surveillance until an ARU unit could be assembled. When the armed officers were in place, she supervised the raid personally, flanked by Mironova, Pearce and DC Andrews. 'Viv, stick by me. You're the only one who has actually seen this Freeman character. That'll make identification easier.'

The raid took the occupants of the house by surprise. In addition to Freeman, two other men were detained, and the detectives discovered a suitcase in the bottom of a wardrobe containing over two-hundred-thousand pounds in cash. Significantly, a considerable amount of the money was inside cash bags emblazoned with the name and logo of Good Buys supermarket. On searching Freeman, they found a paying-in book along with seven-thousand-five-hundred pounds in cash.

'You must have been doing a roaring trade in posters,'

Fleming told Freeman, who maintained a surly silence. 'The trouble with money-laundering from the criminals' point of view is that it has to be done gradually, a bit at a time, to avoid arousing suspicion. Banks have instructions to report suspiciously large transactions. That's obviously what our *Easy Rider* friend here was in the process of doing.'

SIX WEEKS LATER, Nash stood by the rail of the cross-Channel ferry, watching the Kent coastline appear through the slight mist. Alongside him, Daniel was prey to mixed emotions as they neared the English shore. News of the loss of their flat, the only home he'd shared with his beloved papa, had at first been traumatic. Now, the idea of the two of them finding a new place to live excited the small boy.

It would be their house. One which held no conflict of memory for either of them. Not that Daniel viewed it that way. He saw it merely as a great new adventure.

During their absence, the British press and media had been full of the identification and death of the notorious serial killer known as the Cremator. Despite that, Nash felt uncomfortable, dissatisfied.

His feeling had nothing to do with the injuries he'd suffered or the destruction of his home. Although the media had hailed the unmasking of the Cremator as a great triumph, Nash knew that the truth was that it had been down to pure luck rather than good detection. They had gone to interview Dawson about one crime, only to find evidence that linked him to a far worse one.

On top of that, although media and public alike were unconcerned by the inquest findings, which recorded a verdict of murder, Nash felt frustrated that this too remained unsolved. His only solace, at what he knew to be a low point in his career, was that women would feel marginally safer knowing that with Dawson's death, the Cremator no longer prowled the streets. The media would talk about closure for the families of the Cremator's victims. Nash didn't believe there was such a thing as closure. It was the sort of glib phrase used by those who were not closely involved with violent crimes and who didn't witness at first hand the anguish they caused.

Nor had their efforts in the other cases proved much more successful. Although they had arrested three potential suspects in the van hijack and bank robbery, and recovered a substantial amount of money, the rest of the gang remained at large. They had no idea who the other men were: hardly Nash's finest hour.

Before leaving England, Nash had bought a laptop, one of his main aims being to search for properties suitable for purchase. Shortly before he and Daniel were due to return, he had received a long e-mail from Clara containing an item of good news. Viv Pearce had asked Lianne Ford to marry him. 'The girl must be an idiot,' Clara wrote, 'because she said yes. Can you believe it? Viv setting up home and playing happy families? He's already talking about the wedding.'

Her message also contained an item of far less welcome news. It had been decided that the police presence in Bishopton was to end with immediate effect. The small team headed by Fleming and Nash would be responsible for crime prevention and detection over an area that had just doubled in size. It was somewhat ironic that Nash had left the Met in search of a quieter, less stressful existence. Well, that hadn't worked.

Nash looked at his son. He thought briefly of the boy's mother, wondering how much of a struggle it had been for her to raise him alone. Now, Daniel's future lay in Nash's hands. He wasn't one to shirk a challenge, but this would be like no other he had faced before. And perhaps it would be an adventure for him too.

As they turned to walk towards the car deck, Daniel reached out and took his papa's hand. Nash looked down and smiled. Whatever the challenges, he thought the future was going to be that much brighter, for both of them.

'Papa,' Daniel said. 'When we buy a new house, could we get one with a lawn big enough to play cricket on?'

* * * * *

REQUEST YOUR FREE BOOKS!

2 FREE NOVELS
PLUS 2 FREE GIFTS!

MYSTERY WORLDWIDE LIBRARY®

Your Partner in Crime

YES! Please send me 2 FREE novels from the Worldwide Library® series and my 2 FREE gifts (gifts are worth about $10). After receiving them, if I don't wish to receive any more books, I can return the shipping statement marked "cancel." If I don't cancel, I will receive 4 brand-new novels every month and be billed just $5.49 per book in the U.S. or $6.24 per book in Canada. That's a savings of at least 31% off the cover price. It's quite a bargain! Shipping and handling is just 50¢ per book in the U.S. and 75¢ per book in Canada.* I understand that accepting the 2 free books and gifts places me under no obligation to buy anything. I can always return a shipment and cancel at any time. Even if I never buy another book, the two free books and gifts are mine to keep forever.

414/424 WDN F4WY

Name	(PLEASE PRINT)	
Address		Apt. #
City	State/Prov.	Zip/Postal Code

Signature (if under 18, a parent or guardian must sign)

Mail to the **Harlequin® Reader Service:**
IN U.S.A.: P.O. Box 1867, Buffalo, NY 14240-1867
IN CANADA: P.O. Box 609, Fort Erie, Ontario L2A 5X3

Want to try two free books from another line?
Call 1-800-873-8635 or visit www.ReaderService.com.

* Terms and prices subject to change without notice. Prices do not include applicable taxes. Sales tax applicable in N.Y. Canadian residents will be charged applicable taxes. Offer not valid in Quebec. This offer is limited to one order per household. Not valid for current subscribers to the Worldwide Library series. All orders subject to credit approval. Credit or debit balances in a customer's account(s) may be offset by any other outstanding balance owed by or to the customer. Please allow 4 to 6 weeks for delivery. Offer available while quantities last.

Your Privacy—The Harlequin® Reader Service is committed to protecting your privacy. Our Privacy Policy is available online at www.ReaderService.com or upon request from the Harlequin Reader Service.

We make a portion of our mailing list available to reputable third parties that offer products we believe may interest you. If you prefer that we not exchange your name with third parties, or if you wish to clarify or modify your communication preferences, please visit us at www.ReaderService.com/consumerschoice or write to us at Harlequin Reader Service Preference Service, P.O. Box 9062, Buffalo, NY 14269. Include your complete name and address.

WWL13R